THE FIRE-EATERS

THE FIRE-EATERS

JASON MANNING

The characters and events portrayed in this book are fictitious. Any similarity to real persons, living or dead, is coincidental and not intended by the author.

To Grace

CONTENTS

Supper Talk

"You're that army man that's been with the Injuns, aren't you?" Barlow grimaced. Apparently someone had a loose tongue.

One of the men leaned forward, his knuckles on the table, looming over Barlow's plate. "You pass right through here in one day, and spend the better part of a month with them heathens up in New Echota? Makes me think you must be one of them Northern Injun lovers. That shoe fit you?"

"The Cherokees and I fought together in Florida. I have some friends there."

The backwoodsman hawked and drooled spittle into Barlow's food.

As he shot up out of his chair, Barlow overturned the table and drove it forward against the two men, knocking them off balance. The table fell on one of the men, and Barlow turned his attention to the other, who had righted himself against a wall and was charging at him, his bearded features twisted into a snarl of rage....

PART I:
1829

CHAPTER ONE

Timothy Barlow woke up to the sound of battle—and found himself in an all-too-familiar room at the Langford boarding-house in the middle of Washington. There was no battle—no roar of the guns, no drift of bitter powder smoke, no flags flying, no valiant deeds, no dying heroics. He sighed, lying there on his back in the narrow bed, staring up at the ceiling. What a shame. And what good a soldier when there were no battles to be fought? The sound he had heard was that of a drum and fife being played, in very spirited fashion, in the street below his window. He could hear, too, a multitude of voices, some raised in hurrahs. It was a day of great celebration for many in the republic's capital city. For others, Barlow reminded himself, it was a day of great trepidation. March 4, 1829. The day that Andrew Jackson of Tennessee, Old Hickory, the Hero of New Orleans, was to be sworn in as president of the United States.

The people were out early; the weak light angling through the window belonged to a day just now dawning. Somewhere off in the distance roared a thirteen-cannon salute. Barlow swung long legs off the bed, stood, and went to the window.

Washington had changed considerably since he had first visited her, fifteen years ago. Since the conclusion of the War of 1812— or, as many Americans were prone to call it, the Second War for Independence from Great Britain—the young republic had enjoyed unprecedented economic prosperity, and her capital city had gotten its fair share. The three bridges across the Potomac, all of which had been burned when the British marched through Washington, had been rebuilt, bigger and better than ever, connecting the capital with the states of Virginia and the Carolinas, where thriving plantations produced the money crops—cotton, tobacco, rice and indigo—that comprised most of the country's exports. To the north, the road to Baltimore had been widened and improved, and just within the last year the Chesapeake & Ohio Canal and the Baltimore & Ohio Railroad had both been started, promising to connect Washington with the ever-growing region west of the Appalachians. In the city itself, the population had swollen from three thousand during the late war to nearly twenty thousand. There were five banks and a college now, as well as several major newspapers, including *The National Journal, The Daily National Intelligencer,* and *The United States Telegraph*—the latter having been but recently created by pro-Jackson forces for no other reason than that the other two had been firmly in the camp of John Quincy Adams, the man Jackson had vanquished in last year's presidential election.

Still, despite all this progress, Barlow thought as he peered out the window at the city—he had a very good view—Washington was still just a cluster of largely unprepossessing structures squeezed in between a steep ridge to the north and a putrid swamp to the south. The streets were neither paved nor lighted. The most important thoroughfare was the one right beneath Barlow's window. Pennsylvania Avenue connected Capitol Hill with the President's House. It was the street where one found all the good restaurants in town—of which there were not many—and all three hotels as well, including the new National, looming four stories above the street and boasting two hundred rooms. Most of the good boardinghouses were located on Pennsylvania as well, and there were plenty of these, as the vast majority of congressmen preferred not to—or could not afford to—own their own home, and found lodging instead, while Congress was in session, in a room for rent.

Pennsylvania Avenue this morning was already filled with revelers. They'd been at it all night long. Washington had been invaded by Jackson supporters, many of whom had traveled hundreds of miles just so they could say that they'd been there when Old Hickory had been inaugurated. Every hotel room and boardinghouse was filled to overflowing. Barlow was well aware of the fact that he might not have found a place to lay his head had it not been for the fact that the owner of this particular lodging house happened to be his mother-in-law. The new arrivals found themselves sleeping on the floors of taverns and out in open fields, even though the weather— up until today, at least—had been miserable, damp and drizzling for days. Today, though, had dawned sunny and warm. It was as though Nature herself had decided to put on her best attire for the special occasion of Jackson's swearing in.

Barlow turned away from the window, bleakly scanned the room. Sarah, of course, was gone. She usually woke before he did—and Barlow was no slouch when it came to early rising. He assumed she was downstairs, helping her mother with breakfast. Mrs. Langford had nearly twenty guests to feed, and it was not in Sarah's nature to lounge about in bed like a princess while her mother slaved over a hot stove. Of course, Mrs. Langford had some help. She'd been forced to acquire some assistance after Barlow had, more or less literally, stolen her daughter away. Now she had a freed black woman by the name of Harriet to lend a hand around the place. This was just as well. Mrs. Langford was getting on in years, and in Barlow's opinion—one he had been careful to keep to himself—she did not look at all well. It was true, some years had passed since he had last seen her. Only recently had she reconciled herself to the fact that her daughter's marriage was a lasting one, that Sarah would not be coming back to her, admitting to a mistake in running away with the dashing young Army officer. Sarah had begged him to take her away from the drudgery of life as hostess in a Washington boardinghouse, and this he had done, earning from Mrs. Langford what he'd assumed would be undying animosity. But she had greeted him cordially a few days ago. It seemed she was capable of letting bygones be bygones, much to Barlow's surprise.

Going to the dresser, he found fresh water in the porcelain bowl that sat atop it, and splashed some on his face. Then he looked at himself, critically, in the mirror above the dresser. Mrs. Langford, he mused, wasn't the only one getting on in years. He was but a few years shy of forty. There was some gray now in his black hair, and his face was adorned with a good deal more "character"—as Sarah tactfully put it—than had once been the case but five or six years ago. He was still on the lean side, at least, despite years of partaking of Sarah's cooking. What worried him most were the signs of aging one could not see reflected in mirrored glass. He was far more prone these days to falling ill than had once been the case. And he was much slower to heal from an injury than he'd been before. He was no different from anyone else in that he'd taken his youthful vigor for granted. He'd thought himself indestructible. Now, of course, he knew better. His life was more than half over. He had ten, perhaps twenty, years left. His own father had died two years ago, aged fifty-five. That was considered to be a good long life. It helped if a man could look back and say, with conviction, that he'd accomplished what he'd wanted to do. Barlow wasn't sure he could do that. Nearly forty, and a captain in the United States Army, second in command of a garrison force in western New York. The likelihood of a promotion, unless there happened to be another war, was quite slim. He'd been in the army nearly twenty years, and this was as far as he was likely to go. He had seen very little action since accompanying Andrew Jackson on his campaign into Florida to deal with the Seminoles. And that had been—well, much longer ago than Barlow cared to think about. Since then, nothing, apart from dealing with smugglers moving back and forth across the border shared by New York and Canada. That was a pretty dull business, indeed.

Barlow frowned at himself, and turned away from the mirror. Nothing was to be gained by brooding over his fate. He put on his white trousers, a clean white shirt, his blue coatee with the shiny brass buttons—all laid out quite neatly on a chair by his wife. She had even polished his boots for him the night before. Then came the visored cap—shakos were no longer regulation—and the broad white leather belt and the sword in its scabbard. He had been invited to this affair by one of Jackson's men—John Henry

Eaton, Old Hickory's biographer and longtime aide. Barlow did not know Eaton well, but the invitation had been made at the general's request. And Barlow had never been able to refuse Andrew Jackson.

Checking himself once more in the mirror, Barlow nodded his satisfaction and left the hotel room. At that very moment Sarah came storming up the stairs. He could see at a glance that she was furious. Sarah Langford Barlow seldom lost her temper. But when she did it always turned out to be an event worth remembering.

"Good morning, darling," said Barlow mildly.

She was looking at the sword. "I'm of a mind to take that and run the blade right through that insufferable John C. Calhoun!" she exclaimed.

"Calhoun is here?"

"Yes," she hissed. "Come to take breakfast with Henry Clay."

"Ah, I see. Well, I don't think it would be wise to run him through, dear. Mr. Calhoun is our new vice president, after all."

"Oh, is that all he is?" asked Sarah caustically. "Don't tell him that, Timothy. *He* thinks he sits at God's right hand, you know."

Barlow had to laugh.

"It's no laughing matter," she chided him. "Not when someone sits there and smugly informs me that the institution of slavery is actually beneficial to those poor souls who suffer its scourge."

"Oh, so that's what this is all about," said Barlow, stifling a sigh.

It didn't do any good. She could tell by his expression that he was uninterested, if not a little disappointed. Standing there on the top step, her hair in slight disarray, high color in her cheeks, she looked as lovely as ever. But she had her hands on her hips, and Barlow knew that meant he was in trouble.

"Yes, that's what this is all about," she replied. "Slavery. That wicked institution. That indelible black spot on the honor of our country."

"Have I ever told you how pretty you are when you're mad?"

That just ignited fresh fury. "Don't patronize me, Timothy Barlow," she warned. "You know how strongly I feel about this subject."

He nodded. He knew, indeed, all too well. His sweet, gentle Sarah, who once had been passionate about nothing except him, had become a fervent abolitionist. It had happened several years ago, when he was transferred to Fort Perry, and Sarah was befriended by the wife of his commanding officer, Major Hayward. It was Margaret Hayward who had introduced Sarah to her abolitionist group, the Antislavery Society of New York. That had been a turning point in Sarah's life. Barlow had often wondered if she had been particularly susceptible at that point in time to the blandishments of the abolitionist members of the society. For by then she had become far less passionate about her husband.

"Yes, I know," he said. "At any rate, I hope you didn't say anything to Mr. Calhoun that was too...insulting."

"Why do you care?" she asked.

"Because he is the new vice president—and, as such, is my superior."

"He is hardly that."

"You know what I mean."

She relented, somewhat. The hands came off her hips. "Well, you needn't worry, or go down there and apologize for me, God forbid."

"I wouldn't dream of doing that," he said wryly.

"Good. You'd better not. All I said was that, in my opinion, those who owned slaves, regardless of their justification for doing so, performed the devil's work."

Barlow winced. "Oh, is that all?"

"I'm not afraid of Mr. Calhoun," she said hotly. "As you appear to be. Remember, he has boarded here many times in the past. I have washed his clothes and darned his socks. And I will not stand meekly by and allow him to speak such nonsense about such a brutal system."

Barlow nodded. He had a feeling he'd just been subjected to an example of feminine logic; that because Sarah had once done domestic duties for John C. Calhoun, as a guest at her mother's boardinghouse, she now had the right to debate one of the nation's most prominent political leaders on an issue as important as slavery. Barlow wasn't one of those who believed, necessarily, that a woman's place was in the home, her sole duty to attend to her husband's comfort and the proper upbringing of her children. But the majority of men in this day and age did feel that way, and he suspected that Calhoun was probably one of this number. The South Carolina planter had long ago struck him as an old-fashioned type. That was one of the chief problems with abolitionists like Margaret Hayward, mused Barlow. They did not see fit to observe the proprieties; they felt their cause was so urgent that its proponents were naturally exempt from any responsibility to play by the rules.

"As I am under my mother's roof," continued Sarah stiffly, "I shall abide by her wishes, and retire to my room until such time as Mr. Calhoun has left these premises."

With that, she stalked off down the upstairs hallway to their room—and slammed the door.

Barlow smiled wanly and continued down the staircase. He tried to slip past the doorway to the dining room unnoticed on his way to the kitchen, knowing that Mrs. Langford would be happy to feed him there, and thinking it might be best to avoid Calhoun and Clay and the others. But he was found out, and it was Henry Clay's distinctive, somewhat high-pitched voice, perfectly enunciated words cutting like daggers into his brain, that arrested him in mid-stride.

"Ah, Captain Barlow, come and join us, if you please. There is someone here to see you."

Barlow plastered an amiable and carefree smile on his face and entered the dining room. There was Clay, slight, redheaded, with his hawkish features and piercing blue eyes. Sitting to his left was Calhoun, an imposing figure, ramrod-straight, with a leonine head topped by a thick helmet of black hair and the lantern-jawed face with features that belonged to an ascetic—or a zealot; hard and uncompromising features, as though carved from stone. Clay was something of a dandy where attire was concerned; this morning he wore an exquisitely tailored blue swallowtail coat and a silk cravat of robin's-egg blue, to go with yellow doeskin trousers and black boots polished to a high sheen. Calhoun, on the other hand, was dressed like a preacher, in a severe black coat and trousers. He was perusing a special edition of *The National Intelligencer*, and looked up from it only long enough to spare Barlow a glance that betrayed nothing.

There were several other men in the dining room, most of them eating their breakfast while discussing in muted tones the upcoming inauguration or, like Calhoun, reading a newspaper. Barlow knew none of them, and assumed they were all politicians. Mrs. Langford's boardinghouse had a well-deserved reputation for being favored by the brightest lights in the congressional firmament, and birds of a feather tended to flock together. Barlow wondered who Clay might have been referring to with respect to the someone who wanted to see him, and then the politician-lawyer from Kentucky smiled and gestured at a man who sat across the table from him. Barlow realized then that he had met the fellow once before, after all. It was John Eaton.

Eaton rose and extended a hand. He was a man of stocky build and medium height, dark-haired and dark-eyed, with a ready smile and good looks.

"Ah, Captain," said Eaton, "delighted to see you again. I was wondering if you would remember that we had met once before. We had a mutual acquaintance. Major Reid, may he rest in peace."

"Yes, I remember. How have you been, sir?"

"Well. Very well, indeed. And I hope you can say the same?"

Barlow nodded. "I have no complaints worth speaking of."

"I was hoping we might be able to speak privately for a moment?"

"Certainly." Barlow gestured towards the hallway.

"Just don't bring up the subject of slavery, Eaton," said Calhoun, his voice rasping like a file on a horseshoe. "His wife might overhear, and then you'd find yourself under attack, with no quarter given."

Barlow glanced speculatively at Calhoun, trying to gauge whether the South Carolinian was demonstrating disrespect for his wife; if so, Barlow knew he would be honor-bound to do something about it. But Calhoun glanced up again from his newspaper and, meeting Barlow's gaze, smiled faintly. It was enough, permitting Barlow to let the comment go without response.

"After you, Mr. Eaton," he said.

They entered the hallway, and Eaton led the way to the end furthest away from the dining room, which placed them near the front door. The sounds of the street, filled with revelers, intruded, but Eaton didn't seem to mind. In fact, Barlow surmised that he wanted to use the noise from outside to mask their conversation.

"Let me first express how pleased I am," said Eaton, "that you were able to accept the general's invitation to be here today."

"I must confess, I was surprised to receive it."

"You shouldn't have been. General Jackson is not one who forgets those who have served him well. No matter how long ago that service was rendered."

"Frankly, sir, I didn't think the general and I parted on the best of terms."

Eaton made a dismissive gesture. "You're referring to a disagreement over the treatment of the southern tribes. Men of principle are bound to disagree. The general has no quarrel with you." Eaton's smile faded. "There are some in this town, however, who would be wise to fear his wrath, as the general blames them for the tragic death of his beloved Rachel."

"Yes, I heard about that," said Barlow somberly. He had met Rachel Jackson at the Hermitage many years ago, and he had liked her immensely. She had been a gentle, plainspoken woman, without guile or pretension. "I look forward to the opportunity to express my condolences to General Jackson."

Eaton shook his head morosely. "She was a fine woman. The general tried to shelter her from the slanders cast against him— and her good name, as well. But she happened to get her hands on a campaign pamphlet that I and others had prepared to defend the general against all the baseless charges leveled against him. That he was a murderer of innocents, a duelist and womanizer—that both he and Rachel were shameless adulterers."

Barlow nodded. He was aware of the story. Rachel had been married when she and Andrew Jackson first met, to an insanely jealous man who later abandoned her and went to Virginia to seek a divorce—or so everyone thought. Jackson and Rachel had subsequently gone to Natchez and been married there, embarking on what they thought would be a lifetime of joy together. Not long after, however, they had discovered that Rachel's first husband had not acquired a divorce; so, technically, she was guilty of bigamy, and Jackson of adultery.

"As might be expected," continued Eaton, "Mrs. Jackson reacted hysterically to the charges. She began a slow but inexorable decline, physically and mentally, from that day forward, until she passed away on the twenty-second of December last. She suffered terribly at the end. The general was grief-stricken. He was inconsolable. They had been together for thirty-eight years. For thirty-eight years he had loved her as no man has ever loved a woman. He was strengthened by one thing and one thing only. A growing desire for vengeance against those he blamed for Rachel's death. The partisans of John Quincy Adams who had spread the calumnies that broke Rachel's heart and health. One of his house servants told me that every morning the general would kneel before a portrait of Rachel and thank the Lord Almighty that he had been given another day to seek retribution against his enemies."

"It was a terrible loss," agreed Barlow.

"Indeed. But not just for the general, mind you. For the nation. For us all. Because Rachel was the one person who could temper the general's anger, who could reason away his fearsome rages. She was a most benign influence upon him. But now that's gone. And the general will never take another wife. She may rest in her grave, but Rachel will forever be his only love, and I dare say he will not visit a single glance upon another woman for the remainder of his days."

Barlow wasn't sure how to respond—and wondered what all of this had to do with his invitation to the inauguration.

"I understand that you have been happily married for quite some time now, Captain," said Eaton.

"Yes, that's correct."

"To the daughter of our hostess, Mrs. Langford?"

"Yes."

"What a coincidence. I, too, have married the daughter of a boardinghouse owner. Margaret O'Neal consented to become my bride this past January."

"Congratulations, sir."

"Perhaps you and your wife would agree to come to dinner some night this week?"

"We would be honored."

"Splendid." Eaton gave him a long look. "I, um, I take it that you have not heard of the scandal that hovers like a cloud over my head, then? My head, and that of my beloved wife?"

"Scandal? No. But then, Fort Perry is far removed from Washington."

"She was married once before, you see. Yes, my dearest Peggy was the wife of a sailor, who lost his life at sea. Some scoundrels insist he committed suicide, hurling himself over the side, because he knew Peggy was unfaithful." Eaton's features darkened with anger. "Shortly thereafter, she gave over to me the management of her affairs, and the rumors began circulating. Rumors that we had slept together. It was a lie. But there are those in this town, particularly the women, who do not concern themselves overmuch with the veracity of the scurrilous tales they tell. They ripped Peggy's reputation to shreds with their wicked, razor-sharp tongues. Even had I not loved her with all my heart—which, of course, I do—I would have been compelled, by my commitment to honor and justice, to do that which was right and proper, and tender to her the offer to share my life and prospects. I sought counsel from the general, and he agreed that I should do so."

Barlow was still puzzled. "I assure you, sir, that I was not acquainted with any such rumors, and that, even had I been, I would not give them credence."

Eaton beamed at him, relieved. "The Washington women spurn my bride. You and your wife would be doing me a great favor by making her feel … welcome."

"Of course."

Eaton chuckled. "I can see by the expression on your face that you are wondering if this is the one and only reason you were invited here. I can assure you that it is not. The reason, apart from the general's desire to have you here to witness this momentous occasion, is to inquire as to whether you are amenable to a change of scenery."

"I beg your pardon?"

Eaton cast a conspiratorial look down the hall to make sure no one was lurking within earshot. Then he leaned forward, pitching his voice low. "I am the new secretary of war, Captain. As such, it will be within my power to have you transferred here to Washington, to the War Department."

"I see," said Barlow. His initial reaction to the news was ambivalence. While it was true that a position at the War Department might improve his chances of earning another promotion before he reached the age of retirement, it also meant riding a desk. As almighty dull as he found duty at Fort Perry, that looked to be an even worse situation. His first impulse was to gratefully, but firmly, decline the offer. But he exercised restraint. The new secretary of war clearly thought he was doing him a favor by making the offer, and it might not be wise to turn him down so abruptly.

Eaton, apparently, had a talent for reading people. "I fear you may misunderstand my intentions, Captain," he said. "I know enough about you to realize that you are not predisposed to spend the remainder of your career shuffling papers. You would be transferred here to serve the president in a matter that demands the utmost tact, not to mention a brave heart and a familiarity with the southern tribes."

"What matter might that be, sir?"

"It has to do with the Cherokees. And the general tells me that the Cherokees hold you in extremely high regard."

"I fought with them in Florida, against the Seminoles," said Barlow cautiously.

"Exactly. We will discuss this in much more detail over dinner. Unfortunately, I am late for my appointment with the general.

Would you be so kind as to make yourself available as an escort for the general, at eleven this morning, in front of Gadsby's Hotel?"

"I would be honored."

Eaton nodded. "I will see you then, Captain. Good morning."

He turned, scooped up his hat and cloak which hung near at hand, and was out the door, plunging into the press of people filling Pennsylvania Avenue, before Barlow could think of something to say.

Heading down the hall to the kitchen, Barlow was lost in thought. What could Eaton have been talking about when he'd referred to the Cherokees? He knew that, of all the southern tribes, only the Cherokees had managed, thus far, to hold onto most of their ancestral lands. He knew, as well, that white settlers were putting pressure on them to move. There had been isolated incidents of violence. What did Andrew Jackson have in mind for him to do? Barlow had a bad feeling—a sense that, whatever it was, it would not bode well for his Indian friends.

Chapter Two

More than a decade had passed since last Barlow had laid eyes on Andrew Jackson, and he found the general much changed in some ways, and completely unchanged in others. Physically, the Hero of New Orleans and new president of the United States looked quite old and frail. He had always been a rail-thin man, but now his body, once ramrod-straight, was bent and twisted, and his step, once long and forceful, was prone to falter. His face was deeply creased with lines of worry and hardship, his eyes sunken in their sockets, his hair completely white. Yet there remained that blazing, indomitable will reflected in his eyes and echoing in the words he spoke. Andrew Jackson's body would one day fail him completely, but his spirit never would.

As Eaton had requested, Barlow was in front of Gadsby's Hotel a few minutes before eleven in the morning. A company of dragoons was there, some of them afoot and others on horseback, to control the crowd that had gathered in Pennsylvania Avenue. Some of the onlookers had joined together in song, a rousing version of "The Hunters of Kentucky." Barlow had heard it before; it had become the Jackson campaign song, with thousands of copies printed and distributed by Jackson partisans.

> *You've heard, I s'pose, how New Orleans,*
> *'Tis famed for youth and beauty.*
> *There're girls of every hue it seems,*
> *From snowy white to sooty.*
> *So Packenham he made his brags,*

If he that day was lucky,
He'd have those girls and cotton bags
In spite of old Kentucky.

But Jackson he was wide awake
And was not scared of trifles,
For well he knew Kentucky's boys,
With their death-dealing rifles.
He led them down to Cypress Swamp,
The ground was low and mucky.
There stood John Bull in martial pomp,
And here stood old Kentucky.

Oh! Kentucky, the hunters of Kentucky!
Oh! Kentucky, the hunters of Kentucky!

They went on and on, tireless in their enthusiasm, and at the end of each verse the crowd would roar a huzzah! in ragged unison, a raising of voices loud enough to rattle the windows of the hotel.

The escort of which Barlow was to be a part consisted of old Revolutionary War heroes, most of them done up in their Continental Army uniforms, along with warriors of more recent vintage, particularly the officers who had fought with Jackson at New Orleans—Hinds, Call, Patterson, Spotts, Jones, Ross, Robb, Harper and Nicholson. Barlow recognized a couple of them. None were regular army; all had served in the militia of Tennessee or Kentucky. As he had missed the Battle of New Orleans—he'd been in Washington on a special mission for the general at the time—Barlow felt as though he did not belong. But he'd given his word to Eaton, so he lingered, as inobtrusively as possible, near the entrance to the hotel, allowed past the cordon of stern-faced dragoons because of his uniform.

At precisely eleven A.M.—the church bells of the city were pealing every hour on the hour—Jackson emerged from the hotel. His appearance was greeted by a deafening roar of adulation from the crowd of onlookers. The general was dressed in a long black coat and black tie. His head, with its shock of white hair, was uncovered. He was flanked by two aides, Majors Donelson and Lewis. Though Barlow stayed back, without a care as to whether Jackson saw him or not, the general spotted him instantly and veered off his course to take Barlow's hand in his and shake it vigorously.

"Captain Barlow!" he said forcefully. "You honor me with your presence."

"I am honored to be here on such a momentous occasion, sir."

"And how is the noble Thirty-ninth?"

"Glad to a man that you are to be our president, sir."

Jackson laughed, a raspy sound. "Your regiment fought with high distinction at Horseshoe Bend. As I recall, you were grievously wounded in that engagement, leading your men into battle. I hope those wounds cause you no trouble these days."

"None whatsoever, sir."

"Fine, fine. Stay close at hand today, Captain, if you please. When I have a few moments away from the duties imposed upon me, I would have a few words with you."

"Certainly, Mr. President."

Jackson wagged a bony finger at him. "Not yet, Captain, not yet." With that he moved on, followed by his aides.

Jackson headed eastward up Pennsylvania Avenue, flanked by his escort, with a squad of mounted dragoons in advance to clear the way. Barlow hung back, remaining near the rear of the procession. The people streamed along on both sides. A Dutch wagon soon appeared behind him, filled with young women dressed all in white, with flowers in their hair. One of them held Old Glory aloft. They garnered nearly as much attention as the general himself. Barlow noticed that every window and balcony along the route was filled with spectators.

They were nearly to Capitol Hill when Barlow saw Andrew Jackson Donelson drop back and fall into step beside him. Donelson was a tall, slender, handsome young man, Jackson's nephew, and his most trusted aide. Donelson's wife Emily was expected to play the role of White House hostess, or so Barlow had heard, since the president was a widower and his Emily was his niece.

"Captain," said Donelson, with an urgency in his voice, "can I rely on your loyalty to the general?"

Barlow was taken aback by the question. "What do you mean?"

Donelson gave him a very direct stare. "Would you give up your life to save his?"

"Of course," said Barlow. He didn't take the time to explain to Donelson that his motivation for doing so would have little to do with his personal feelings about Jackson; it was his duty as an officer in the army to lay down his life for his commander in chief.

"Then take this," said Donelson. Reaching beneath his coat, he brandished a pistol and handed it to Barlow. As he did so, Barlow noticed that another pistol remained lodged beneath Donelson's belt.

"Is the general in some sort of danger?" asked Barlow, taking the pistol and concealing it beneath his coatee as best he could.

"There are rumors," said Donelson, looking about. "There are many men who fear Jackson, and what he might do as president."

"Fear him in what way?"

"We will have to discuss the details at a later date. Stay as close as you can to the general until this day is over, if you please."

"Of course," muttered Barlow.

Arriving at the Capitol, Jackson visited the Senate chamber, which was so packed that Barlow had a difficult time getting in. He had to push and shove his way through a press of men blocking the doorway, and found a spot, his back against the wall, where he could clearly see the goings-on. That suited him; he was quite content to remain at the back of the room, as from here he could watch the galleries as the vice president, Mr. Calhoun, was sworn in. He was somewhat relieved that Sarah wasn't with him. There was no telling what she might have said about a slaveholder—and, worse still, one of the most prominent and influential of the defenders of the peculiar institution of slavery—becoming the second most powerful man in the republic. Barlow did manage to catch of glimpse of Jackson inside the Senate chamber, seated in front of the secretary's desk. The general's somber black outfit was in stark contrast to the diplomats, resplendent in their ribbons and gold, who sat to his left, along with the black-robed justices of the Supreme Court. The galleries that encircled the chamber were filled with representatives from the House and their families.

Precisely at noon, with the vice president sworn in by the president pro tem of the Senate, a procession of officers and congressmen escorted Andrew Jackson to the East Portico. Barlow was astonished at the size of the crowd that had gathered around the Capitol to watch the swearing in of the republic's new chief executive. He figured that, conservatively, there had to be twenty thousand people in the crowd. As soon as the massive rotunda doors swung open and the distinctive figure of Jackson appeared to them, all those people raised their voices as one in a cheer that was unlike any noise Barlow had ever heard. A Marine band positioned to the right of the doors struck up "The President's March," but though it was only thirty paces away, Barlow could barely hear the tune, so loud was the assemblage. Two artillery companies were positioned in a field a stone's throw away; they fired a twenty-four-gun salute. The people seemed compelled to raise the level of their cheering, as though they were in some sort of competition with the musical instruments and the instruments of war.

Barlow glanced at Jackson. Stern of visage, the old man scanned the sea of upturned faces. Then he bowed quite low to the people who had come to wish him well. This gesture of humility stirred the crowd into an even greater fervor than before. They cheered hysterically. Women seated on sofas along the Portico waved their handkerchiefs. Men tossed their hats into the air. Flags and banners were waved. Fresh flowers were thrown upon the steps leading up to the Portico.

Jackson moved to a table covered with red velvet placed between the two central columns of the Portico. Jackson took his seat. John C. Calhoun took the chair to his left, while the chief justice, John Marshall, seated himself to the general's right. Barlow managed to

position himself not far behind Jackson's chair. He was still somewhat perplexed by Donelson's enigmatic words about a threat to the
general's life, but he assumed that if that threat was real, and an
attack made, that it would most likely come from behind.

Eventually the crowd, having shouted itself hoarse, began
to quiet down. Now Barlow could hear distant cannon. He had
read that artillery at the Navy Yard and the Arsenal were going to
fire salutes during the swearing in. Once he was satisfied that he
would be heard, Jackson lifted his lanky frame out of the chair and
adjusted some spectacles on the tip of his nose, the better to read
his inaugural address from a piece of paper. Barlow noted that the
general's hand was shaking slightly. Was that a sign of frailty? Or
was the old hero, for once, suffering from a case of nerves?

The crowd was hushed now—and while he might look frail,
Andrew Jackson's voice was stentorian.

"My fellow citizens," he said, "about to undertake the arduous
duties that I have been appointed to perform by the choice of a
free people, I avail myself of this customary and solemn occasion
to express the gratitude which their confidence inspires and to
acknowledge the accountability which my situation enjoins. While
the magnitude of their interests convinces me that no thanks can
be adequate to the honor they have conferred, it admonishes me
that the best return I can make is the zealous dedication of my
humble abilities to their service and their good.

"As the instrument of the Federal Constitution it will devolve
on me for a stated period to execute the laws of the United States,
to superintend their foreign and their confederate relations, to
manage their revenue, to command their forces, and, by commu-
nications to the Legislature, to watch over and to promote their
interests generally. And the principles of action by which I shall
endeavor to accomplish this circle of duties it is now proper for me
briefly to explain.

"In administering the laws of Congress I shall keep steadily in
view the limitations as well as the extent of the Executive power
trusting thereby to discharge the functions of my office without

transcending its authority. With foreign nations it will be my study to preserve peace and to cultivate friendship on fair and honorable terms, and in the adjustment of any differences that may exist or arise to exhibit the forbearance becoming a powerful nation rather than the sensibility belonging to a gallant people.

"In such measures as I may be called on to pursue in regard to the rights of the separate States I hope to be animated by a proper respect for those sovereign members of our Union, taking care not to confound the powers they have reserved to themselves with those they have granted to the Confederacy...."

Barlow glanced at John C. Calhoun. He could see the South Carolinian's face only in profile, and it was as animated as a slab of stone. But Barlow figured Jackson's words had to be music to Calhoun's ears, as they had to be to the ears of all Southerners. In recent years they had increasingly used the concept of state's rights to shield the institution of slavery, and they were leery of a national government that might grow too powerful—and, at the same time, monopolized by the North. During the administration of the Massachusetts-born John Quincy Adams, who believed strongly in a powerful central government, Southerners had grown more and more vociferous in their defense of state's rights. But Jackson was a Southerner himself, and a slaveholder. And he was making a point now of reassuring other Southern slaveholders that he would not tamper with their concepts or institutions.

"...Considering standing armies as dangerous to free governments in time of peace," continued Jackson, "I shall not seek to enlarge our present establishment, nor disregard that salutary lesson of political experience which teaches that the military should be held subordinate to the civil power. The gradual increase of our Navy, whose flag has displayed in distant climes our skill in navigation and our fame in arms; the preservation of our forts, arsenals and dockyards, and the introduction of progressive improvements in the discipline and science of both branches of our military service are so plainly prescribed by prudence that I should be excused for omitting their mention sooner than for enlarging on their importance. But the bulwark of our defense is the national militia, which in the present state of our intelligence and population must render us invincible. As long as our Government is administered for the good of the people, and is regulated by their will; as long as it secures to us the rights of person and of property, liberty of conscience and of the press, it will be worth defending; and so long as it is worth defending a patriotic militia will cover it with an impenetrable aegis. Partial injuries and occasional mortifications we may be subjected to, but a million of armed freemen, possessed of the means of war, can never be conquered by a foreign foe. To any just system, therefore, calculated to strengthen this natural safeguard of the country I shall cheerfully lend all the aid in my power."

Barlow grimaced. He had been in the regular army too long to put much faith in the militia. While it was true that he had admired the fighting prowess of the Tennesseans that his regiment, the Thirty-ninth, had fought alongside at the Battle of Horseshoe Bend, he didn't agree with Jackson that a "patriotic militia" was sufficient to protect the republic with an "impenetrable aegis." He wasn't sure Jackson really believed it, either. Yet no politician who hoped to earn the support of the people could come right out and support a stronger standing army. So the army would remain as it had been—a few thousand officers and men scattered thinly across the nation as garrisons of forts and arsenals.

"It will be my sincere and constant desire to observe toward the Indian tribes within our limits a just and liberal policy," said Jackson solemnly, "and to give that humane and considerate attention to their rights and their wants which is consistent with the habits of our Government and the feelings of our people."

These words had Barlow wondering all over again what task Jackson and Eaton had in mind for him involving his friends, the Cherokees. Attention to their rights and wants consistent with the feelings of our people? That meant the tribes would have no rights, nor would their wants be attended to.

"The recent demonstration of public sentiment inscribes on the list of Executive duties, in characters too legible to be overlooked, the task of reform, which will require particularly the correction of those abuses that have brought the patronage of the Federal Government into conflict with the freedom of elections, and the counteraction of those causes which have disturbed the rightful course of appointment and have placed or continued power in unfaithful or incompetent hands. ...."

Barlow was not all that familiar with Washington politics, but he had heard that Jackson had earned many enemies through his determination to do away with the civil servants who had established themselves, more or less permanently, in their offices since the time of Thomas Jefferson. He claimed that they put their own interests before those of the people, while they warned that his true intent was to fill the bureaucracy with his cronies.

"...A diffidence, perhaps too just, in my own qualifications will teach me to look with reverence to the examples of public virtue left by my illustrious predecessors," said Jackson, "and with veneration to the lights that flow from the mind that founded and the mind that reformed our system. The same diffidence induces me to hope for instruction and aid from the coordinate branches of the Government, and for the indulgence and support of my fellow citizens generally. And a firm reliance on the goodness of that Power whose providence mercifully protected our national infancy, and has since upheld our liberties in various vicissitudes, encourages me to offer up my ardent supplications that He will continue to make our beloved country the object of His divine care and gracious benediction."

He was finished. The crowd roared its approval. The address had been short—by Barlow's calculation, not longer than ten minutes in duration—but it had been a good speech, chaste and patriotic and reassuring.

Chief Justice John Marshall rose to administer the oath of office. Looking quite solemn and thoroughly dignified, Jackson laid one hand upon a Bible, raised the other, and repeated after the chief justice, swearing that he would faithfully execute the office of president, and that he would preserve, protect and defend the Constitution. The oath taken, he kissed the Bible and shook hands with Marshall. The crowd exploded into a delirium of joy, and Jackson turned to face the multitudes and bow humbly. It was, thought Barlow, a nice touch. During the campaign, Jackson had consistently portrayed himself as a man of the people—the man who would wrest the reins of power out of the hands of the American aristocracy (which John Quincy Adams, said Jackson partisans, so perfectly represented) and give them back to the citizens of the republic, where they rightfully belonged.

And then, suddenly, the crowd surged forward and broke through the first cordon of marshals and dragoons at the foot of the portico, rushing toward their hero. Jackson stood his ground, but Barlow didn't. He rushed forward, very nearly colliding with Chief Justice John Marshall in all his gray eminence, and taking the liberty of clutching the arm of the president.

"You must retire at once, Mr. President," said Barlow firmly.

"They mean no harm," replied Jackson confidently.

"A mob doesn't know its own strength. Please, sir."

Several men reached them, their faces illuminated with the ecstasy of adulation, their hands groping for Jackson, and Barlow moved to block their way. He was jostled roughly, and pushed back even more roughly. "Stand back," he warned, slipping a hand under his coatee to grasp the butt of the pistol Major Donelson had given him, and with the major's words ringing in his ears. If there really was a plot to do harm to the new president, this would be a perfect opportunity for the conspirators.

Several other officers and aides had surrounded Jackson, and Barlow heard the president, slightly annoyed, saying "Yes, yes, all right, I'll go. Just unhand me, sir!" He threw a quick glance over his shoulder and saw that the president was being hurried into the Capitol building, encompassed by a protective phalanx of men. Barlow followed in their wake, and didn't relax until the heavy doors were shut behind them; his last glimpse of the Portico was of a swarm of citizens, shouting and shoving and in general wreaking havoc, scattering the ladies who had, only moments before, been seated so primly, in their Sunday finest, in orderly rows of chairs.

Barlow and the others caught their breath, and then the United States marshal, Tench Ringgold, was informed by one of Jackson's aides that the new president had a public reception scheduled at the White House. The big, gruff Ringgold grimaced. Then he asked for ten minutes—and, casting a keen survey round the room, spotted Barlow.

"Captain, I require your assistance."

"You have it, Marshal."

Ringgold explained his plan. The Revolutionary War heroes in all their finery, as well as some of the other dignitaries, along with the dragoons, would depart out the north entrance and hurry away; hopefully this would fool some of the crowd outside into believing that the president was among them, and they would follow. A few minutes later, Jackson would exit by way of the west entrance, where Ringgold would have several horses waiting. One would be for Jackson, a second for the marshal, and the third for Barlow. They would hasten to the White House by a circuitous route, avoiding Pennsylvania Avenue and, with any luck, deliver the chief executive to his mansion without mishap.

"Sounds fine to me," said Barlow, "except for the last bit. Andrew Jackson will not sneak into the White House by a back alley. He'll insist on going straight up Pennsylvania, and the devil take the hindmost."

That was precisely what Jackson insisted on doing. He was still convinced that the people would do him no harm, accidentally or otherwise. Some of his aides were uncomfortable with Ringgold's plan, but Jackson adopted it instantly, with modifications. He did not put much stock in pomp and ceremony, and was quite willing to eschew a large entourage.

And so it was that a few minutes later Barlow found himself mounted at Jackson's side, with Ringgold on the other, and the three of them leaving Capitol Hill and entering Pennsylvania Avenue. The street was packed with pedestrians, carriages, men on horseback, wagons, even carts. The sidewalks were slow-moving rivers of humanity. All along the way people recognized their new president and cheered him. They fell in line behind the three horsemen, and before long a great procession was wending its way along the avenue to the White House. In spite of their number and their enthusiasm, the crowd was well behaved. Jackson was highly pleased. But Barlow never relaxed his vigil. He kept an eye peeled for a would-be attacker.

By the time they reached the White House, every room on the first floor was filled with revelers. There were townspeople and country folk, gentlemen and farmers, blacks and whites, men, women and children of every description. They were going in and out the windows as well as the doors. Jackson observed all of this activity with a calm eye. Not nearly as calm was Joseph Story, an associate justice of the Supreme Court, who met the new president upon his arrival. The short, stout Story was flustered.

"Mr. President, I must protest! This is an outrage! A rabble has invaded the presidential palace, sir! It is a most gross and vulgar display. The reign of King Mob has triumphed, and I fear there will be nothing left of this hallowed house when the day is done."

"A palace, you say?" asked Jackson. "If this be a palace, sir, then I have no business here."

He appeared to Barlow to be quite satisfied that Story huffed off, thoroughly offended. They dismounted, and Barlow and Ringgold were able to turn the duty of protecting the president over to a detail assigned to the White House. Nonetheless, both Barlow and the marshal kept a close eye on Jackson while the reception took place. It was utter pandemonium. Stewards carried out barrels of orange punch, which were carried off by gangs of revelers. Wine and ice cream were brought to the ladies. Glasses and china were broken, and muddy boot prints marred the furniture upholstery and the fine carpets laid out upon the once clean and polished floors. Jackson stationed himself near the south entrance, flanked by stern-faced soldiers, and endeavoring to shake the hand of everyone who wanted to meet him and wish him well. Barlow could see that he was exhausted, but the stalwart old soldier persevered, convinced, Barlow was sure, that he owed it to the people. He endured for several hours. Then, at four in the afternoon, he made good an escape and returned to his temporary quarters at Gadsby's Hotel. Barlow had seen quite enough of the spectacle at the White House, and went with him. Eaton was there, and asked Barlow if he intended to be at the inaugural ball that evening. Barlow said yes, and Eaton was pleased, telling him that the president would seek a few private words with him.

While Jackson went to dinner with Calhoun and several members of his cabinet, Barlow returned to the Langford boardinghouse. It appeared as though all of the other lodgers were out on the town at this hour, and Barlow sank wearily into a chair in the empty parlor, relishing the peace and quiet and isolation. Sarah found him there, and brought him a cup of tea.

"How did it go?" she asked him.

"It was … memorable." He remembered the pistol under his coatee, and pulled it out, placing the weapon on a nearby table.

Sarah stared at the pistol. "Why on earth did you carry that?"

Barlow explained that Major Donelson had loaned him the weapon, and warned him that an attempt might be made to harm the new president. "I know nothing more about it," he said, "and no such attempt was made. But both the president and Colonel Eaton wish to talk to me privately."

"On what subject?" asked Sarah warily.

"It has something to do with the Cherokees, I think."

"Oh, I see."

He peered at her. While many wives might have been thrilled that their husband would be so honored as to have the confidence of the president, Sarah could only remember that the last time her spouse had answered a call from Andrew Jackson it had taken him into the swamps of Florida, on a hazardous campaign against the Seminole Indians, and away from her arms for many lonely months.

"There has also been mention," continued Barlow, "of my being transferred to the War Department. How would you feel about living in Washington? You and your mother are reconciled now, and, if I may say so, she is growing old."

"Yes, she is," allowed Sarah, "but my first instinct is to remain at Fort Perry."

"I didn't know you liked it there."

"I don't," she admitted bluntly. "But violence follows Andrew Jackson, and I fear his presidency will be a very violent time, filled with intrigue and danger. Especially for you, Timothy, if you become one of his circle."

Barlow nodded and sipped his tea. He couldn't deny that what Sarah said was most probably true. But neither could he deny that he was an officer in the United States Army, and if his commander in chief required something of him, he was duty-bound to serve to the best of his ability, all personal considerations aside.

CHAPTER THREE

The inaugural ball was held in the elegant and spacious Washington Assembly Rooms located at C and Eleventh Streets. An immense flag was draped from the ceiling, and well-appointed tables covered with the very finest in refreshments lined the walls. Barlow noticed that there was no "rabble" here, as Justice Story would call them; it was a shame that the justice had chosen not to attend. But the vice president was there, along with his wife, Floride, as were most of the cabinet members and their wives, and the Jackson aides and their wives. Major Donelson was present and accounted for with his lovely bride Emily, the designated White House hostess, and she was a very graceful and vivacious presence. So was Colonel Eaton's wife, Peggy—indeed, Barlow thought that, with the exception of his own Sarah and Emily Donelson, Peggy Eaton was far and away the most attractive woman in the assemblage. He watched her with interest, having become acquainted, through her husband, with her notoriety in certain circles, and after a time he thought he could detect a definite coolness displayed by most of the other women where she was concerned. Sarah noticed it, too, and without any urging from Barlow or, as far as he knew, any knowledge of the details surrounding Peggy's failure to find acceptance in Washington's polite society, she made an effort to associate with Peggy Eaton. They did, after all, have something in common—they were both daughters of women who owned boardinghouses.

Sarah's initiative freed both Barlow and Eaton, and the two men soon met in the large and crowded room.

"It seems our wives may become friends," said Eaton, the relief evident in his voice. "My thanks to you, Captain. You and your wife have done us a great service."

"Sarah did it on her own. If she has anything it's a very strong sense of fair play."

"You can see what I mean about the other women. Mrs. Calhoun, there, is one of the ringleaders, I'm afraid. And Margaret Smith, over there, is yet another."

"Yes, I've noticed their reaction," said Barlow. The topic was an uncomfortable one for him, and he sought to change it. "I've mentioned your offer, regarding the War Department, to my wife, by the way."

"And what was her reaction?"

"She would prefer to remain at Fort Perry. And so would I, I think."

"I see." Eaton was clearly taken aback, and uncertain for a moment as to what his response should be. At last he said, "I needn't point out, I'm sure, that the opportunity for your advancement would be much enhanced if you accepted the transfer."

"If I'm to retire a captain, then I'll be satisfied," said Barlow, knowing that it was a lie, but hoping that he was convincing in the lie.

"Will you at least still speak to the president?"

"Of course. I am at his service."

Eaton nodded. "I will go and tell him as much." He glanced again at Sarah and Peggy, in animated conversation across the room. "But first, you must give me your word that you'll accept my dinner invitation. If you so desire, we'll not discuss business."

"We would be honored to accept your invitation."

Eaton drifted away. Barlow whiled away the time watching the people dance. Then dinner was served in the room downstairs, and was as splendid a feast as any Barlow had ever sat down to. Afterwards, the guests returned to the room upstairs and continued to dance. Barlow did a few turns with Sarah, even though he was quite self-conscious about it, painfully aware that he was an atrocious dancer, and made to appear all the more so by the grace and skill exhibited by his wife.

It was approaching midnight, and a great weariness had swept over Barlow. It had been a long and eventful day and he was ready to bring it to an end. He needed to find Eaton and tell the man that he and his wife were about to retire, and he'd just begun his search when Major Donelson found him.

"Captain, if you have a moment?"

"Certainly. And I am also still in possession of your pistol, sir. I will have it returned to you tomorrow."

Donelson made a dismissive gesture. "At your convenience. I'm just relieved that you did not have to put it to use today. The president would like a word with you in private."

"Of course."

Donelson led him to a door that gave access to a short hallway, at the end of which was a window and a steep flight of steps. To the right was another door, and upon this Donelson rapped his knuckles. A gruff and familiar voice bade him enter. Donelson opened the door and motioned for Barlow to enter.

"I will make sure your wife is made aware of your situation, Captain," said Donelson.

Barlow thanked him, and entered a small, spartan room. Andrew Jackson was the only other occupant. The old soldier sat slumped in a chair by a stove in which a warm fire crackled. A black cloak was wrapped around his bony shoulders. His features, thought Barlow, exhibited a deep and abiding weariness. He looked gaunt and pale, but when the eyes rose to fasten upon Barlow, the army officer could see that the spirit still burned hot and unquenchable within Old Hickory.

"Ah, Captain," said Jackson, his voice raspier than usual. "Would you care for a glass of port?"

"No thank you, Mr. President."

Jackson nodded and poured himself a glass from a bottle that stood on the floor beside the chair. "I don't blame you. Ghastly stuff. But I was told long ago that a glass a day would benefit my health. I am not sure that it has worked, but in my present state I can hardly afford to stop now." He smiled ruefully. "It has been a bloody long day."

"But a great day for the country, sir."

Jackson spared him a wry, sidelong glance. "Just being polite, Captain? I wasn't sure you approved of my ascension to the highest office in the land."

"Well, I didn't vote for you, General. But then, I didn't vote for your opponent, either."

Jackson threw back his head and laughed heartily. He laughed so long and hard that Barlow began to fear he might pass out from lack of breath.

"That's what I've always admired about you, Barlow. You're honest with me. I can rely on you to tell me how you feel, and you don't concern yourself with the consequences. Donelson is like that. Eaton, too. I try to surround myself with honest men, not sycophants."

"A wise decision, Mr. President."

"I understand Colonel Eaton spoke to you earlier today?"

"Yes, he did. He offered to transfer me to the War Department. I told him this evening that I was predisposed to decline the offer."

Jackson sipped his port without enthusiasm. "By the Almighty," he groused, "you'd think after thirty years I would develop a tolerance for this Godawful stuff." He fastened his piercing gaze upon Barlow. "I hope you will reconsider, Captain. And I hope you will agree to undertake for me a special mission that is of the utmost importance to the republic to which we have both devoted our lives."

Barlow sighed. Andrew Jackson hadn't changed. He'd never been a man who knew how to take no for an answer.

"It has to do with the Cherokees, I take it," he said. It was as noncommittal a response as he could come up with.

Jackson nodded. "That it does. Your friends. I'm sure they still think highly of you. During the Seminole War they displayed an inclination to follow you into Hell, if required."

"It's been many years, sir."

"It's not the Indian way to forget a friend, any more than they will forgive an enemy. In fact, I am told your good friend Mondegah has become a chief. I want you to go down there and see him."

"For what purpose, sir?"

Jackson leaned forward. "You know where I stand where the southern tribes are concerned."

"Yes, sir. It is your policy towards the Indians that has been the sole reason for any disagreement that might have existed between us in the past."

It had started, Barlow mused, in 1814, when Jackson had coerced the Creeks—not just the Red Sticks against whom he had fought the Battle of Horseshoe Bend, but the friendly ones as well—to sign the Treaty of Fort Jackson, which ceded 23 million acres of land to the United States. Some of this land had been previously claimed by the Cherokees as spoils of war in the aftermath of their earlier conflicts with the Creeks. But Jackson ignored their claims, and proceeded to have the Creek Cession surveyed by his crony, John Coffee. Though he had no authorization from Washington to do so, Coffee went ahead with a survey that was sharply criticized by the Cherokees, who were particularly incensed because they had fought faithfully at Jackson's side against the Red Sticks.

When the secretary of war, William Crawford, learned of Jackson's activities, he'd denounced the Treaty of Fort Jackson as well as the survey, and returned much of the disputed land to the Cherokees. This, in turn, had outraged Jackson, who refused a direct order from Crawford to remove white squatters from Cherokee soil. He then proceeded to bribe and threaten some Cherokee leaders into signing another treaty at the Chickasaw Council House in 1816, which took all Cherokee lands south of the Tennessee River. That agreement was ratified by the Cherokee national council, though many Cherokees cried foul, charging that Jackson had again used bribery, this time coupled with forgery, to achieve his ends.

Through it all, Barlow had thought this a dishonorable way to treat former allies. Despite their treatment at the hands of Old

Hickory, however, the Cherokees had once again taken up arms to fight alongside Jackson's troops in the campaign against the Seminoles. It was during this campaign that Barlow had earned the loyalty of the Cherokee warriors. They did not trust Jackson, but they trusted him completely. Why would they fight for Jackson considering what had happened in the past? The answer was simple. Not to do so would give Jackson the opportunity to brand the Cherokees as enemies of the United States, and give him ammunition in his schemes to seize all Cherokee land.

"White men and red," said Jackson gravely, "cannot live together in peace. This has been demonstrated time and time again, despite what those Northerners in their Indian-loving societies say—people who, I might add, have never lived cheek by jowl with the red man, as those who have tamed the frontier have done. It is impossible, too, to turn the red man into a white man, to 'civilize' him, as they say."

"Not to mention that it's wrong to rob the Indian of his ways," remarked Barlow.

"The only recourse for the tribes, therefore, short of annihilation, is removal."

Barlow grimaced. In 1817, Jackson had served as commissioner for another treaty of cession with the Cherokees, this one for a tract of land in Georgia. Included in the treaty were provisions for "removal." Some three thousand Cherokees had already moved west of the Mississippi; Jackson had not been the first president to recommend Indian removal—Thomas Jefferson had done likewise, and had prevailed upon some of the Cherokees of the Lower Towns to send a delegation westward to find a new home, with the result that the first group of Cherokees had moved. Jackson's treaty provided for the acquisition of land near them for any others who chose to make the trip. It was Barlow's understanding that some six thousand Cherokees had taken advantage of that offer, and abandoned their ancestral lands. In the years to follow, Jackson had used bribery and intimidation to acquire most of the land belonging to the Choctaws and the Chickasaws. These tribes had, for the most part, reconciled themselves to removing west of the Mississippi. Now, only the Cherokees remained—and Barlow was sure that Jackson, like so many Southerners, saw them as the last great impediment to the settlement of what was called the Dixie frontier.

"I am not an Indian-hater, Captain," said Jackson, reading the expression on Barlow's face. "It is true that as a child I adopted the prejudices of my elders. Few in the Waxhaws trusted the red man, for they had given us nothing but trouble. But as I grew older, and became better acquainted with the Indians, I came to understand that they are no worse—and no better—than we. After all, I want to remind you that I adopted a Creek orphan boy after a battle against the Red Sticks. I took him home, and named him Lincoyer, and raised him with as much affection and tenderness as I would my own flesh and blood."

"I heard he passed away recently," said Barlow. "My condolences, sir."

"Yes, he fell victim to consumption at the age of seventeen." Jackson's eyes grew bleak, and Barlow felt sorry for the old man, sensing that he was remembering his other personal loss—Rachel. "But the point is that I do not wish the Cherokees ill. It is a simple fact, however, that they is a conquered and dependent people. Their leaders do not do them justice. They are men who did not always have the best interests of their people at heart. It is true that I had to resort, on occasion, to bribery, to get the chiefs to sign my treaties. It is because they are an avaricious gang who would not do what in my heart I know is the best for their tribes. The object, Captain, is to remove them from harm's way. It is the only recourse other than extinction. And their extinction will be inevitable if they remain. All the more so because of the recent discovery of gold on the Cherokee lands."

"Gold? I wasn't aware. ..."

Jackson nodded. "Discovered last year near Dahlonega. Do you know where that is?"

"Yes, sir. Near New Echota, in the middle of the Upper Towns of the Cherokee."

"That is correct. A nugget was found in Ward's Creek by a slave, and before long the news was everywhere. And from that time on, removal of the Cherokees became inevitable. I have been told that the representatives of the people of Georgia intend to pass through Congress a law that will render null and void all Cherokee land claims within the borders of that state. It will also prevent any person with Indian blood in his veins from taking action in a court of law against a white man."

Barlow was shocked. "Surely you would not sign such a bill into law, Mr. President!"

Jackson's eyes flashed with anger. His lips thinned. Barlow realized he had fired Old Hickory's mercurial temper. It wasn't the first time he'd managed to do that. He braced himself for the storm he expected would follow.

"By the Eternal, sir, do not presume to tell me what I will or will not do!"

"So not only will you countenance the stealing of Cherokee land, you will take away their opportunity to legal recourse against the theft." Barlow shook his head, too disgusted to say more.

Jackson fumed, fighting to control his temper. "I have a grave responsibility, Captain. It is to keep this republic together, even as there are forces, which grow daily stronger, which seem ever more committed to tearing it apart. I will sign such a bill into law, yes. Not because I want to, but because it will be in the best interests of the United States."

"You would sacrifice the Cherokees, who have always fought alongside you, who have always responded to your call to arms, just to placate Georgia."

"Not just Georgia, but all of the southern states."

"I see," said Barlow bitterly. "I would prefer, sir, not to be a party to this, if you don't mind."

"Don't do it for me, Captain, but rather for your Cherokee friends. If they do not all remove to the territory west of the Mississippi, there will be bloodshed. Go, and convince them of the wisdom of a new beginning far away from the settlements of whites who consider them adversaries."

"Someone else would be better suited for that task, Mr. President."

Much to Barlow's surprise, a slow smile spread across Jackson's deeply creased face. "I see you haven't changed. You're mule-stubborn, Captain. But so am I. Take twenty-four hours to consider the assignment."

"As you wish," said Barlow. He didn't think twenty-four hours would make any difference, but he would humor the old man.

Jackson rose, with considerable effort, from the chair. "I should get back to the festivities and say my goodbyes. I will expect to hear from you tomorrow night, Captain."

"You will, Mr. President."

Barlow found his wife still in the company of Peggy Eaton. It was late, he told Sarah, and suggested that they go home. They left Peggy with a promise to come to dinner some night soon. As the Langford boardinghouse was but a few blocks away, they decided to forego one of the carriages for hire that loitered in front of the Washington Assembly Rooms and walked, arm in arm. Only then did Sarah ask him if he had had a private meeting with Andrew Jackson, and, if so, what it had been about. The query caught Barlow off guard. Rarely did Sarah inquire into his affairs, and seldom was she so blunt.

"He wants to send me on a mission to the Cherokees," he said. He was not in the habit of doing anything but telling Sarah the unvarnished truth.

Her expression, caught in the uncertain throw of light from a street lamp, told him that this was the realization of her worst fears.

"But I told him I wasn't inclined to accept the mission," he added hastily. "And I informed Colonel Eaton—well, I suppose that would be Secretary Eaton now—that I would prefer not to be transferred to the War Department."

She looked vastly relieved, and squeezed his hand. "Thank you, Timothy."

"Of course, as secretary of war, Eaton has the power to transfer me whether I want to be transferred or not."

"And if he does, what will you do?"

Barlow hesitated before answering. Sometimes he got the distinct impression that were he to inform her that he would resign his commission rather than do this or that it would be music to her ears. So he suspected that his response would be a disappointment to her.

"I would do my duty, and go where I was told. I'm a soldier, Sarah. I don't know anything else. I don't want to do anything else."

"I understand," she said quietly.

They walked the rest of the way in silence. Once in their room at the boardinghouse, Barlow shed his sword and cap and boots and coatee and heaved a deep sigh. It had truly been a long and eventful day, and he was heartily glad that it was drawing to a close. He glanced across the room at Sarah, who stood at the window, and he came up behind her, wrapping his arms around her slender waist, breathing deeply of her hair's fragrance, and then brushing his lips against the warm silken skin at the nape of her neck. She pulled away, twisting in his grasp, freeing herself, not violently, but with a grim determination, and he didn't try to hold on to her.

"I think I shall go see if my mother is asleep," she said, averting her eyes. "If not, I will tell her good night. I suppose ... I suppose we will be leaving soon, and it will be a long time before I see her again."

"Of course," said Barlow, keeping all emotion out of his voice.

She hurried out, still carefully avoiding his gaze. Once the door had closed behind her, Barlow sat down in a chair and sighed. He loved Sarah, and knew that she loved him. But somewhere along the way, something had happened. He wasn't sure what that something was, but the end result was painfully clear—the intimacy was gone from their marriage. More often than not, these days, she spurned his advances, albeit gently. He thought perhaps it had something to do with her inability to bear him children. Ever since the miscarriage she had been burdened with a profound sense of guilt, and no matter how often and earnestly he tried to assure her that it did not change his feelings for her one whit, it was as though she felt she had let him down in the worst possible way, in a way that could not be reconciled or forgotten. And it was true—he still desired her, as much now as he had in the beginning. But he had to smother that desire these days, and when thoughts of her in that way intruded he had to occupy his mind with other things.

He sat there for a while, brooding, and listening to the revelers who still filled the streets, even at this late hour. Andrew Jackson was president—and Barlow could not honestly say whether he was happy or alarmed. One thing was certain: things would never be the same. Old Hickory made things happen. Momentous things. Barlow's thoughts turned to the Cherokees. They had to be filled with foreboding at the prospect of a Jackson presidency. They had never fought at his side out of a sense of loyalty, but rather in self-interest, for they'd been wise enough to understand that the only way to placate Jackson and the frontiersmen he represented was to prove themselves staunch allies. Even so, in the long run this would change nothing. If anything, it had merely prolonged the inevitable. And the inevitable, mused Barlow, was about to descend upon his Cherokee friends. With a vengeance. He had not wanted to be a party to the victimization of the Cherokees. On the other hand, what kind of friend was he to turn his back on Mondegah and all the others? Wouldn't it be better that a friend brought them the bad news? Perhaps there would be some way he could soften the blow. And there were likely to be some Cherokees who would want to stand and fight. Perhaps he could convince them of the futility of standing against Andrew Jackson.

Barlow stripped off the rest of his clothes and went to bed. He'd taught himself to go to sleep as soon as he turned over on his right side. In spite of all the things that were troubling him, he slept soundly. That was another habit he had developed thanks to his years of service in the army. When you had the opportunity to sleep you didn't want to squander it.

He slept so soundly that he did not hear or feel Sarah come to bed. But in the morning, as usual, he awoke to see that, while she had lain beside him, she was now gone. As usual, there was fresh water in the pitcher. He poured some in the bowl, then splashed some on his face. He shaved, dressed, and went downstairs. Sarah was in the kitchen helping her mother with breakfast. She looked up at him and smiled, as though nothing were the matter. It was all an act, for Mrs. Langford's benefit, thought Barlow crossly, and he was tired of the acting.

"Breakfast will be ready in a few minutes, Timothy," said Mrs. Langford.

"I won't be eating here this morning, thank you," said Barlow briskly. "I must go to the White House and speak to the president."

"About what?" asked Sarah, a scared look on her face.

"I've changed my mind. I'm going to visit the Cherokees."

He turned away from her crestfallen expression and left the kitchen. Immediately he was stricken with guilt. He was just getting back at her. There were better ways of breaking the news to her.

He was met at the White House by Major Donelson, who took him upstairs at once to see Jackson. The mansion, thought Barlow, shocked, looked as though it had been hit by a hurricane. There was a pile of broken furniture piled up in the foyer. Servants were sweeping up refuse, cleaning up spills.

Old Hickory was in his office, a suite of three rooms on the south front, adjacent to the oval parlor. The first room, through which Barlow and Donelson passed, was a sitting room. Jackson was in the next chamber, the centerpiece of which was a long table that had been introduced into the mansion by Thomas Jefferson. In one corner was a small desk, and along the walls were assorted cabinets and bookcases. An oilcloth painted in a carpet pattern covered the floor. The silk curtains on the windows were crowned by gilded-eagle cornices. A Russian stove stood in another corner, in its sandbox, its pipe fed through a sheet of wood covering a fireplace. Through an open doorway in the opposite wall, Barlow could see the third of the three rooms—a rather small enclosure containing a narrow field cot and a water closet. He marveled at how quickly someone had worked to make the suite of offices functional for the new president.

Jackson was bent over the small desk, busily scribbling a letter. He did not seem to be aware of their presence until Major Donelson discreetly cleared his throat. For the first time Barlow wondered if, on top of all his other sundry ailments, the old general was growing hard of hearing.

"Ah, Captain, good morning to you, sir," said Jackson. He looked rested, and his voice was strong and steady. "You've come to give me your answer, I take it?"

"Yes, Mr. President. I'll go."

"Splendid. I thought you would. The major will prepare some letters of introduction for you, which will make clear to all concerned that you are acting on my authority. I ask of you only one thing, Captain."

"Yes, sir?"

"In your zeal to do right by your Cherokee friends, do not make any promises you know I would not want to keep."

Barlow had to smile. "I wouldn't dream of it, sir."

Chapter Four

Barlow felt sure he was only a few miles shy of the town of Athens, Georgia, but night was falling fast, and a few miles in the Blue Ridge mountains could take many hours to travel, so he selected a high mountain meadow about fifty yards west of the trail for his camp. It provided him with a stunning view of the mountains, their summits wreathed with cloud, the dark blue shadows of coming night in the valleys between them. They seemed to go on forever, rolling on to the horizon, and they were beautiful, much less severe than the craggy heights of upstate New York. For a fortnight he had been gazing at the mountains, first from the window of a stagecoach that had carried him from the capitol through Charlottesville, Virginia to Greensboro, North Carolina. There he had purchased a horse and saddle, using scrip provided him by Major Donelson at the president's behest, and traveled the rest of the way on horseback. So he had seen plenty of vistas as spectacular as the one that greeted his admiring gaze that evening. Still, it filled him with wonder. In the past month he had traveled from New York to Georgia, and he marveled now at the sheer magnitude of the republic, at its natural bounty and its grandeur. It was surely a land worth dying for. He could only hope that the Cherokees would not decide to die for it.

Tomorrow, upon arrival in Athens, he was to meet with William Tolliver, a highly respected judge who had, like Jackson, been a commissioner on several of the treaties hashed out with one or another of the southern tribes. Tolliver was supposedly an expert on Indian affairs, and one of the letters Barlow carried would introduce him to the judge. It would request that Tolliver give him any assistance he might require. Barlow didn't think he required any, but he felt obliged to at least let his presence and intentions be known to the judge. So he would stop off in Athens and then proceed to New Echota, where he hoped to find his friend Mondegah.

He built a small fire—while the early spring days had been warm and sunny since his departure from Washington, the nights were still quite cool. He unsaddled his horse and tethered it in some tall grass. Then he sat back and dined on strips of smoked venison and a couple of biscuits; he'd purchased the food from a settler two days back along the trail. His stomach full, he rolled up in his blanket, his head resting on the saddle, and dozed off watching the fire burn down.

A gunshot jerked him awake. The pearly light of dawn colored the eastern sky. His fire had long since died, and was now a mound of ashes. He noticed that his breath vaporized in the cold air, and that a fine dusting of frost lay upon the tall grass where the horse was tethered. The mountains he could see from the high meadow were thickly shrouded with clouds. But he spared little time admiring the scenery—there was noise coming from the direction of the trail, the sounds of a struggle, men shouting, a horse snorting in terror. Without a moment's hesitation, Barlow leaped to his feet, swept up his saber and pistol, and ran in that direction.

As he broke through the undergrowth, the scene on the road gave him pause. Two men were accosting another, who lay in the dirt, trying to fend off their blows. One of the assailants had a pistol, which he was using as a club, and the other wielded a knife, which the unarmed man on the ground was desperately trying to keep at bay. Another man was trying to catch up a handsome black stallion, which was snorting and shying away from his every lunge. Barlow immediately assumed that the man with the gun, the one with the knife, and the one cursing a blue streak as he tried to capture the stallion were all colleagues in crime, a gang of road bandits that had waylaid a solitary, unsuspecting traveler. Barlow had been warned back in Greensboro about the robbers one was all too likely to meet.

The man who was after the horse saw him first—he'd just gotten one of the dangling reins, but he took one look at Barlow, and at Barlow's weapons, and let go, turning to scamper into the brush with a warning shout to his cronies. But they were too busy trying to finish off their intended victim—until Barlow charged forward. Then the one with the knife whirled, brandishing the blade. With plenty of free time on his hands as part of the Fort Perry garrison, Barlow had polished his sword work, and with a flick of the wrist he'd cut the bandit's forearm, causing his adversary to drop the knife. Clutching at his wounded arm, the man backed away, giving Barlow time and space enough to launch a kick that sent the other assailant sprawling. When he got to his feet he froze, realizing that Barlow had him covered with the pistol.

"Please don't do anything foolish, gentlemen," said Barlow. "I prefer not to kill a man before breakfast. It ruins my appetite."

The road bandits exchanged glances, then glowered at Barlow—but they didn't try to jump him, or try to run, either. They just stood there, under the gun. Barlow spared their intended victim a glance.

He was a young man, well-dressed, though his clothes, at the moment, were covered with dirt and blood. So was his face, though Barlow could tell right away that the bleeding resulted from nothing more serious than a split lip. He was a bit bruised and battered, but did not appear to be too much the worse for all of that. Still, the polite thing to do was to ask.

"Are you badly hurt?" asked Barlow.

"No. No, I don't think so." The young man sounded shaken. He got to his feet, wiping at the blood on his chin and then looking at the smear of it on his hand as though he couldn't figure out what it was. He looked up at Barlow, then at the road bandits. "They . . . they got the jump on me. One of them actually took a shot at me." He sounded offended.

"We'll take them into Athens," said Barlow. "Turn them over to the constable there."

"No, let them go."

"Let them go?" Barlow was astonished. "They were trying to kill you, sir."

"But they failed, didn't they?"

"Wasn't trying to kill nobody," said the one who'd been brandishing the pistol. "Just wanted that horse is all."

"Shut up," said Barlow. "And what about the next unsuspecting traveler?" he asked the young man.

"We all have to look out for ourselves."

Barlow studied the road agents a moment. Did he really want to be saddled with the responsibility of herding these two ruffians all the way to Athens? The answer was no.

"Fine, then," he said curtly. "The two of you can go. But be warned. I'm going to make a report of this to the constable in Athens. I suggest you find a new vocation. This one is going to get you killed, or at the very least thrown in a jail for a very long time. And besides, you're just not very good at it."

"Yes, sir," said the wounded knife wielder. "Don't you fret now. We'll turn over a new leaf, I swear."

"Of course you will," said Barlow wryly. "Now get going."

They disappeared into the brush.

"I should have been on my guard," said the young man, with plenty of self-disgust. "I knew this road was dangerous. But I thought it would be Cherokee raiders that I'd have to deal with."

"I wasn't aware that the Cherokees were a threat to travelers."

"Rest assured, they are a threat to us all." The young man extended a hand. "I want to thank you for coming to my aid, sir. Allow me to introduce myself. My name is Claybourne. John Ashley Claybourne, at your service."

Barlow stuck the pistol under his waistband and shook the proffered hand. "Captain Timothy Barlow, Thirty-ninth Regiment of Infantry, United States Army."

"I am honored to make your acquaintance, Captain. Where are you bound, if I might ask?"

"To Athens. I'm to meet a Judge Tolliver there."

"Why, I know Judge Tolliver very well. I am from the Athens area myself. My father has recently relocated here from South Carolina."

"And what does your father do?"

"He is a planter, sir. I hope you will consent to be our guest during your stay in Athens."

"Well, I don't know. I won't be there long. I'm just…"

"I insist, for however long your stay may be. I would like to introduce you to my father. He will want to meet the man who prevented the theft of his prize stallion."

Barlow thought he detected a trace of bitterness in John Claybourne's tone, but he couldn't be sure of it. *And what about saving his son from a band of cutthroats?* Perhaps it was pride that prevented Claybourne from mentioning that particular debt. Or perhaps it was something else.

"Thank you," said Barlow. "I gratefully accept your invitation."

"Splendid. Just let me catch up Belarus and we'll be on our way."

"Fine. And I'll go put on my boots." Barlow realized that he was only half-dressed; his boots, coatee and cap remained in the camp he had departed in such haste a few minutes before.

It was early in the afternoon of yet another warm, sunny spring day when Barlow and Claybourne arrived at the latter's home. The house was a two-story affair flanked on either side by a one-story wing, and with a veranda, adorned with four fluted columns, running the full length in front. The structure was whitewashed, with blue shutters, and as he drew closer Barlow could see that it had only recently been erected—the cypress roof shingles were brand-new, and the mortar in the brick chimney had not had time to weather. The house was built on the summit of a gently sloped hill, and to the west of it, at the bottom of the slope, were various outbuildings and, beyond these, the slave quarters. They approached the residence up a wagon trace with fields of tobacco on either side, and Barlow counted about two dozen slaves working in the fields. Claybourne told him that there were over 240 acres in cultivation, and they were in the process of clearing another 160 acres to the north of the house.

When they arrived in front of the house a barrel-chested man in a rust-colored frock coat emerged. One of the sleeves of the frock coat was empty. Barlow could tell at once that this man had, at some time in the past, been a soldier. It was in the way he carried himself, and it was unmistakable.

"What happened to you, son?" asked the man gruffly. "One of Belle's whores rough you up a bit?"

"Father!" This came from a young woman who came out of the house just as the elder Claybourne spoke.

Barlow was struck by the woman's beauty. Her hair was as black as a raven's wing, her eyes as green as emeralds, her lips as red as a ruby. She was of medium height, slender in build, and moved with a gracefully light step. Her taffeta dress, pale yellow in color, was tastefully adorned with delicate lace. When she looked at Barlow their eyes locked, and somehow Barlow felt as though he had known this woman whom he had never met his entire life.

"Sorry, Rose," growled the elder Claybourne. "But you know I don't approve of your brother gallivantin' off to Shelbyville to waste his time and money on those … those loose women at Belle's bordello."

"From what I've heard," said John Claybourne, "you spent some time with Belle herself, in your younger days. She speaks fondly of those times, by the way."

"Watch your tongue, boy," warned Claybourne. "And tell me what happened to you."

With a sidelong glance at Barlow, John Claybourne said, "Belarus threw me. Captain Barlow here came along and gave me some assistance. I invited him to stay with us. He is here to see Judge Tolliver. Captain, may I introduce my father, William Claybourne, and my sister Rose."

"Sir. Miss."

With a smile that took Barlow's breath away, Rose executed a small curtsy. "Captain."

Claybourne switched his steely gaze to Barlow—and Barlow, by dint of great effort, managed to stop looking at Rose long enough to meet it squarely.

"Is that what happened, Captain?"

Barlow grimaced. He didn't appreciate being placed in the position of having to lie to his host, but on the other hand he was not inclined to show John Claybourne up to be a liar. Clearly, the relationship between John and his father was complicated, and Barlow's fervent desire was to stay out of it.

"Your son was laying in the road when I found him, sir," he said. Well, it wasn't exactly a lie. "I inquired after his well-being, that's all."

"I thank you, just the same," said Claybourne. "And of course you are welcome under my roof."

Barlow was about to reiterate to the elder Claybourne what he had earlier told the younger—that he did not wish to impose. But then he made the mistake of glancing at Rose again—she was still watching him in a very intense, speculative way that, for some reason, sent a tingling sensation down his spine—and he knew he had no choice but to accept the offer.

"I would be honored, sir."

"Fine, fine." Claybourne looked around. "Now where is that blasted boy? Jericho!"

A young slave came dashing around the corner of the house. "Yessuh, Massuh, I's right here."

"See to these horses. Captain, please come in."

Barlow stepped down out of the saddle, handed the reins to Jericho, and mounted the veranda. Watching every move he made, Rose waited until he was an arm's length away before giving him a faintly saucy smile and then, with a rustle of petticoats, whirled and preceded the men inside. Barlow found himself led into a downstairs parlor. The furniture was quite elegant by frontier standards. Clearly, Claybourne had done well for himself in South Carolina, and Barlow wondered what had compelled him to pull up stakes and start all over again in Georgia. He was offered a drink—crystal decanters, filled with port, sherry, brandy, whiskey, lined a side-board—and gladly accepted a glass of the latter. It was a fine bourbon, a mellow liquid flame that seared his throat and eased some of the tension of long travel out of his body. Claybourne bade him take a seat, and he eased his lanky aching frame onto one of the sofas with an audible sigh of relief, apologizing in advance for the trail-stained condition of his clothing.

"You've come a long way, then?" asked Claybourne, pouring himself a whiskey and sitting in a big armchair facing Barlow. Rose stationed herself behind his chair, so she could gaze unabashedly at the army captain without her father noticing, while John went to the sideboard to pour himself a drink, since his father had not offered to do so for him.

"From the capital city," said Barlow, nodding.

"Your business with Judge Tolliver is official?"

Barlow hesitated. His mission was not a secret one, and he did not want to be rude to his host, but he saw no practical reason for Claybourne to know the details of his task. The planter recognized Barlow's reluctance to reply, and smiled.

"Just idle curiosity, Captain. Nothing more sinister than that, I can assure you. You don't have to tell me. I'll warrant, though, that it has something to do with the Indians. The judge was, after all, a treaty commissioner at one time."

"Indians," muttered John. "When is the army going to send them packing? They're just in the way."

Barlow looked coolly at the younger Claybourne. "I believe we are the interlopers here, sir," he said. "In fact, in the first treaties between the Cherokees and the republic, the latter promised to keep white settlers off Indian land, and to use the army to do so, if necessary."

"But the truth of it is that they claim far more land than they have any use for," said Claybourne reasonably. "It is a waste of the forest and of the field, which God created for man's use."

"They use it," said Barlow. "They just use it differently than we do."

Claybourne shrugged. "Clearly, we see things differently."

"I fought with the Cherokees, when they allied themselves with the republic to put down the Red Stick uprising, and the Seminole threat. Without their help, things might not have turned out to our advantage. For me it's simply a matter of fair play. To remove them from their homeland seems to me an improper way to deal with friends and allies."

"Former friends and allies, perhaps. We've been having a spot or two of trouble with young Cherokee hotheads from the Upper Towns. Livestock killed or stolen. Fields burned. No one killed yet, that I know of. But things seem to be headed in that direction, I fear."

"I'll tell you what the problem is," said John truculently. "It's that man Worcester. He should be jailed. Or, better yet, hanged."

"John!" scolded Rose. "I wish you'd stop being so melodramatic."

"I'm serious," he shot back. "He's the one who is stirring up those young Cherokee bucks. He's a traitor to his own kind, that Worcester is!" Finishing off his drink, he returned to the sideboard to pour himself another.

"Who is Worcester?" Barlow asked Claybourne.

"A missionary. The Reverend Samuel Worcester, sent down here by the American Board of Foreign Missions. He is publishing a newspaper for the Upper Towns. It's called *The Phoenix.* In it, he and a fellow by the name of Elias Boudinot editorialize against the attempts by the state of Georgia to remove the Indians, and he chastises the government in Washington for failing to keep settlers and gold hunters off Cherokee lands." He glanced at his son. "Rumor has it that Worcester and Boudinot go even further in private, urging young Cherokee warriors to commit the crimes I have previously mentioned."

"I see," said Barlow.

Claybourne put down his glass. "But enough of this unpleasant talk. Supper will be ready soon, and I'm certain you'll be wanting to freshen up before sitting down to table. I will have one of the servants bring fresh water to your room, and direct Jericho to bring your belongings to you. Rose, dear, would you be so kind as to show the captain to the guest room?"

"It would be my pleasure," said Rose.

"Thank you again for your kind hospitality," said Barlow, rising.

"It's the least we can do for someone who offered to render aid to my son here, and you are welcome here for as long as you desire to stay." Claybourne glanced sidelong at John. "Perhaps tomorrow you would like to take a ride around the property. Your services may be required again, as John seems unable to keep his seat while on horseback."

John just glowered at his father and knocked back another glass of whiskey.

"Thank you for the offer," replied Barlow, "but I should ride into Athens first thing in the morning and meet with Judge Tolliver." He bowed slightly. "If you will excuse me?"

He followed Rose out of the parlor and up the main staircase— trying very hard not to fixate on the mesmerizing sway of her hips. During the ascent she looked back at him, a smile of delight on her face, and he smiled back dutifully, half-dazed by the faint fragrance of lavender that she trailed behind her. At the top of the stairs she gestured and said, "Right this way, Captain," and led him to a door, opened it, and breezed right on inside. Barlow paused one step across the threshold, aware of the impropriety of remaining long in a room alone with an unmarried woman, especially when that room was a bedroom. The chamber was as well appointed as the rest of the house.

"I hope this will suit you, Captain," she said, from all the way across the room at one of the windows. "This room has a very nice view of the hills to the north." She held the curtains aside, an invitation for him to draw closer and view the scene she had just described.

Barlow didn't dare budge. "These are by far the best quarters I've enjoyed for a very long time, Miss Claybourne, thank you."

"Oh, please, not Miss Claybourne. Call me Rose."

"Well, I'm not sure I should. ..."

"Nonsense. I insist." She let the curtains fall and came towards him. "I should warn you. I usually have my way. Just ask my father if you don't believe me."

"I believe you."

"Is there anything else I can do for you?"

"Urn, no, thank you."

"Then I shall see you at supper." She brushed past him, and her fingers touched his hand, and Barlow was sure that incidental contact was by design rather than accident.

Once the door had closed behind her, Barlow remembered to breathe.

Supper consisted of pork and lamb and fresh vegetables, bread with jam, and blackberry cobbler for dessert. They sat at a long table in the dining room, and the table was covered with a snowy-white cloth and some excellent English china. Fresh flowers around a silver candelabra formed the centerpiece. The walls were adorned with family portraits, and Barlow detected a definite family resemblance. Claybourne informed him that his great-great-grandfather had come to the Carolinas as one of the first settlers. His great-grandfather had served with distinction in the French and Indian Wars. His grandfather had fought in the revolution. And his father had been a distinguished representative for the state of South Carolina in the United States House.

"Then you must have been reluctant to leave the land of your forefathers," said Barlow.

"Not at all," replied Claybourne. "I do not put much stock in all of that, really." He scanned the portraits. "I tend to look ahead, not behind. It's the future that matters to me, Captain. The past is past. If I have my way, the Claybourne name will be as highly respected in Georgia as it already is in South Carolina." He looked down the table at his son—and grimaced; Barlow doubted that Claybourne was all that sanguine about the future, especially with a son for whom he seemed to have nothing but contempt. "And what about yourself, Captain? Where is your home?"

"Well, I was born in Philadelphia. But my home, I suppose, would be with my regiment. The Thirty-ninth Infantry."

"So you intend to make the army your career."

"I'm not cut out for anything else, sir."

"It's refreshing to meet a young man who knows what his talents are and where his interests lie. As opposed," said Claybourne, with a telling look in his son's direction, "to those who waste their youthful energy in frivolous pursuits, whose only talent seems to be a knack for debauchery."

"Oh, Father," sighed Rose, "I do wish you wouldn't be so hard on Johnny."

John Claybourne threw his napkin on the table and got up so quickly that he knocked his chair over. "I've had enough of this for one night," he said, and left the room with angry strides.

"My apologies, Captain," said Claybourne, with more than a trace of sadness. "I sometimes let my disappointment get the better of me."

Barlow wasn't sure what to say. Rose came immediately to his rescue.

"Perhaps the captain would enjoy a walk in the garden? I know I would. The nights this time of year are so lovely."

Barlow didn't want to be left alone to carry on a conversation with Claybourne, so he accepted with alacrity. He thanked the old man for his hospitality, rose and went round the table and extended his arm; she took it with delight and they left the dining room.

The garden was behind the house, a serpentine walkway of bricks that took them past flower beds which Barlow surmised were the handiwork of the young woman accompanying him. The fragrance of flowers filled his nostrils—or was it the heady fragrance of Rose Claybourne that beguiled him?

"I want to apologize for my father and brother," she said softly.

"There is no need for apologies, Miss ... I mean Rose."

She smiled up at him. "Why, thank you, Captain."

"See? You *can* teach an old dog new tricks."

54

"You're not old!"

Quite a bit older than you, thought Barlow. He wondered at her age—but of course it would be impolitic to ask. He suspected that she was no more than twenty years old, and probably younger than that.

"That's kind of you to say."

"But I feel I must explain. My poor brother has found it so very difficult to follow in our father's footsteps. From earliest childhood it seems he's never been able to do anything to Father's satisfaction. It's so very unfair. My heart hurts for him every day. Eventually Johnny gave up trying to meet Father's standards. He rebelled, and now all he seems to care about are racehorses and loose women and gambling. All of that infuriates Father, of course. That's why Johnny does it, I'm sure."

"I hope they will be able to resolve their differences someday."

"Mmmm, yes," she murmured. "Someday. So tell me, Captain— are you married?"

"Yes. For ten years now."

"What a lucky woman your wife is. Children?"

"We have no children."

Something in his voice warned her that this was a topic he preferred not to open for discussion.

"Father thinks I should marry soon," said Rose, and it was obvious by the tone of her voice that she didn't agree. "He says I could have any man I wanted."

"I expect you have plenty of young men courting you."

She laughed. "Oh, yes. I won't deny that. The problem is, I don't want any of them. Father says I'm foolish to talk about love. He doesn't think love need have anything to do with it. He says that if I wait for my 'true' love I shall probably have to wait forever. Or, when I do find him, he'll be spoken for. As far as my father is concerned, marriage is a business arrangement."

"And your mother? Where is she?"

She turned her face away from him—to conceal, he assumed, the anguish his thoughtless query had caused.

"She died when I was young. An outbreak of cholera in Charleston claimed her life. That was years ago and I must confess I still miss her terribly."

"I shouldn't have brought it up. I'm sorry."

She squeezed his arm. "It's all right. Really it is."

"I disagree with your father," said Barlow. "Love *does* matter."

She stopped walking and turned, standing very close to him, her face upturned. "It must be awful to be separated for so long from the one you love. I don't think I could stand you being away for weeks on end. I think I would go insane with loneliness and longing."

Barlow thought about his parting from Sarah; it had not been on the best of terms, and he felt guilty for having acted the way he'd acted, simply because she had spurned his advances the night before. And he was too ashamed to tell Rose that in fact he'd been relieved to leave Sarah—or, more particularly, their strained relationship—behind in Washington.

"I'm sure you must miss her terribly," said Rose.

"Yes. Yes, of course."

"Will you be able to return to her soon, then?"

"I'm not sure how long I'll have to remain in Georgia."

"Oh, Georgia's not so bad, Captain; really it isn't. Rather more hot than you're accustomed to, I suspect, and a little on the wild side still."

He looked at her, wondering if he was reading correctly the meaning of her words. An inner voice cried out a warning. *Watch yourself, mister*, it told him. *There is something about Rose Claybourne that is bewitching. Something that makes it so easy for a man to go down the wrong path.* It wasn't that she intended to be this way, Barlow was certain. It wasn't something she had worked to develop; no, her mesmerizing appeal was wholly natural. She'd been born with it, and he doubted that many men would be able to resist her charms.

"I'm … sure I'll manage," he replied.

"I'm sure you will, Captain." She continued walking, and since his arm was still captured by hers, he was obliged to fall in alongside her. "Must you really go into Athens tomorrow? Why not stay here with us for a day or two and recuperate from your long journey?"

"I wouldn't feel right imposing on you and your family that way."

"It wouldn't be an imposition, silly. We get so few visitors here, you realize. Especially brave and dashing army officers."

He smiled. "You flatter me. Regrettably, though, I really must continue on my way in the morning."

Rose Claybourne pouted, and Barlow found his resolve crumbling.

"Then you must at least promise me that you'll come back by before you leave Georgia," she said sternly.

"Well, I..."

"Come now, Captain. I would just like to see you once more. Is that asking too much?"

Barlow thought that it probably was—but he knew it wasn't in him to deny her request. "Very well, then," he said. "I promise I'll visit again when my job here is done."

She stood up on tiptoe and gave him a quick peck on the cheek, and the caress of her soft warm lips against his skin made Barlow blush furiously. He thanked God it was night.

"I'm going to hold you to that," she whispered. Then she stepped back, released his arm, and with a satisfied smile turned towards the house. "We'd better go back inside," she said. "Before Father comes looking for us."

She led the way, and all he could do was follow, and she looked back once, her eyes bright, a saucy curl to the corners of her mouth, and her ruby lips slightly parted—and Barlow decided he would have fled the Claybourne plantation that very day had there been any way he could do so without offending his hosts.

Chapter Five

For a town that a few years earlier hadn't even appeared on the map, Athens had grown by leaps and bounds. Despite the fact that most of its wide streets were still dirt, there was one that had cobblestones for a length of several blocks. It was the one that Barlow rode in on, accompanied by the elder Claybourne. It led into the town square, which was encompassed by substantial buildings, with a handsome, steepled courthouse shaded by majestic oaks as its centerpiece. The streets were bustling with people, the shops with commerce. Barlow lost count of the number of structures that were under construction. Clearly Athens was thriving, and its inhabitants had great hopes for the future. But he couldn't escape the fact that if these people were to prosper, the Cherokees who lived in the forests and mountains that surrounded Athens would have to suffer.

Claybourne led him to a house one block off the square, accessible by a narrow lane lined on both sides with offices and homes. The Tolliver office and home were included in the same building, and a prominent sign with elegant script out front informed the public that this was the workplace of a very important man. Only important men had such signs. The ringing of a brass bell dangling from the frame of the front door summoned an elderly black man clad in a well-tailored black suit, his gray hair close-cropped, his expression amiable, his eyes noncommittal. Claybourne inquired if the judge was in. The black man recognized Claybourne, and did not hesitate in replying that, in fact, he was, and would be highly pleased to see Massuh Claybourne. They were escorted into a richly appointed parlor, where they waited, but not for long.

Judge Tolliver was a tall, florid, beefy man. He had considerable presence, and carried himself like a man who understood his elevated station in life, and all the responsibilities that went with it. He greeted Claybourne with a reserved warmth, and when introduced to Barlow, scrutinized the army officer gravely even as they shook hands. The black man was standing in the doorway, and the judge gestured in his direction as he asked his guests if they cared for a libation.

"Some other time, Benjamin," said Claybourne. "I've come merely to introduce you to the captain, who was kind enough to be my guest last evening. As I understand it, he has a letter of introduction to you from the president, but as I was coming into town anyway on some other matter..." Claybourne shrugged.

He took his leave, after agreeing with Judge Tolliver that they would have to meet again soon over supper, and after Claybourne had repeated his invitation to Barlow to stop by the plantation before he left Georgia. Barlow said that he would. His head told him that he would be better off staying as far as possible from that place—or, more particularly, from Rose Claybourne. His heart told him that he had no choice in the matter.

She had not been there that morning, when he had taken his leave; Claybourne extended her apologies to him, saying that she was feeling a bit under the weather, and was remaining in her room. Of course, her absence resulted in his thoughts being completely occupied by her, and he had to wonder if that had been her intent. Was she really ill? Was she so sorry to see him go that she could not trust herself to maintain her composure as he took his leave? Or was she simply indifferent to his coming and going now? He could hardly accept that the latter would be the case, considering the interest she had taken in him the night before, but then he'd never pretended to understand the first thing about women. They were, from his perspective, unfathomable. So was the feeling he'd had as he rode away from the Claybourne place—a tightness in his chest that made him extremely uncomfortable. He knew it was wrong—he was a married man, after all—but he missed her. She was so full of life, so alluring, so much the woman-child, that most fascinating of all females. And she was so dangerous—that was part of the allure, too. So, in spite of his best judgment, he knew he would make every effort to visit the Claybourne plantation once more, if only to catch a last glimpse of her. He could still feel her soft lips and warm breath on his cheek...

Barlow turned down the offer of a drink from Judge Tolliver, who in turn dismissed the black man. The doors closed, leaving them alone in the parlor, and Barlow produced the letter written by Andrew Jackson. Tolliver accepted it, nodded, and went over by the window for better light by which to read it. Barlow waited patiently until the judge had finished and turned back to face him.

"So it's about the Cherokee problem, is it? I should have suspected. It says here you are here for the president to assess the situation. He trusts that I, as one who is knowledgeable regarding the southern tribes, will be able to provide you with any information you might need."

"Yes, sir. I'm here to listen to both sides. As soon as I'm done in Athens, I intend to proceed to New Echota."

"It's quite simple, really," said Tolliver briskly. "The Cherokees—those who have not already seen the light of reason and moved westward—are determined to stay. And we are just as determined that they must go. White men and red cannot live together in harmony, Captain. I would think that you'd understand that. You fought the Red Sticks at Horseshoe Bend, did you not?"

"That I did, sir."

Tolliver nodded. "I thought so. I recall reading about you. You were one of the heroes of that conflict. And did you also serve with Jackson in Florida?"

"Yes, sir."

"Then you know something about the Indians. Enough, at least, to know that they must go."

"I'm told there's already been some confrontations."

"Yes. A few Cherokee renegades have stolen horses, burned crops, that sort of thing. And just a fortnight ago, a farmer who lives but a half-day's ride to the north shot and killed a Cherokee buck who was lurking around his place."

"I didn't know it had gone that far. What will happen to the farmer?"

"Happen to him?" Tolliver frowned. "What do you mean?"

"Is he to be charged with any crime?"

"Certainly not."

"But how do you know what the Indian's intentions were? Perhaps he meant no harm. Perhaps he was only out hunting."

Tolliver snorted. "Or perhaps he was out picking flowers. Come now, Captain. He was up to mischief, and he was killed before he could undertake it."

"I see," said Barlow.

"You don't approve."

"Not entirely, no, sir. If his intentions were peaceful, the Cherokees will expect justice to be done. And if we don't see it done, they might take it upon themselves."

"And then we'll have a full-scale shooting war on our hands," said Tolliver.

"Exactly."

"I would welcome it," said Tolliver bluntly. "At least it would resolve this business, once and for all. The Cherokees would have no recourse but to move."

Barlow nodded. "If I'm not mistaken, Judge, the treaty between the United States and the Cherokee Nation which is currently in force does not require them to move. In fact, it gives them the choice to go or stay. And that, by implication, recognizes their rights to this land."

"The State of Georgia," said Tolliver stiffly, "does not see fit to recognize the authority of that treaty, or any treaty made by the national government with Indians residing within our borders."

Barlow stared at him, not certain that he had heard the judge correctly. "You mean you would refuse to accept as binding a treaty made by the United States?"

"In this instance, that's precisely what I mean. It should be up to the individual states to determine what agreements its citizens will be required to adhere to."

"It's written in the Constitution, Judge—the right of the federal government to negotiate treaties with foreign entities."

"The Cherokees cannot be treated as though they were a foreign nation. As they reside in Georgia, they are subject to Georgia law. And I hardly think, Captain, that you need lecture *me* on the Constitution. I would remind you that two of our most prominent founding fathers, Thomas Jefferson and James Madison, penned the Kentucky and Virginia Resolutions, which clearly stated the inalienable rights of the individual states to nullify any federal law that was deemed injurious to its citizens. I think we can safely apply that same rule to a treaty."

Barlow was flabbergasted. As far as he was concerned, what Tolliver proposed was nothing short of treason. But he held his temper in check and exercised tact.

"My apologies, sir. I did not intend to lecture you."

Tolliver nodded his acceptance of the apology. "I only hope you will be able to persuade the Cherokees, as the envoy of their old friend, Andrew Jackson, that it is in their best interests to go. And go soon. Our patience is running thin. Every day I see a new family arrive in Athens, all of their belongings packed in a wagon, their eyes set on a new land where they can make a new beginning. The best land still available is currently occupied by the Indians. We must have that land, Captain, and sooner rather than later."

"And the gold, too."

"Personally, I am not at all interested in that aspect of it, except to the extent that gold hunters will not be deterred from seeking their fortune just because that which they seek happens to be on land held by the Indians. Soon enough they will be coming by the hundreds, if not the thousands, and then, I think I can guarantee you, sir, there will be more shed blood. It is an irreversible tide, Captain, and anyone who tries to stand against it will be swept away."

Barlow decided it was a safe bet that Judge Tolliver spoke for the vast majority of whites in the region. There was no reason, then, to make further inquiries in Athens. And if this man, who supposedly believed in the law, in a justice that was blind, could long for a war that would drive the Cherokees out by force of arms, there was no hope for a reconciliation. Suddenly, Barlow felt the urgency of reaching Mondegah and warning his old friend of the storm that was gathering.

"I will trouble you no further," he said. "Thank you for your time, Judge."

But Tolliver wasn't finished with him.

"I know the president fairly well from the time we served together on a treaty commission. I am confident that he feels as I do—that it is in everyone's best interest that the Cherokees be removed. Now that he is our chief executive he has the power to make that happen. Is that his intention?"

"I do not know the president's intentions, sir. He did not see fit to confide them in me."

It wasn't exactly true—Jackson had made it plain enough that he thought the Cherokees needed to go. But Barlow wasn't about to act as the president's proxy and make commitments that Old Hickory might be called upon to honor.

"Well, when you return to Washington and report your findings to him, be sure to tell him, for me, that Georgia is watching. What he does to resolve this Cherokee problem will plainly indicate to us whether we now have a man in the White House who will respect the rights of the states."

"I will be sure to tell him, sir." *Even though*, mused Barlow, *it will be telling him something he doubtless already knows.*

He rode all day towards New Echota, all too aware that the killing of the Cherokee had made his task more dangerous. He had served with about one hundred Cherokee warriors in the campaign against the Seminoles. Of those, how many would remember him on sight, after so many years had passed? He was fairly sure that he would be hard pressed to know many of the young warriors beside whom he had fought in that long-ago war. To most of the Cherokees he was an unknown quantity. All they would know for certain about him was that he was a white man, a bluecoat soldier, and they would have no reason to expect him to be a friend. In fact, if everything Barlow had heard was true, they would have plenty of reason to suspect that he was up to no good. Bloodshed usually begat more bloodshed, so he had to be conscious of the fact that the first he might know of a Cherokee's presence could be when he was under attack.

Most of the day was spent traversing Cherokee land, and yet he saw no one. As a precaution he built no fire for his night camp. A further precaution entailed moving his camp about fifty yards deeper into the woods from where he'd settled down before darkness fell. That way, if he was being watched by someone intent on sneaking in on him under cover of the night, he would have a surprise in store for him. He spent the night sitting up with his back against the trunk of a large pine, dozing off now and then, sleeping lightly, so that the slightest movement or sound awakened him. All of those movements and sounds, though, turned out to be ordinary elements of night in a southern forest, the hoot of an owl on the hunt, the distant lament of a coyote on a high mountainside, the whicker of his nearby horse after, perhaps, catching the faint scent of bear or panther or some other predator on the night breeze.

The next morning, however, he picked up a companion. It was a solitary Cherokee, mounted on a pony, shadowing him from deep in the woods but making no effort to conceal his presence. Barlow stuck to the wagon trace and did not try to approach the Indian. He did not try to hide the fact that he knew the Indian was there, but neither did he demonstrate that the man's presence bothered him in any way.

An hour or so later he noticed that he had another shadow—another Cherokee warrior, also mounted, but on the other side of the road. Barlow worried more than ever that their intentions were hostile. But he forged ahead. It didn't even occur to him to turn back. He felt as though the fate of his old friend Mondegah, and hundreds of other Cherokees, women and children among them, depended on his getting through to New Echota.

A short while later he took a bend in the road and checked his horse sharply. There were four Cherokee warriors, all mounted, arrayed in front of him, waiting for him. He looked to his left and then to his right. The Cherokees who had been shadowing him moved forward through the trees to join their brethren. Their bows and long rifles remained sheathed, but Barlow could take only small comfort in that. For the first time Barlow began contemplating the possibility that he would have to fight the Cherokees. It was something that hadn't even occurred to him when he'd chosen to accept the presidential mission, or all during his trek south. Still, he felt no animosity towards these six braves who posed so clear a threat to him. Their tribe had been backed into a corner, and they were fighting for their very survival.

He was somewhat surprised when they did not charge him en masse. Instead, one of the warriors advanced, holding his pony to a walk. He was older than the other men, and Barlow wondered if he might be one of those who had fought in Florida. If so, Barlow could not remember his face, much as he wanted to. The warrior stopped his horse when it was nose to nose with Barlow's and examined the army officer gravely.

"I am Attakulla," he said, in English.

Barlow knew he was expected to identify himself, and state his reason for being there, and wasted no time in doing so.

"My name is Barlow. I have come to speak to Mondegah. He and I fought together against the Seminoles."

Attakulla's eyes narrowed. "You are the White Warrior?"

"Some called me that, yes."

"You have come from the camp of our enemies."

Barlow nodded. "You mean Athens. Yes, I was there. The president of the United States has sent me to learn all I can of the difficulties down here."

"Then you have much to learn," said Attakulla. "Come. I will take you to Mondegah."

Barlow followed as Attakulla turned his pony and rode back to the warriors. As Attakulla spoke briefly to his companions in their

own tongue, Barlow realized that he had forgotten nearly everything he'd learned, fifteen years ago, of the Cherokee language.
The younger braves looked at Barlow with a mixture of curiosity
and wariness. White Warrior or not, they did not trust him, nor
could he blame them.

As they neared New Echota, Barlow found that the wagon trace
began to run parallel to a river, and that on either side were farms
that looked every bit like those of white settlers. Their well-tended
fields were producing what appeared to be healthy crops of corn,
tobacco, oats, indigo and potatoes. There was even a peach orchard
or two. And New Echota could have been mistaken for a white settlement—with sturdy log cabins lining wide dirt streets. In the center
of the town was the octagonal meeting hall, and around the square
were various enterprises—a blacksmith shop, a store, a school and
the office of *The Cherokee Phoenix*, which Barlow had heard about at
the Claybourne supper table. The Cherokees, he noticed, were clad
in a way that combined their traditional garb and those of the white
man—stroud trousers and a beaded hunting shirt were common
attire for men, and for every woman who wore a calico or deer-
skin dress there was another who apparently preferred gingham.
Barlow was struck by how much things had changed since his last
visit among the Cherokees.

Their arrival drew a crowd toward the center of town, so that
by the time Barlow was dismounting in front of the meeting house
there were nearly a hundred men, women and children congregated. He searched the crowd for a familiar face, and thought he
recognized a few of the men. Some of the people stared at him,
silent, a few even sullen; others engaged in excited conversation
that Barlow could only assume centered on him and speculation
as to his reasons for coming. And then Mondegah arrived—the
crowd parted to let him pass—and the aging warrior smiled
with delight at the sight of Barlow, and extended his arms. They
embraced.

"Timothy Barlow," said Mondegah, nodding. "It is good to see
you again."

"It's good to see you, my friend. You haven't changed much."

"Yes, I have." Mondegah looked about him. "As you have surely noticed, *much* has changed. But come, we will go to my home. It is not far. Walk with me."

According to what Barlow had heard, Mondegah was the head chief in New Echota, but his cabin was a modest affair, no larger than or better than or different in any discernible way from most of the others in the Cherokee town.

They sat at a table in the common room, and Mondegah's wife discreetly left. herding two children, a boy of about twelve and a girl a few years younger, out with her, leaving the men alone. Mondegah offered Barlow some tea. Barlow declined. The Cherokee chieftain explained that he had acquired a taste for the beverage a few years before, and liked it sweet. Barlow watched with amusement as Mondegah dropped chunks of brown sugar into the tea before drinking it. Only after he'd doctored the drink to his liking did Mondegah ask Barlow what had brought him to New Echota.

"The new president sent me. Andrew Jackson wants me to use the influence he thinks I have with you and your people to persuade you to abandon these lands and move west, to join the other Cherokees who have established new homes along the river they call the Arkansas."

"So you have come to do Sharp Knife's bidding?" Mondegah seemed surprised.

"No. I've come mainly to see for myself what has been occurring here," replied Barlow. "I have heard many rumors. They made me concerned for my friends, the Cherokees."

Mondegah nodded. "There is much to be concerned about." He looked about him at the interior of the cabin. "As you can see, many of us have adopted the white man's ways. We decided we ought to do this, because then the white man might leave us alone, might treat us with respect, might let us live in peace. That is what they said to us, once upon a time. That if we became like them that we could be as neighbors. But that is not the case. It didn't make any difference. They still want to drive us out."

"I know." And Barlow proceeded to tell Mondegah what he had heard in the White House, at the Claybourne plantation, and in the judge's home in Athens. Mondegah listened gravely. And when Barlow was done he sipped his tea for a moment, reflecting on all that he had heard.

"I have tried to keep the peace. But it grows more difficult with each passing day. It is true that some of our young men, resentful of the treatment we receive at the hands of the whites, have burned a few fields and stolen a few cows or horses. But, so far as I know, they have not killed anyone. That may soon change, however, now that one of our own has been struck down."

"They have no intention of bringing the farmer who did that to trial," said Barlow. "I don't know if you were expecting them to or not. But Judge Tolliver will have none of it."

"I have learned to expect very little from the whites," said Mondegah bitterly. He peered a moment, speculatively, at Barlow. "So, my old friend, what do you suggest we do?"

Barlow had anticipated that question, and responded without hesitation. "Much as I hate to think of it, I don't believe you have any choice. Not if you want your people to survive."

Mondegah sighed, nodded. He didn't need Barlow to spell it out for him. "It will not be easy to persuade the others that they must go," he murmured, glancing out the open door at the town beyond.

"Those who remain are doomed," said Barlow. "I'm sorry to have to say it, but we both know it's true."

"Will Sharp Knife send the army?"

Barlow shrugged. "If the situation worsens. If people start dying. If the state of Georgia requests the aid of the national government. Yes, he would. Right now, though, the state of Georgia thinks it can handle the Cherokees quite handily all by itself."

"And if he sends the army, what will you do?"

"I don't want to think about it. I just hope it doesn't come to that."

They looked at one another a moment, friends reflecting on the possibility that one day they might be enemies.

The room darkened—a man's shape filled the doorway.

"Excuse me," said the newcomer. "Am I intruding? If so I will come back later."

"You are welcome, Samuel," said Mondegah. "Captain Timothy Barlow, Samuel Worcester."

Barlow rose as Worcester came forward and they shook hands. Worcester was a tall, rail-thin man; he was young, in his mid-twenties by Barlow's estimation, but his gaunt, ascetic face was that of someone much older.

"Pleased to make your acquaintance, Captain," said Worcester. "By your accent I take it you are from the North?"

"Philadelphia. And you are from New England. Boston, perhaps?"

Worcester chuckled. "You're right on the mark, sir!"

"Samuel was sent to us last year by the American Board of Commissioners for Foreign Missions," said Mondegah. "He was supposed to convert us to Christianity, I think."

"I thought they would send me somewhere like the Sandwich Islands, to be honest," said Worcester. "I confess I was a bit dismayed when they handed me this assignment. But now I can honestly say I wouldn't trade places with anyone. These are a magnificent people, Captain."

"They fight well, I can say that much," agreed Barlow.

Worcester scowled. "I fear a calamity is going to befall them now that that…that…beast, Andrew Jackson, sits in the Executive Mansion. Has the republic gone mad, sir?"

"The captain," said Mondegah, amused, "is here on behalf of the beast, Samuel."

Worcester was mortified. "I've put my foot in it, haven't I?"

"At least I'll never have to wonder where you stand, Mr. Worcester," said Barlow, and laughed.

"I'm sorry. It's just that these Jacksonians are so thin-skinned. Say one bad thing about their hero and they're likely to cut you from stem to stern. And speaking of saying bad things—I received this from the mail rider yesterday, Mondegah."

He handed a letter to the Cherokee chieftain, who read it slowly before returning it. Worcester then proffered the missive to Barlow, who took it.

"It's from your employers, I see," said the army officer. "The American Board. Jeremiah Evarts?"

"The Board secretary."

Barlow nodded and read:

We received yesterday, from Col. McKenney, a letter containing a charge against you, forwarded to this office from the nation. The charge was, interfering with the press, & writing scurrilous articles respecting officers of government & other public men. The letter was answered & the charge declared by us to be unfounded. The number of The Phoenix containing your disclaimer was forwarded to him. Col. McKenney gave no opinion as to the credit attached to the article in the War Department. Do what is right and you need not fear.

Barlow returned the letter to Worcester. "Sounds to me like you've made some powerful enemies. What did you write that so incites them?"

"I wrote the truth," said Worcester, with surprising ferocity for one who looked so bookish and frail. "That there is a great conspiracy that reaches all the way to the hallowed halls of our national government, designed to deprive all the Indian tribes of their lands. That those engaged are, to a large degree, from the South. Men who are wedded to the brutal institution of slavery as the means by which they grow fat and rich, profiting from the sweat and blood of the poor African who is put in chains and lives the rest of his life in bondage. The Indians are simply in the way, Captain, of these Southern slaveholders. They want all the land, so that they may build their plantations, and import more slaves. So the Cherokee must suffer, as well as the African. And all for the good of a few."

"I see," said Barlow.

"Since the inception of this republic, sir, the national government has done everything in its power to placate the Southern slavocracy. It will continue to do so, I fear, especially now that a Southern slaveholder, Andrew Jackson, is in the White House. Tell him, Captain, when you return to make your report, that we know what he is up to. We know what is in his heart. And, as I've said, great calamities await these people as a result."

"Mondegah and I were just discussing that when you arrived," said Barlow.

"The captain believes that only by moving westward can we save ourselves," said Mondegah.

"Do what you must," said Worcester stiffly. "But I shall not retreat one inch. They can jail me. They can kill me. But I will not surrender to such tyranny. I have come only to show you this letter, Mondegah, my friend. Mr. Evarts says to do right, and I will have no reason to fear. Of course I shall do what is right, but because I do it I will have *much* to fear—not from the American Board, but from the evil and greedy men who lurk all around us. They have targeted me."

"You would be well advised to remain in New Echota. Do not stray far afield. They would not dare come in here after you."

"Don't be so sure," said Worcester gravely. "One day they will come. And it will be with gun and sword in hand." He turned to give Barlow a stiff bow. "If your duties allow it, please come and visit me at *The Phoenix*. And perhaps you will consent to supper with myself and my wife, Ann. We would be quite happy to have someone with whom we can reminisce about life in the North. I must confess, I do miss it sometimes."

"Thank you," said Barlow, noncommittal. Once Worcester had taken his leave, he turned to Mondegah. "So what now?"

"I will ask for a council of the clans. Many who will sit at such a council will remember you as the White Warrior. Your words will have much weight."

Barlow nodded. "If you do agree to go west, I feel confident I can persuade the president to send the army down to assist you."

"Would you go with us?"

Barlow didn't hesitate. "I would gladly accept such a duty."

Chapter Six

Even in times of crisis, things took time in Indian society. Much concern—in Barlow's opinion, overmuch—was given to appearances and ritual. It wasn't sufficient for Mondegah to call for a council; there was a particular etiquette attached to the messages he sent to the chieftains of the other Upper Towns. These chieftains then sent envoys to negotiate time and place and subject matter with Mondegah, as well as details of the council itself—who would be allowed to speak, and in what order. The impression that Mondegah could merely snap his fingers and summon the other chiefs could not be permitted. Nor could any one leader have undue advantage over another, for the Cherokees had no head chief. Aware of this from his previous experiences with the southern tribes, Barlow exercised patience—it was not, ordinarily, one of his virtues—and stayed in New Echota for the fortnight that Mondegah required to organize the council, talking to men who had been with him in Florida, learning where they stood on the matter of the current troubles with the whites and on the subject of a removal westward. What he learned did not give him much in the way of encouragement. Those inclined to move west had already done so; by and large, the Cherokees who remained were determined to hold onto their lands. They had no illusions. They knew that if the national government got involved, if the army was sent against them, they would meet the same fate as the Red Stick Creeks and the Seminoles. But some things were more important than victory. Like honor. And Barlow was well aware that, if nothing else, the Cherokees were an honorable people.

He spent much of the time with Samuel Worcester. The office of *The Phoenix*, like most of the other structures in New Echota, was a log cabin about thirty feet long and twenty feet wide. The press and type had been shipped all the way from Boston to Augusta and then carried overland by wagon. Printing paper had to be shipped from Knoxville. The press itself was the latest model, made of cast iron, with spiral springs. Worcester was proud of it, but even more proud of the cases that had been built to accommodate the Cherokee alphabet—no pattern had previously existed. There were over one hundred boxes in all.

Worcester's partner in the enterprise, Elias Boudinot, was a Cherokee who had been educated at the Foreign Mission School at Cornwall, Connecticut, a school run by the American Board. His Cherokee name was Galagi'na, but he had been allowed to take the name of his sponsor, Dr. Elias Boudinot of the American Bible Society. He had married a white girl, Harriet Gold of Cornwall. This had not gone over well with many of the Cornwall residents; Boudinot and his bride both were burned in effigy on one side of town even while they were being wed on the other. At Harriet's insistence, the Boudinot home was no log cabin, but rather a spacious two-story frame home that would have seemed quite acceptable in the better part of Cornwall.

At first *The Phoenix* had been devoted largely to preaching the Christian faith and converting the Cherokees to it. That was, after all, the reason the American Board had dispatched Worcester there in the first place. But Worcester was incensed by the whites' efforts to take Indian land, and now the newspaper was filled with denunciations of the state of Georgia as well as the national government—along with scathing attacks on individuals, including Andrew Jackson. Barlow whiled away the time reading some of the recent issues. He thought Worcester had ample reason to believe he was going to be the target of retribution, and in Barlow's opinion, the man had, to an extent, brought it upon himself. A white man defending Indians would be considered by many of his own kind a traitor to his race. And he compounded this sin with another, attacking the Hero of New Orleans, the Man of the People. Worcester expected them to come for him like thieves in the night, to steal him away from home and family, to make him the centerpiece of a show trial that would turn the pursuit of justice into a farce, and then to cast him into a dank jail cell and throw away the key. Boudinot thought that even worse was in store—that they would send assassins to silence both Worcester and himself. Barlow thought that either scenario was quite possible, considering how high feelings were running.

The day of the council finally arrived. As Mondegah's guest, Barlow was privileged to speak first. He performed the duty Andrew Jackson had asked him to—and he did so with more conviction than he had thought he'd have. But what he had seen and heard these past few weeks had persuaded him that the only hope for the survival of the Cherokee Nation was its voluntary removal.

After Barlow spoke it was the turn of Womankiller, from the town of Hickory Log. He spoke eloquently in favor of resurrecting a law that would inflict the death penalty on any Cherokee who sold his land to the white man without the consent of his tribe, and he did so in English for Barlow's benefit. "Permit me," said Womankiller, "to call you my children, as I am an old man and have lived a long time. I love your lives, and wish our people to increase and prosper on the land of our fathers, as is our right. The law will punish only wicked men, those who may want to cede away our country contrary to the wishes of the tribe. It is a good law. It will not harm the innocent, only the guilty. Men of renown, once members of this council, who now sleep in the dust, spoke in the same language, and I now stand on the verge of the grave to bear witness to their love of country. My sun of existence is now fast approaching to its setting, and my aged bones will soon be laid underground, and I wish them laid in the bosom of this earth we have received from our fathers who were given it by the Great Being above. When I sleep in forgetfulness, I hope my bones will not be deserted by you."

Mondegah rose to object to Womankiller bringing up the law he had spoken about, for that had not been on the council's agenda. He was followed by the chieftain of another of the Upper Towns, who defended Womankiller's right to discuss the law. It was, he said, relevant to the issue of whether they would keep their lands or surrender them to the whites.

"I am told," he said gravely, "that the government of the United States will spoil their treaties with us and sink our council under their feet. It may be so, but it shall not be with our consent, or by the misconduct of our people. We hold them by the golden chain of friendship, made when our friendship was worth something, and if they act like tyrants and kill us for our lands we shall, in a state of unoffending innocence, sleep with thousands of our departed people, and sleep easily knowing we have not sacrificed our honor. I can say no more, but before I sit, allow me to tell you that I am opposed to leaving this land, and am in favor of the law spoken of by Womankiller."

Another council member rose. "I am not sure that it can be called honorable to stand by while our lands are stolen, our farms and fields and towns destroyed, our women and children made to become wandering beggars, our men disarmed and humbled and treated with contempt by the white men. Either we should be willing to fight for what belongs to us, or we should give up these lands and go west."

Barlow glanced at Mondegah with brows raised in a silent query, and the New Echota chieftain understood; he informed the council that their guest wished to have more words with them, and it was unanimously agreed that he should be allowed to do so.

"There can be honor in fighting a war you cannot win," Barlow conceded. "But what happens to the women and children of the brave warriors who fall fighting for a lost cause? They will still become wandering beggars. Only they will not have their men to provide for them. They will be completely at the mercy of the white men you call your enemies. No one questions the bravery of the Cherokee. It has been proven on countless battlefields. But many might question their wisdom if their families were left to fend for themselves."

He paused, sighed, and pondered his next words for a moment.

"It seems to me," he said, at last, "that life is a succession of challenges, and all too often the options we are given are not the ones we would wish for. At the end of life a man is worthy of praise if he has done the best he can under the worst of circumstances. The man who expects a pleasant life is subjecting himself to endless disappointment. The man who strives to make his life tolerable in the face of all its adversity is the one who succeeds." He looked around him at the somber faces of the Cherokee leaders—and decided that was all he needed to say. He thanked them for allowing him to speak, and sat down.

A half dozen other leaders spoke, some of them at length. Barlow sat motionless, appearing to be attentive to all that was being said. But in fact his mind wandered. He thought of Fort Perry, and of Sarah, and wished that he had never gone to the presidential inauguration in Washington, for if he hadn't, he wouldn't be here now, with a knot growing in the pit of his stomach as he realized that something tragic, something bloody, something irrevocable was going to happen before these people he liked and admired would get it through their stubborn heads that they had but one viable option. And, too, had he remained in New York, he would not have met Rose Claybourne, and he would not be feeling, as he felt now, an irresistible urge to see her again.

When, at last, it was over, he told Mondegah of his intentions to depart the following morning. The New Echota chieftain nodded, peering speculatively at Barlow.

"And what will you tell Sharp Knife?"

"I'll tell him the truth," said Barlow. "At least what I perceive to be the truth of what I've seen down here. That neither the Georgians nor the Cherokees are inclined to bend. That there's more trouble on the horizon. More bloodshed, in all likelihood."

"And what will be his response to your report?"

"I honestly don't know, my friend."

"Perhaps you'd see fit to let us know when you do find out what Jackson intends," said Samuel Worcester, coming up behind

Barlow, having overheard most of the exchange. "Or perhaps I should say, when he plans to act, as I think we all know what he will do, ultimately."

"I'm not sure I can do that," confessed Barlow. "If you're asking me to inform you about military plans, I'd not be inclined to do that."

"So, if it comes down to your having to make a choice, you'll side with Jackson?" asked Worcester, in disbelief. "You know he's looking for an excuse to remove these people. What you tell him will give him the justification he needs. Then he'll be able to accomplish his goal under the guise of preventing a war."

Barlow nodded. "That's quite possible."

"The captain is a man of honor, Samuel," said Mondegah. "He will do his duty. He always has—whether he's liked it or not. I only hope," he said to Barlow, "that if Sharp Knife sends his army, you will come, too."

"I would not care to be put in the position of having to fight the Cherokees."

"But if you come, at least there will be one man whose word we know we can rely upon."

He left New Echota at sunrise the next day, and by sundown had reached Athens, Georgia. His arrival in the town seemed to go unnoticed. The day's business had been concluded, the hustle and bustle had died down, and the wide, dusty streets were quiet. Deciding that it was too late to continue on to the Claybourne plantation—he didn't care to come calling in the middle of the night—Barlow resigned himself to spending the night in town. He went to a tavern located near the edge of town, and was glad to learn that the proprietor was able to supply him with a meal of mutton and bread. The man told him of a boardinghouse down the street that would take him in. Barlow thanked him and took his trencher of food to a table in a back corner of the establishment so that he could eat in peace, well removed from the half dozen men who lined the tavern bar.

Two of those men, with the look of backwoodsmen about them, were drinking ale and giving him over-the-shoulder looks. Barlow pretended not to notice, hoping that if he ignored the men they would leave him be. But eventually they worked up the nerve to approach his table, and stood over him, glaring, until he looked up and acknowledged their presence.

"Evening," he said, cordially. "Can I help you boys?"

"You're that army man that's been with the Injuns, aren't you?" asked one.

"That's right."

"Then you be the one ol' Andy Jackson sent down here," said the other.

Barlow grimaced. Apparently someone had a loose tongue—Judge Tolliver or one of the Claybournes. They were the only people he had enlightened regarding the reason for his presence in Georgia.

"Right again," he said. "Now, if you don't mind, I'd like to finish my supper."

One of the men leaned forward, his knuckles on the table, looming over Barlow's plate. "You pass right through here in one day, and spend the better part of a month with them heathens up in New Echota? Makes me think you must be one of them Northern Injun lovers. That shoe fit you?"

"The Cherokees and I fought together in Florida. I have some friends there."

"We don't want no Injun lovers hanging around these parts," said the backwoodsman. "So you'd best just get on your horse and ride on out of here now."

"I think I'll finish my meal."

The backwoodsman hawked and drooled spittle into Barlow's food. "Finish it now, why don't you?" he asked, leering.

As he shot up out of his chair, Barlow overturned the table and drove it forward against the two men, knocking them off balance. The table fell on one of the men, and Barlow turned his attention to the other, who had righted himself against a wall and was charging at him, his bearded features twisted into a snarl of rage. Barlow ducked under the man's wild roundhouse swing and plowed a fist into his adversary's midsection. It was like hitting a tree trunk, and pain shot straight up Barlow's arm into his shoulder. The back-woodsman doubled over and Barlow brought the back of his elbow down as hard as he could on the man's back, right below the nape of the neck. The Georgian collapsed in a heap. Barlow just had time to whirl and duck—the other man had regained his feet and was in the process of attacking with a hunting knife in hand, exe-cuting a lateral stroke that might have taken Barlow's head off had it connected. Instead, the knife whistled harmlessly through the air and Barlow hit the man low, plowing into him with his shoulder, knocking the wind out of him. The backwoodsman sprawled, losing his grip on the knife. He scrambled for it. Barlow reached it first, planted a booted foot on the blade and then placed the point of his drawn saber in the vicinity of the man's Adam's apple.

"You don't want to do that," rasped Barlow.

"No," muttered the backwoodsman. "Reckon I don't."

"Get out of here—and don't come back."

The backwoodsman got up gingerly—the tip of the saber remained at his throat—backed away a few steps, and then, with a final sullen look at Barlow, turned and left the tavern.

Barlow noticed that the first man was trying to get up. With con-siderable relish, the army officer walked over and kicked the man right below the ribcage. Wheezing, the backwoodsman rolled over and just lay there, clutching his midriff. Barlow figured it would be a while before he was able to breathe right, much less stand.

Checking the tavern's other patrons—they were all grouped together over at the bar—Barlow judged that there were no further threats to his well-being under this roof, at least, and sheathed the saber. On his way out, he thanked the proprietor for his dinner.

The accommodations he rented at the boardinghouse were just fine. The room was clean, the bed comfortable and free of pests. But Barlow slept poorly, tossing and turning. He dreamed of a garden maze, made with thick hedges as had been popular in the previous century. He was trying to catch up to Rose Claybourne. It was neither day nor night, but somewhere in between, and the gloom was deepened by the presence of a cottony haze. She was running from him, laughing, and the looks she threw back at him were full of promise. She wore some sort of gauzy, diaphanous gown that revealed much of her taut young body. Though he was gripped by a vague disquiet, Barlow followed her deeper into the maze, turning so many corners that he was soon completely lost. She was too far ahead of him now for him to see her, but he could still hear her laughter, and he let this guide him to the fountain at the center of the maze. The fountain looked quite old and weathered, the water that lay in its base black. Rose was nowhere in sight. He hesitantly approached the fountain and looked down into the water. Instead of his reflection he saw countless faces twisted into the rictus of agony, and frozen in death. They were the faces of Cherokees. At that point he awoke, sitting bolt upright in bed, drenched with perspiration. He spent the rest of the long night trying to get back to sleep, without success.

He left Athens early the next morning, heading for the Claybourne plantation, a persistent sense of impending doom hanging over him. It seemed clear to him now that it didn't really matter how far he tried to run from the situation in which he now found himself. He would be drawn back into it. He was no longer the master of his own fate. He tried to tell himself he was just very tired, and depressed about the situation he'd found in New Echota.

Whatever the reason, he was so preoccupied with his thoughts that he failed to remain alert to the possible dangers of the trail. Otherwise he might have seen one of the backwoodsmen with whom he had tangled the night before, moving among the trees that grew thickly on a slope above the road. He might have seen the man pick his spot and kneel, bracing the barrel of his percussion rifle in the fork of a tree, drawing a bead—and allowing himself a slow grin as he squeezed the trigger.

Barlow felt the impact—it was like a blow from an ax handle against his side—and it had such force that he found himself falling sideways out of the saddle. He braced himself for the impact with the ground that he knew was coming. But he never felt the ground. He lost consciousness before he finished falling.

When he came to the first thing he saw was Rose Claybourne's face—and he thought he must be dreaming again. Then the pain seeped into his consciousness, and kept growing, and growing, and he realized he was awake even while wishing that he wasn't. It came back to him—the last thing he remembered, falling off his horse—and he groped at his side reflexively. His midsection was tightly wrapped with a dressing. He'd been shot—that was the only explanation for the pain that he was experiencing. Unfortunately, he knew what being shot felt like. It was an experience he had fervently hoped to avoid having again. He tried sitting up, but the pain intensified, and he gave up the effort.

Rose laid a gently restraining hand on his shoulder. "Lie still, Captain. You've been badly hurt."

"I was shot," he said, and his voice, a croaking travesty of its former self, startled him. "Water…"

There was a pitcher and a glass on a table beside the bed; Rose poured water from the former into the latter and held the rim of the glass to his lips so that he could sip from it.

"Yes," she said, gently, and he could hear the emotion in her voice; it gladdened him, and banished forever any doubts he might have entertained previously that she did not care about him. "Three days ago, in fact. You must have lain there on the road for hours, the doctor says, because you lost a great deal of blood. Fortunately, Jericho had gone into town early that morning, and he found you when he was returning home. He recognized you, of course, and brought you here." She placed the empty glass on the bedside table and then sat on the edge of the bed and touched his cheek with her fingertips. "My dear captain, I was worried sick."

"That she was," said the elder Claybourne, as he entered the room. "She has scarcely left your side, day or night. But now, my dear, as you can see, he has regained consciousness, and that is an excellent sign. I was right—he is a strong fellow, not easy to kill."

"Has the man who shot me been caught?"

Claybourne shook his head. "My overseer, Richman, rode out that afternoon, accompanied by my son. John can't read sign—he wouldn't be able to tell you if a herd of elephants passed through the front yard. But Richman can. He says it was Indians. Cherokees, by the way the moccasin was shaped."

Barlow shook his head. "Not possible."

"There was horse sign nearby—and the horse was unshod. I don't know of any white men who wear moccasins and ride unshod ponies, do you?"

"All I know is I had a quarrel with two men in a tavern in Athens the night before. I believe one of them was probably responsible. Waited for me to ride out of town, circled ahead of me, and set up the bushwhacking."

"A quarrel, yes. I heard about that. What was it over?"

"They thought I'd partaken of Cherokee hospitality a little too long," said Barlow dryly.

"No one seems to know their identity, Captain. They must have been passing through. Gold hunters, maybe."

"No Cherokee would have done this," insisted Barlow.

"Now really, Captain. Be logical. I know you have friends among the Cherokees. But not all the Cherokees are your friends, I'll wager. There are plenty of young bucks in the Upper Towns who hate all white men. And, as I expect you did your duty and told them that it was in their best interests to move westward, I'm sure there were some who did not care for your message."

Barlow grimaced. He couldn't deny that Claybourne's scenario could, possibly, be accurate. But he still preferred to believe that it had been one—or both—of the backwoodsmen he had bested in the Athens tavern the night before.

"At any rate," said Claybourne, "we'll sort all that out later. Right now you must concentrate on recuperation. Get plenty of rest, Captain. If you need anything, ring the bell that you see there on the table. That is, assuming my daughter ever sees fit to leave you alone." The planter looked wryly at Rose. "Get plenty of rest. The doctor says you should remain bedridden for at least a fortnight."

"A fortnight!" Barlow shook his head. "Impossible. I must return to Washington. It's important that I make my report as soon as I can."

"You wouldn't make it five miles, much less to Washington. Write your report, and any private letters you may wish sent. I will see that they arrive at their destinations, and guarantee their confidentiality."

Barlow wished he could trust Claybourne. But he just wasn't sure about anyone now. Except for Mondegah. He thanked Claybourne, and informed the planter that he would likely take him up on his offer. Claybourne advised his daughter to get some rest and then left the room.

"You will want to write a letter to your wife, of course," said Rose, unable to quite conceal the sadness in her voice. "She will be worried if you are overdue, and she's received no word from you."

Barlow didn't tell her that, in fact, Sarah was accustomed to seeing him go for weeks—or, as had been the case during the Seminole campaign, for months—at a time without hearing from him, without being able to say with any certainty whether he was alive or dead. He was an abysmal letter-writer. But he made no mention of this to Rose. Instead he nodded, and said, "Yes, that would be a good idea."

She rose from the edge of the bed. "I shall get you pen and paper," she said, suddenly very brisk and businesslike, and left the room.

That left Barlow alone with his thoughts, and these turned immediately to what Claybourne had said about Indians having been the perpetrators of the ambush that had nearly taken his life. He just didn't believe it. Something was wrong. It all fit too neatly into the plans of the Georgians, those plans centering on agitation for war with the Cherokees. The two backwoodsmen were just drifters? Unknown to anyone in Athens? That was awfully convenient.

And if they were just passing through, what stake did they have in whether Barlow favored the Cherokees in the present situation? Assuming that he was right, and that Cherokees had not ambushed him, then the Claybourne plantation overseer—what was his name? Richman, yes, that was it—and John Claybourne himself were conspiring to stir feelings against the Indians to fever pitch. If the Cherokees killed an army officer, the War Department would have no recourse but to act. And if he was right, then the fact that he might actually survive the attempt on his life must be an inconvenience for them. Barlow smiled to himself. He could appreciate the irony of being bedridden in the house of people who would have preferred to see him dead. With the exception of Rose, of course.

It was clear now that Rose Claybourne was in love with him.

CHAPTER SEVEN

Barlow wrote his letters, both official and private. The former, addressed to John Eaton, secretary of war, said only that he had been wounded by person or persons unknown as he was about to make his return trip, and that he would proceed as soon as his injuries had healed. He suspected that Eaton—and the president— would be disappointed at the paucity of information enclosed in his missive, but despite Claybourne's assurances, Barlow was working under the assumption that his mail—at least his official correspondence—would be read. Someone had a stake in perpetuating the fraud that he had been shot by Cherokees, and would want to know if he was going to refute that fraud.

As for his private correspondence, he dutifully penned a letter to Sarah, care of the Langford boardinghouse on Pennsylvania Avenue. At first he thought to conceal from her the fact that he had been shot. Then he realized that it was probably futile to do so—it was likely that Secretary Eaton himself would call upon her, assuming that she had received the same news as he, to offer his assurances and services during Barlow's absence. And he wasn't about to ask Eaton to keep the news from her—it was hardly appropriate for an army captain to ask the secretary of war to become a co-conspirator in a personal matter such as that. So he told her the truth in his letter. That he had been ambushed on the trail, by whom or for what reason he did not know. That he was fine, not seriously hurt, and recuperating nicely at the Claybourne plantation outside Athens, Georgia. That he loved her, missed her, trusted that she and her mother were well, and was looking forward to being with her again.

He doubted that Claybourne—or his son, or overseer—would be so crass as to read his private letter, but he couldn't be certain, so he said nothing more about the Cherokees, or his suspicions that someone was trying to use his bushwhacking to start a war with the Indians. It was usually wise to keep the enemy in the dark as to exactly what you knew, and what you intended to do about it.

Not that he had any idea what he could do. Were he able to ride he might have had a notion about going out to find the backwoodsmen with whom he had fought. The "findings" of Mr. Richman—the moccasin and unshod-horse sign—were printed in the local newspaper, along with a nicely timed editorial that raised the alarum that the Cherokees were becoming more bold and bloodthirsty with each passing day; that the fact that they would risk attacking an officer of the United States Army was proof positive that they were a desperate and dangerous crowd; that all citizens must be on their guard; and that all good men must be prepared to take up their rifles in defense of their women and children, their homes and state, and the honor of the republic itself. All were in jeopardy now, as the savages painted themselves for war and prepared to decorate their lodge poles with the scalps of Americans. Et cetera, et cetera. Barlow could not resist commenting to Claybourne, after reading this purple prose, that the Cherokees neither took scalps, as a rule, nor lived in lodges.

A week later Barlow learned that the Georgia state legislature had passed a law that extended the jurisdiction of the state to the Cherokees who lived within its borders. That meant its laws, its police powers, and its courts. This reversed an earlier statute that had recognized the Cherokee Nation as a state within a state, and therefore permitted to make its own laws and police itself without interference from Georgia. The new law, mused Barlow, opened the way for a challenge to the Cherokee ownership of certain lands. They had no title—at least not a white man's title, recognized by the courts. And even though they occupied the land, Barlow suspected that in this case that old rule of thumb—that possession was nine-tenths of the law—would not apply.

"I wouldn't be surprised," he told Claybourne dryly, "if the Cherokees start running into white men who have title to the land of their forefathers. Paper issued by some white judge, with the ink barely dry on it, giving ownership to men who probably will never have stepped foot on land that, by the stroke of a pen, has become their property."

Claybourne shrugged. "One must have clear title to his land, Captain. That's the civilized way. Prevents conflict, you know."

Barlow smiled. "It will be blatant thievery. If the English Parliament passed a law stating that the king of England owned all the land in the original thirteen colonies—which would include this land, by the way—and that to prove otherwise you would have to present an English title recognized by English courts, in person in England, and that if you failed to do so the British army would come and take the land away from you, what would you do?"

"I'd take up my guns and tell them to come and take it, if they thought they could."

"And do you suppose the Cherokees will do any different?"

Claybourne gave him a long, somber look. "I'm not one of these fire-eaters, aching for a war, Captain. War is bad for business. Neither does the government of the state of Georgia seek a war. The law was passed, in my opinion, to bring matters to a head, in the hopes that the president would intervene, and remove the Indians. That is why your mission here has been of such great interest to so many people. By now everyone knows President Jackson sent you down here to appraise the situation. And they're curious to know what you will report back to him."

"I'm afraid what I will report to the president must be for his eyes and ears only."

"Of course." Claybourne chuckled. "Relax, Captain. I'm not trying to loosen your tongue. I am content to sit back and let matters take their inevitable course. I have the land I want. I desire no other, especially no land claimed by the Cherokees. Personally, I would not care if they remained, except to the extent that they may pose a threat to me or my family."

"They pose less of a threat than the editor of your newspaper would have everyone believe."

Claybourne laughed, made a dismissive gesture. "Nathan Moore is an excitable fellow. He tends to be over-dramatic in his speculations."

"Your son seems to feel a good bit more strongly about the Cherokees than you," observed Barlow. "In all the time I've been here I don't believe I've heard him say one good thing about them."

"Pay him no mind," said Claybourne briskly. "I don't."

Barlow tried not to, but it became increasingly difficult to ignore John Claybourne. As the days passed he seemed to display more and more animosity toward the army officer, and did a poor job of concealing his feelings. Barlow assumed John's attitude towards him was based on envy. He thought the younger Claybourne was one of the many young hotspurs in these parts who longed for a campaign against the Cherokees so that they might be afforded an opportunity to prove their courage. And having Barlow underfoot—a man who was acclaimed a hero, particularly by Rose at every opportunity—had to be galling. Worst of all, the elder Claybourne treated the uniformed hero with impeccable respect—something he did not give his son.

Barlow's wounds mended well. There was no infection; the doctor summoned to the plantation on the day that Jericho had discovered him had removed the bullet from his side and done a fine job of cleansing the wound. It was more a matter of recovering his strength—the loss of blood had been extreme, and his body needed time to make up that loss. There was no way, of course, that Barlow was going to remain bedridden for two weeks, and he was pleasantly surprised when Rose proved wise enough to understand him in this, for she did not give him trouble about testing his strength that first week. At first it was all he could do to make it from the bed to the chair by the window before feeling faint. In the following days he grew impatient with what he considered slow progress. He cursed his weakness, as he always had before during times of illness; he expected his body to perform whatever he asked it to. He took strength and stamina for granted. Every day he tested himself a little more, and within another week he was negotiating the stairs to get outside on the veranda—an effort that, initially, left him so exhausted that Jericho and another slave had to carry him back to his room, a humiliating experience for Barlow. Soon, though, he was regularly going downstairs for some fresh air and to feel the sun of the warm, fine spring days on his face.

And of course there was Rose, who made it far more bearable than it would have been otherwise. She was consistently of good cheer, and especially so on those occasions—which happened entirely too frequently to suit him—when he became cross and impatient with his progress. "Why, someone might think you're in a hurry to get well just so you can leave me," she would say, or something to that effect, and always with a mock pout. Invariably he would smile, and remind himself that many a man would gladly suffer a wound to be in his position. Rose was with him almost constantly. She was there in the morning when he woke, greeting him with that bright, slightly breathless smile of hers. She would fuss over him when one of the housemaids brought him breakfast, and again at lunch, and once more at supper. She would be by his side when he ventured to stand and walk, and would sit beside him on the veranda for as long as he cared to be outside. She allowed no one else to change his dressing. The only thing she did not do for him was give him a sponge bath—at his insistence she left that to one of the black house servants, albeit reluctantly. "I have a brother, you know," she said. "It isn't as though I've never seen *it*." But she bowed to his wishes, knowing that he was embarrassed. Another time she asked him how he could be sure she hadn't taken a peek while he slept. "Rose!" he exclaimed, shocked—and she just giggled.

The day finally came when he felt strong enough to climb into the saddle. Jericho brought two horses around to the veranda—naturally, Rose insisted on being the one to accompany him. Fresh pain lanced through his mid section as he climbed into the saddle with an assist from Jericho. When the horse began to move he felt more pain, but it was bearable. They did not go far that first day, but on every day after that they took a ride, and each excursion was of longer duration. Until, more than three weeks after he had awakened in the Claybourne house, Barlow was able to ride at a gallop without feeling too much discomfort. He was thrilled. His wound was nearly healed. His recuperation was nearly over. But Rose wasn't thrilled. He could tell—he seemed to be able to know what she was thinking all the time. He just didn't know what to say to cheer her up. What *was* there to say? The day when they would part company was fast approaching. Barlow had tried not to think about it. Rose, apparently, had been thinking about it a lot. There were traces of melancholy in her voice, and in her silences, and in the glances she threw his way.

They rode several miles down the lane, and when Rose suggested they turn back he said no, that he was enjoying the ride and the day—and the company—far too much. Just the thought of spending one more hour in that bed made him cringe. She didn't argue with him. Abruptly, though, the day darkened, as rain clouds blotted out the sun, and almost without warning the deluge came. Rose cried out in shock and delight as the cold downpour drenched her to the skin, and she called to Barlow to follow her, and set her horse to a gallop down the lane. Lightning flashed on all sides, and the thunder rolled. A half mile further on they came to a derelict structure—what appeared to him to be an old frame church. One of its doors hung sideways off a hinge, and part of the roof had been taken off by a falling oak tree. Rose didn't hesitate—she leaped from the saddle and ran inside. Barlow followed, making sure their horses were tethered to a post outside. The interior of the church was littered with debris. Several huge limbs of the fallen tree, now devoid of leaves, filled the back of the church. The rain poured in through the hole in the roof back there, but up front it was quite dry.

"This place was built a few years ago," she told him. "But a tornado did all that damage, and it was never rebuilt. Rumor was that this church was cursed, because the preacher was sleeping with a member of his flock—a fourteen-year-old girl. They said the tornado touched down right here and then disappeared back up into the clouds, damaging nothing else. They said it was God's vengeance. The people had their vengeance, too. They rode the preacher out of the county on a rail. After they tarred and feathered him. They didn't know then that the girl was pregnant. She died giving birth to a stillborn child." Her teeth chattered, and she hugged herself. Lightning struck again, this time very close by—so close that Barlow could smell the singed air. The thunder that followed seemed to shake the foundations of the building.

"You're soaked right through," he said, and shed his jacket, draping it over her shoulders. She pushed stray tendrils of black hair away from her eyes and looked up at him in that breathless way that stirred the longing deep inside him. He quickly removed his arms from around her shoulders. Just as quickly she captured him, her arms around his neck, and pressed her warm soft lips against his. He responded instinctively with a hard kiss full of passion, and as she pressed her lithe young body against his he could feel the heat of her own passion through their wet clothes.

Then he came to his senses and detached himself from her embrace, stepped away.

"No," he breathed. "This isn't right. We can't do this, Rose."

"I know," she whispered. "It's a sin. But this is a place of sin, isn't it?"

He looked about him at the wreckage of the church, and then, when he gazed again into her bright, emerald-green eyes, he saw reflected there the wreckage of his own life if he gave in to his desires. He wanted her more than he had ever wanted anything; he wanted to become one with her, to explore every inch of her body, to feel her writhe in ecstasy beneath him, to hear her small cries of joy as he joined his body with hers, wanted to share that very special moment with her, as he had shared nearly everything else in the past weeks. He could do it, and no one would have to know. It could be their secret. Sarah would never know the truth. But, of course, *he* would know. He would have to live with the fact that he had betrayed the trust of another woman. He could try to tell himself that it was Sarah's fault for spurning his advances in recent months. But that was not a sufficient excuse for doing what he now contemplated. And, more than that, he was going to have to leave soon. That was going to be hard enough—for himself as well as for Rose. If they did what they wanted to do here and now it would be a hundred times more difficult.

"I want you," she said, her voice husky with passion. "Here and now. Don't worry about tomorrow. Tomorrow may never come. I want you—and I know you want me." She reached up and grabbed the bodice of her dress and tore at the lace and fabric, ripping it open to reveal her firm, proud breasts, the dark brown nipples hard with desire. He reached for the jacket that had slipped to the ground, and as he draped it again over her now-bare shoulders she captured his right hand by the wrist and pulled it down until the palm cupped the tip of her breast. Barlow faltered—long enough for her to kiss him again, and as she kissed him she slid his hand down over her belly, down between her legs, and he realized that she had raised her skirt with her free hand. His touch seemed to send a jolt of electricity through her body. Her lips still pressed against his, she began to gasp into his mouth, tiny quick little gasps culminating in a sobbing moan, and before he could collect his thoughts her entire body was convulsing. In the grip of violent pleasure, she banged her head against his chest so hard it hurt, then suddenly arched her back and bit him, fiercely, on the chin, her eyes blazing like those of a wild animal. Then the passion subsided. She let go of his hand and slumped against him, and he caught her, held her tightly, the mounds of her breasts pressed against his midsection. He could feel the rapid gallop of her heart.

"My God," she breathed, at last. "If just your touch can do that to me I can only imagine what…"

"Don't," he groaned.

She lifted her face, gazed earnestly at him. "I love you, Captain. And even if we are never together again, even if I never see you again, I will always love you, with all my heart."

She spoke the words with such ferocity that no one—least of all Timothy Barlow—could have doubted their sincerity.

"Even if I wanted to ..." he began.

"I know you want to," she said. "And you should take me. Now. It will be something you will never forget."

"I know," he said miserably. He could only imagine. Sarah had been a quiet lover. Obviously Rose was made of entirely different cloth. "But I can't," he added, with a sigh.

She stepped back, away from him, and stood there a moment, gazing at him with that wild light burning in her eyes, wet and half naked in her torn dress, her chest heaving, her cheeks full of color—and he thought she had to be the most desirable, the most sensuous woman in the world.

"You don't belong to me," she murmured. "But one day you will. One day we'll be together, and the next time I won't let you go. We'll make love every day, anytime we want to, anywhere we want to. And I'll make you the happiest man alive. You'll see."

All Barlow could do was stare. He'd never heard a woman talk in such a way. But Rose wasn't just talking—she meant every word.

"I'm going home," she said suddenly, and turned to the door.

"You can't go back like that," he said. "What would your ..."

"I don't care what they think!" she said defiantly, standing on the threshold, the rain glistening on her face, rivulets of rain running down the seductive curve of the breasts she did not bother to cover. She smiled at him. "Are you coming, Captain?"

Barlow grimaced. There would be trouble if he brought Rose home in this condition. But he could not leave her to make the trip back alone.

He stepped outside the derelict church. It was still raining, a steady downpour now. The front edge of the storm had passed on. The thunder was distant. The lightning no longer struck so close. She was already in the saddle, riding like a man now, her breasts still uncovered, that wild look still in her eyes, and Barlow thought that perhaps in these past few moments Rose Claybourne had done what she had longed to do—she had escaped the strict confinement of what society expected of her. For a while, at least, she no longer had to play at being the meek Southern belle. It was a role, he imagined, that had to be a real burden for a young woman so full of curiosity about life as she, and so for her sake he was glad she had managed her escape—even though he could foresee that it would come at some expense to him.

Climbing into the saddle himself, he followed her as she kicked her horse into a spirited gallop down the lane.

When they reached the plantation the rain was nothing more than a drizzle, but, as had been the case with the lane, the trace leading up to the house between the soggy fields was a morass of mud and pools of standing water, so that when they checked their horses in front of the big house both of them were splattered with mud. One of the black house maids was the first through the door—and she took one look at Rose Claybourne and her hands flew to her gaping mouth and she cried out to the Lord. Barlow leaped from the horse—even though such exertion caused him severe pain in his side—and tried to reach Rose before she could climb the steps of the veranda, intent on attempting once more to drape his jacket around her shoulders and cover her nakedness, but she eluded him and bounded up the steps and stalked archly into the house, her chin tilted upward at a defiant angle. He grimaced and followed, only to be met at the door by John Claybourne, red-faced, fists clenched as he charged straight at the army captain. Barlow was in no mood for John's shenanigans; he deftly deflected a flailing fist and, bracing himself, inserted a shoulder right into the center of the younger Claybourne's reckless attack, sending the young man sprawling.

"I advise you to stay down," rasped Barlow crossly.

"Go to hell, you bastard!" raged John, and leaped to his feet, taking another swing at Barlow. Barlow could have blocked that blow and struck one for himself that would probably have rendered John unconscious. But he refrained. He told himself that John was acting the way any brother would act if his sister arrived home in

Rose Claybourne's present condition. So he grabbed John's arm just below the elbow, gave the young man a hard shove with his free hand, and pushed him back against the door frame.

"Be still," he said, pinning the struggling John.

"What's the meaning of this?" roared the elder Claybourne, appearing at the other end of the downstairs hallway.

Rose was halfway up the staircase. She had turned to see her brother attack Barlow, and now she spoke up. "Stop fighting this instant!" she snapped. "The Captain did not force himself upon me, John, you fool. I wanted him to take me, but he did not."

Coming to the foot of the stairs, Claybourne looked up at Rose, and his face grew hard and cold as he surveyed her condition. "Go cover yourself at once," he growled. "You've brought shame down upon yourself and your family."

"There's no shame in wanting to be with the man you love."

"Go to your room at once!" bellowed Claybourne.

Rose angrily stomped up the stairs and disappeared into her room, slamming the door.

Claybourne turned to Barlow. "I would thank you to release my son, sir," he said icily.

Barlow did as he was told, and stepped back. Once freed, John immediately slapped Barlow across the cheek.

"I demand satisfaction," he said, eyes blazing. "We shall meet on a field of honor, sir—assuming you *have* any honor."

"No you won't," said Claybourne.

"You can't let him get away with this, Father!" exclaimed John. "If you do, you'll be the one who shames us."

"He would kill you, John," said Claybourne bleakly, looking at Barlow, seeing a man who had killed before and could do so again, a man for whom mortal combat held no fears. "Besides, you heard your sister. She invited him to have his way with her. And he refused. Is that not so, Captain?"

Barlow thought about it. He had kissed her, had let her slide his hand between her legs, and he had touched her there, bringing her to the peak of pleasure. Could he have stopped it? Of course. But if he told all of this to Claybourne one thing would lead to another and he would have to kill John, or be killed. He had wanted to do more, so much more than that, so in a way Rose was right—he had refrained from having his way.

"That's correct," he said stiffly. "Now, if you don't mind, I will collect my belongings and be on my way."

"Yes," breathed Claybourne, "I think you would be well advised to do just that."

With a final warning look fired at John, Barlow headed up the staircase.

"I won't forget this," John called after him. "One day we shall meet again, Captain, and then we'll have our reckoning."

Barlow let him have the last word. He didn't turn, or in any way acknowledge that he had heard the threat. But he believed it. Knew, somehow, that the day to which John Claybourne was referring would come. Because, despite the events of the day, and the cloud under which he was leaving, he felt sure he would see Rose Claybourne again. In fact, in spite of himself, he hoped to.

Within the hour he was ready to go, mounting his horse in front of the big house, with Claybourne alone on the veranda to watch him go. The planter had no words for him, and that suited Barlow. Unlike the last time he had taken his leave from this place, he did not wonder where Rose was, or why she was not downstairs to see him off. He was sure that, even if she wished to be, her father would have forbidden her. He was about to set off down the wagon trace when Jericho came bundling round the side of the house with some leather panniers slung over his shoulder. He started for Barlow, but Claybourne's stern voice stopped him in his tracks.

"What have you got there, boy?"

Jericho grinned at his master. "Just some vittles for the Cap'n, massuh. We knows you ain't the kind would send a man up the trail without some vittles, no matter what."

Claybourne nodded, and Jericho slung the panniers across the haunches of Barlow's horse, securing them to the saddle. When he was done he looked up at Barlow with a crooked smile and patted the left-side pannier. "You be wantin' what's in here first," he said, and then turned and loped away, disappearing around the side of the house whence he had come.

With a final look at Claybourne, Barlow rode away.

He waited until he was out on the lane, heading north, before checking his horse and reaching back to lift the flap of the left-side pannier. Within there was food wrapped in cloth—and a folded piece of paper. He opened the latter, and read:

I LOVE YOU WITH ALL MY HEART AND SOUL
AND WILL WAIT FOR YOU UNTIL THE GRAVE CALLS ME
AND THEN I'LL WAIT FOR YOU STILL—ROSE

Barlow heaved a deep sigh, crumpled up the letter, and threw it by the trailside. He rode on twenty or thirty yards before checking the horse again and returning to the spot where he had previously stopped. He drew his saber and pierced the crumpled piece of paper, lifting it from the ground. Then, sheathing the saber, he smoothed the letter out on the plane of his thigh, folded it neatly, and secured it beneath his coatee before riding on.

CHAPTER EIGHT

When Barlow was escorted into the office of the secretary of war he had high hopes that John Eaton was about to order him back to his former posting at Fort Perry. He'd spent months twiddling his thumbs in Washington, D.C. Worse still, he'd been sitting idly about in the heat of summer—and summers on the banks of the Potomac River were insufferable. Returning from Georgia, he had made his report to the president himself, and then gone directly to the Langford boardinghouse to help Sarah finish packing their bags. That very afternoon, orders had come from Secretary Eaton. They were not what he'd been hoping for. *You are to remain in Washington at the convenience of the president.* The words were etched into his brain. His first assumption was that Andrew Jackson intended to act immediately upon the Cherokee problem, and Barlow had already resigned himself to the fact that, like it or not, he would be involved in the campaign. But Jackson had not acted. In fact, Old Hickory had been entirely too consumed with the so-called "Petticoat War" raging right in the nation's capital to even contemplate embarking on a war against the Indians.

At the center of the conflict was Peggy Eaton, the secretary of war's pretty wife, whom Barlow had met—and whom Sarah had befriended—at the inaugural ball. During Barlow's absence, the refusal of the Washington wives to accept Peggy into their circle had ballooned into a political crisis that, as insane as it might seem, threatened to tear the Jackson administration apart. It quickly became clear that Peggy Eaton was being shunned; she was treated so badly at one soiree that many of the social commentators of the day assumed she would remove herself from society lest she suffer again the humiliation of such neglect and indignity. Indeed, Peggy considered doing just that. But then the president stepped in. Somehow he equated the treatment Peggy was receiving with the abuse his beloved Rachel had received at the hands of his political opponents during the recent campaign for the presidency. He ordered his cabinet officers to *force* their wives to treat Peggy Eaton with the respect she deserved. Some tried—to little avail. Others, John C. Calhoun chief among them, took offense at the president's presumption that he could dictate to their spouses. In fact, it was Calhoun's wife, Floride, who appeared to be the leader of the group of women who adamantly refused to associate with Mrs. Eaton.

The "Eaton Affair" even threatened to rupture the long friendship between Andrew Jackson and one of his most trusted aides, Major Andrew Jackson Donelson, whose wife, Emily, was the White House hostess in Rachel's absence. Emily Donelson did not like Peggy—she thought the latter to be a coy troublemaker who secretly enjoyed being the center of controversy, and she was incensed when Peggy got back at her by writing a personal note to Jackson declining his invitation to dine at the White House owing to the "unkind treatment" she had previously received from Mrs. Donelson. When called on the carpet by Old Hickory, Major Donelson staunchly defended his wife, and the shouting match that followed, or so Barlow was told, could be heard throughout the Executive Mansion. Only fierce loyalty to Jackson prevented Donelson from packing his bags and taking his wife back home to Tennessee.

The only member of the cabinet who did not need to worry about defending his wife's behavior, or about cajoling her into accepting Peggy Eaton, was Secretary of State Martin Van Buren. The wily New York politico was a widower. He was also clever enough to realize that the Eaton Affair could work to his advantage. His chief rival in Jackson's inner circle was none other than the vice president, John C. Calhoun. Not only did the he not see eye-to-eye with Calhoun on most of the major issues of the day, but he and the South Carolinian competed for the role of Old Hickory's heir apparent. There were many who believed that the frail old man who occupied the White House would serve but a single term, and Van Buren was ambitious enough to believe that he ought to be Jackson's successor. He saw in Peggy Eaton a way to ingratiate himself with the president. Jackson's blessing would go a long way in the Democratic Party; it might even ensure that Van Buren would be the party's next candidate for the highest office in the land.

Barlow had met Van Buren on a couple of occasions, and while he understood that the New Yorker was a staunch supporter of Old Hickory, he didn't trust the man. Van Buren was sly like the fox, a man who always measured a situation for the advantage it might gain him. It seemed to Barlow that you could never be altogether sure where Van Buren stood. It all depended on which way the political winds were blowing. One of his nicknames was the Little Magician, and Barlow thought it apropos, as Van Buren was quite adept at making it appear to you as though he were doing one thing when in reality he was up to something else entirely. Calhoun, on the other hand, was a man who stood firmly upon his convictions. Barlow had to admire that, even while he disagreed with Calhoun on a number of fundamental issues. All in all, though, the army officer was just glad he wasn't involved in the political war that was being waged in Washington during the summer of 1829. And he had no apprehension whatsoever that the summons to the office of the secretary of war might embroil him in it.

When Barlow entered the office, Eaton was already on his feet, coming around from behind a desk cluttered with documents and maps. They shook hands.

"Ah, Captain, it's good to see you looking so well. Your wound is fully healed, then?"

"Completely, thank you, Mr. Secretary."

"And your lovely wife? How is she?"

"She's well." Barlow didn't feel he ought to burden Eaton with his latest complaint where Sarah was concerned. During his long absence, Sarah had become involved with a group of abolitionists headquartered in the nation's capital. From what she had told him, these reformers were far more militant in their views than their New York counterparts, with whom she had previously associated. This group advocated a federal law mandating the immediate emancipation of all slaves, without recompense to the slaveholders. Unlike the American Colonization Society, which was attempting to establish a country called Liberia, to which freed slaves could be transported on the western coast of the African continent, the Washington abolitionists insisted that all freed slaves be given a mule and a section of land, compliments of the republic responsible for their bondage. They were a bold bunch, Barlow gave them that. Washington was a Southern town when all was said and done, and apparently numerous death threats had been leveled at the group's leader, a man by the name of Marten. Sarah had been unable to tell Barlow much about him, other than that he came from Europe and was very educated. What she didn't have to tell him was that she was completely under Marten's spell. Sarah spent nearly every waking hour in the service of the group, attending meetings, distributing pamphlets on street corners, writing letters to newspapers, and assailing slaveholders with her cant about how holding a people in bondage was a violation of the letter as well as the spirit of the Declaration of Independence, et cetera.

Barlow had tried to reason with her, to advise her against becoming too enmeshed in the activities of Marten's group, because he was worried about her safety. But she misconstrued his warning, and accused him of being concerned only with his own career. It simply wouldn't do, would it, for an officer in the United States Army to have an abolitionist for a wife. It would be detrimental to his future, she said. Barlow was more concerned with her welfare than his career, but he was old enough now, and sufficiently experienced where women were concerned, to recognize the futility of trying to correct her misapprehension. So he dropped the matter altogether and fretted in silence every night she failed to come home until very late.

"I apologize," said Eaton, returning to his chair, "that I have not yet had the time to extend to you and your wife an invitation to dinner. I had no idea how busy this job would keep me." He gestured at his cluttered desk with an expression that mixed amusement with dismay. "But rest assured, I have not forgotten the kindness you and Mrs. Barlow showed myself and my beloved wife Peggy."

"Think nothing of it, Mr. Secretary."

"Please, call me John. Or, if you can't see your way clear to doing that, then Colonel will do. I still hold a commission in the Tennessee volunteers, by the way."

"Thank you, Colonel."

"And please, feel free to sit down."

"I'll stand, if you don't mind."

"Suit yourself." Eaton sank wearily into his chair. "Captain, I suppose you've been wondering why you've been left hanging, as it were, in limbo all these weeks. It was in part to make sure you got a well-deserved rest, so that you could completely recuperate from the injury you sustained down in Georgia. It was also, partly, to keep you close at hand. I—and the president—had a feeling we would soon require the services of a man with your unique qualifications."

"I'm afraid I don't follow, Colonel. What unique qualifications are you referring to?"

"Your courage. Your integrity. Your discretion."

"Does this have anything to do with the Cherokee situation, sir?"

Eaton shook his head. "Unfortunately, events here in Washington have preoccupied all of us, the president most of all, diverting our attention from matters that one could argue are more pressing. But they are not more vital to the interests of the republic. We have a situation, Captain, that threatens to destroy this administration. It could shatter the Democratic Party into irreconcilable fragments. It is a conspiracy that reaches all the way into the inner sancta of the White House, and reaches back an entire decade."

"I don't think I understand what situation you mean, Colonel," said Barlow, all the while thinking that, whatever it was, he didn't really want to know about it.

"Let me begin by relating to you the events of the dinner held at the Indian Queen Hotel on the occasion of Thomas Jefferson's birthday. That was on April thirteenth last, and I believe you were still away on your mission to Georgia. It was mere days after that tremendous debate on the floor of the Senate between Mr. Daniel Webster and Mr. Robert Y. Hayne. The latter, I might add, being a close friend and associate of his fellow South Carolinian, Mr. John C. Calhoun."

"Yes, sir, I've read the entire debate. All the newspapers printed it."

"It was, I daresay, a defining moment in the brief history of our young nation. Hayne enunciated the doctrine of nullification as eloquently as anyone has ever managed, arguing that an individual state had the right, even the responsibility, to declare any federal law or order inoperative within its boundaries, if said law or order was perceived to be injurious to its citizens. He warned that the Southern states viewed nullification as a defense against federal interference with its institutions. And threatened that if nullification was not recognized, the only recourse might one day be secession. Webster's answer took all of two days. I was myself present on the second day, to see him shake his finger at the vice president, who was presiding over the Senate as was his duty. He knew, as do we all, that Calhoun is the great articulator of the doctrine of nullification. Perhaps not the author. It is said that Thomas Jefferson and James Madison perpetuated the notion in the Kentucky and Virginia Resolutions. But Calhoun is the chief nullifier these days, and it was to him that Webster retorted that the republic was made up of people, not states. The Constitution belonged to the people, as did the government, made by the people, and answerable to the people, not to the states. He was for the Union, indivisible."

Barlow nodded. He was quite familiar with the high points of the Webster-Hayne oratorical duel. It was still the talk of the town, even now, months after the fact.

"The president was shocked and saddened by Senator Hayne's remarks about secession," continued Eaton, "particularly since Hayne's brother was, at one point, one of his military aides. It seems nearly everyone expected the president to side with Hayne and the Southern states when it came to the idea of states' rights. The president is no Federalist in disguise. He would probably agree with Senator Hayne that the possibility of a central government endowed with too many powers is a great threat to the republic. But he also believes that this talk of nullification and secession is a greater threat. It also borders on treason. Would you not agree, Captain?"

"I would prefer to leave to you and the president," said Barlow, treading carefully, "the determination of what constitutes treason. But if and when the president points to a man and declares him a traitor it will be my duty to deal with that man."

Eaton nodded. "Fair enough." He smiled faintly. "You see? Your discretion *is* commendable. It's a shame, really, that you weren't present at the Jefferson Day dinner. In addition to the president and the cabinet, at least a hundred congressmen were in attendance, as well as high-ranking officers of the government and distinguished citizens who had been invited to the affair. The dinner was splendid, and followed by the toasts. There were scheduled to be twenty-four of these in all. Senator Hayne was there, being chairman of the Committee on Arrangements, and he spoke long and eloquently of the Kentucky and Virginia Resolutions. He made mention of the state of Georgia, and its claim of sovereignty over the Indians within its borders. Called it, if memory serves, 'a great and glorious victory.' He then proposed a toast to 'the union of the states, and the sovereignty of the states.' I remember glancing across at the president at that moment. Anyone who knew him well could tell that he was about to explode. He later told me that in his opinion Hayne's comments bordered on sedition. But that night he bit his tongue, waited until it was his turn to make a toast. Then he stood, raised his glass, looked the vice president squarely in the eye, and said, 'Our Union; it must be preserved.'" Eaton chuckled. "You could have heard a pin drop. No one doubted that the president was issuing a challenge to the nullifiers and states'-rights men. Mr. Calhoun was next. He rose and toasted 'The Union. Next to our liberty, the most dear.'"

Barlow shook his head. What Eaton was telling him gave him cause to worry about the republic he had devoted his life to defending.

"Needless to say, the president was incensed by what had transpired in that room. He told Amos Kendall that his toast was intended as a stern rebuke upon the seditious sentiments that were expressed in his presence. He felt as though the entire affair had been arranged as a celebration of the nullification sentiment, and as a means to maneuver him into coming out in opposition of the Tariff of 1828, which has so incensed the South Carolinians. A few days later a congressman from that state paid the president a call. I was present, and I remember every word of the president's response when the man asked if he had anything he wished to convey to his friends in South Carolina. The president said, 'Yes, I have. Please give my compliments to my friends in your state, and say to them that if a single drop of blood shall be shed there in opposition to the laws of the United States, I will hang the first man I can lay my hand on engaged in such treasonable conduct, upon the first tree that I can reach.' He later told me, in private, that he thought John Calhoun ought to be the first one hanged."

Barlow was feeling very uncomfortable now. There was no reason that he could see for Eaton to be telling him all this other than as a prelude to embroiling him in the matter. And it sounded to him like a matter he wanted to stay as far away from as possible.

Realizing that the army officer standing before him had no comment, the secretary of war cleared his throat and continued. "Now we come to the letter written by John Forsyth, the governor of Georgia. It seems that Mr. Forsyth is a close friend of Mr. William H. Crawford, who was, with Mr. Calhoun, a member of the cabinet of President Monroe. On the occasion of General Jackson's march into Florida to chastise the Seminoles, the governor claims that Crawford told him it was Mr. Calhoun who urged the president to have the general arrested and tried for treason."

"What?" Barlow couldn't believe his ears. "Surely there must be some mistake."

Eaton shook his head. "The letter has come to the president's attention. He is now convinced that the vice president harbors a personal animosity towards him, and that this animosity has motivated Mr. Calhoun to be the cause of most of the troubles that have vexed this administration from the beginning. That includes the unpleasant matter involving my wife. The president is of the opinion that Mr. Calhoun used the rumors about Peggy to stir up controversy that, he hoped, would drive me out of Washington, as he knew that I was a staunch supporter of the tariff to which he is just as staunchly opposed. The president has composed a letter addressed to the vice president. It is his wish that you deliver that letter, Captain."

"Why me, Mr. Secretary?"

"As I said, because you are discreet. That is a foremost consideration in this instance. And, while you have served with the general, you are not generally perceived to be a 'Jackson man.' Perceptions will be all-important in this matter."

"Do you know what the president's letter contains?"

Eaton nodded. "I and Major Lewis were permitted to read it after he had finished composing it. The president has laid out the charges against Mr. Calhoun as enunciated in the Forsyth letter. He requests that if they be true, that Mr. Calhoun refrain from any further communication with him."

"I know Mr. Calhoun fairly well," said Barlow. "He was rooming at the Langford boardinghouse when I spent a summer there. When he receives such a letter he will feel it necessary to resign the vice presidency."

"That is the result the president is hoping for."

There was more to his being chosen for this unpleasant task than Eaton was telling him, of that Barlow was sure. He had a hunch it had to do with the fact that he was an officer in the army. His uniform would be a not-so-subtle reminder for Calhoun that the president wielded the power to have him arrested for treason. With any other man but Andrew Jackson such an act would be unthinkable. But one never knew what Old Hickory would do. He wasn't very close to John C. Calhoun—while they had been fellow boarders at the Langford place, Calhoun had always maintained a quiet, dignified reserve. He had a way of keeping everyone at arm's length without seeming rude. Still, Barlow felt sure that Calhoun was not short on intestinal fortitude. He was not a man who would be easily cowed.

"Are you ordering me to perform this duty, Mr. Secretary?" asked Barlow.

The question—and the curtness with which it was posed—startled Eaton. "I didn't think I would have to *order* you to do it, Captain. I assumed you would recognize the danger Mr. Calhoun and his fellow nullifiers pose to the republic, and that you would readily agree that such a man should not be one step away from the presidency."

Barlow's eyes narrowed. "At the inauguration, Major Donelson gave me the impression that there was a threat against the president's life. He even gave me a pistol, and made me to stay close to the president. What do you know about all of that?"

"There were rumors that some were desperate enough to kill the general rather than see him assume office. That's all I know."

"Has there been an investigation into those rumors?"

"Nothing has come of it," replied Eaton,

"And you don't, personally, suspect that the vice president would be involved in such a business."

"I would not go that far."

"I'll deliver the president's letter," said Barlow. "I would ask a favor in return."

"What is it?"

"I want to go back to Fort Perry."

"Are you sure?"

Barlow was absolutely sure. This unpleasant business with Calhoun had convinced him that Washington was not the place for him. Even his concern for the fate of his Cherokee friends could not keep him there any longer. Besides, if he was ordered back to Fort Perry, Sarah would have no choice but to part company with

Marten and his band of merry abolitionists. And that would be the best possible result for her.

"I am, Mr. Secretary."

"The president and I both will be sorry to see you go. But I'll grant your favor. You may expect the order to be delivered to the Langford house no later than in the morning." Eaton opened a drawer of his desk and withdrew an envelope. Barlow took it, recognized Andrew Jackson's scrawl of the vice president's name.

"Thank you, sir," he said flatly. "And good luck to you and to your wife."

"I expect with Mr. Calhoun gone, we'll have far fewer problems around here than has been the case."

Somehow Barlow doubted it. He had a feeling the entire republic was going to have more problems from here on.

An hour later he stood in Calhoun's presence, in the front parlor of the vice president's house. The South Carolinian was reading Jackson's letter by the light that came through the chintz curtains draping the windows. Barlow watched Calhoun's face for some sign. But there was no sign. Calhoun's gaunt, lantern-jawed face might as well have been carved from stone for all the emotion his features betrayed.

Finally Calhoun slowly raised his leonine head and looked bleakly at Barlow. "Are you privy to the contents of this letter?"

"I have not read it, sir, but I know the gist of the message."

"Then you should also know that your president is a fool."

"He is your president, too, sir."

Calhoun smiled coldly. "I am painfully aware of that fact, Captain. But he is still a fool. He thinks that by crushing the nullification doctrine beneath his heel he will save the Union. Instead, he secures its doom." The vice president tossed the letter, with contempt, upon a nearby table. "He thinks I am a traitor."

"I wouldn't know about that, sir."

"Yes, yes, of course," said Calhoun impatiently. "You're just a good soldier, doing his duty. But I am not a traitor! I am a patriot—as much a patriot as the Hero of New Orleans. At least I am well acquainted with the basic foundations upon which this country was built. And at least I can see that a recognition of states' rights is the only way to preserve the Union. Without nullification as a defense against the potential tyranny of the North, the Southern states would have no recourse but to leave the Union."

"I doubt very much that the president will stand by and let that happen, sir."

Calhoun shook his head. "The use of force has always been Jackson's first recourse. He cowed the Spanish dons in Florida by marching his army against Pensacola. Perhaps he forgets that Southerners do not quake in their boots at the prospect of an invading army. I would remind you, Captain, that during the War for Independence, the British strategy, as it eventually developed, was to conquer the Southern colonies. They were, after all, the ones most dear to the British empire, the ones that made a profit for the mother country with their crops of tobacco and sugar and indigo. We had no Continental Army to defend our homes and families. No, we gathered together in small bands of partisans, and we proceeded to harass the redcoats. We did not stake all on a single battle, but rather fought a thousand skirmishes, and in so doing denied the British the victory they needed. It happened once. It could happen again."

Calhoun's version of the southern part of the war did not mesh with what Barlow knew of it—for one thing, the vice president had apparently, and conveniently, forgotten the battles of King's Mountain and Guilford Courthouse, among others. But Barlow had not come here to argue military history with this man.

"I have never questioned your devotion to your country, sir," he replied. "And I trust that, as a patriot, you will not allow this unfortunate situation to widen the rift that seems to be growing between the two sections."

Calhoun looked again at the letter, then went to an armchair and wearily lowered his long, lanky frame into it with a sigh. "I do not care about this for myself. I do not seek fame or fortune, and any political ambitions that I might entertain exist solely for the purpose of protecting the state—and the republic—which I love. This is a personal matter. Andrew Jackson has made it so. He has misconceptions about me, has believed rumors that are simply not true. So be it. I will not make an issue of this. I will resign my position quietly. But there will be no concealing what has happened here from the people of the South, and nothing anyone can say—not even myself—will be able to convince them that this is anything but a blow struck against the doctrine of nullification—the first blow against the institution of slavery upon which the economy, the very survival, of the Southern states depends." He gazed grimly out the window. "It may not come next year, Captain, or the year after that. The Lord God knows that I pray daily that it will never come. But now I am persuaded that it is inevitable."

"What is inevitable, sir?"

"Secession, Captain. And with secession will come war." Calhoun glanced at Barlow, and smiled wanly. "I hope I am wrong."

"So do I, sir," said Barlow fervently. "So do I."

PART II:
1832

CHAPTER NINE

L ying in a hammock that gently swayed with the motion of the ship, Timothy Barlow felt so bad that he would have welcomed death just to put the misery behind him.

Ever since the departure of the USS *Constellation* from the upper Chesapeake Bay in the vicinity of Fort McHenry a week ago, Barlow had been wretchedly seasick. The *Constellation*'s captain and members of the crew assured him that he would have his sea legs soon enough, and feel better as a result. That hadn't happened. Three days before Barlow had stopped trying to keep food in his stomach. All he'd had since was water, and sometimes even that didn't stay down. He had vomited so often that his stomach muscles ached constantly, as did the small of his back, and he had a continuous headache to boot. His situation was only marginally better when he remained in a prone position. Everything about his surroundings contributed to his illness—the sound of the sea slapping against the warship's hull, the smell of the sea heavy on the air, and the rank stench that perpetually exuded from the belly of the ship. The one good thing about the voyage was that it had instilled in him a new appreciation for life in the army. He'd thought that such a life—his life—was one of considerable hardships. But it was nothing compared to the life led by sailors. The work was backbreaking, the food was awful, and the living conditions were equivalent, he thought, to what the conditions in the Tower of London had to be like.

Now, on the seventh day of his voyage, he could at least look forward to the hour that would see him depart the *Constellation*. The frigate had just dropped anchor in Bulls Bay, some miles north of the city of Charleston, South Carolina. He thought he could actually smell the blessed land on the breeze that whispered through the gun port located directly beneath his berth. He had been quartered among the frigate's midshipmen; there were seven young men of this rank aboard. A full complement was eight, but one had perished prior to the *Constellation*'s arrival in Chesapeake Bay. It was his hammock that Barlow now occupied.

As the frigate approached the South Carolina shore, Captain Hawkes had ordered the guns on the starboard side run out; as a consequence, Barlow had been forced to endure the clamor of a gun crew working feverishly around him to load and then run out the twelve-pounder cannon. That done, the crews lounged about, talking in hushed tones in the darkness—another of the captain's orders were to extinguish all unnecessary light. Barlow knew that this was for his benefit; tonight the *Constellation* was to deposit him ashore to meet with a band of Unionists. And although this was South Carolina's shore, it had become, owing to recent events, enemy territory.

Barlow was vaguely aware of the sailors rustling about, mumbling their respects as Captain Hawkes entered the midshipmen's quarters, lighting his way with a lantern that had been blacked out on three sides. Hawkes was a stocky, broad-shouldered man of the sea, his face dark and craggy, his eyes a washed-out blue and narrowed into the perpetual squint of one who has spent a lifetime surveying the horizon. Though Barlow had been too wretched to pay much attention to the goings-on aboard the frigate, he had the impression that Hawkes was a stern taskmaster, hard but fair, who had the respect of most if not all of his crew; a man who knew his business and who was *all* business. Out of respect for the man, Barlow tried his level best to roll out of the hammock so that he could greet the captain on his feet. But as soon as he embarked on the maneuver his stomach performed a slow, sickening roll, and it was all he could do to keep from vomiting over the edge of the hammock onto the captain's shoes.

"They told me you were still a bit under the weather," remarked Hawkes. He had greeted Barlow courteously enough when the latter had been piped aboard ship from the dingy that had transported him away from Fort McHenry. Barlow had dined that evening in the captain's cabin, with the *Constellation*'s four lieutenants. Since then, however, Hawkes had left the care of their special passenger to his midshipmen, and focused his attention where it needed to be, on the sailing of his ship to its destination. "You'll be happy to know, I suppose, that you'll be standing on dry land in a couple of hours."

"It won't be a moment too soon, Captain."

Barlow thought he saw the ghost of a smile on the captain's face. "So you would rather be on land, even though you know that if the wrong men discover your true identity, and your purpose for being in South Carolina, you'll likely be killed outright?"

"A risk I will most happily accept."

Hawkes nodded. "You're a brave man, Captain. We could use men like you in the Navy. Too bad you wouldn't last a month on the open sea."

Barlow looked blearily at Hawkes—and realized that the captain was actually trying to make a joke. From what he'd heard the midshipmen say about this man, Hawkes was an individual entirely devoid of humor. Apparently that was not so. And even though the humor was at his expense, Barlow didn't mind. He liked what he'd seen of this capable, no-nonsense seafarer.

"We're waiting on the signal from Bulls Island," continued Hawkes. "We'll lower the boat immediately upon seeing it. Be ready."

Barlow assured the captain that he would be. He could only hope that the signal would come, as arranged; he didn't fancy the prospect of spending another day aboard the frigate.

Once Hawkes had departed Barlow gingerly removed himself from the hammock. He wore ordinary stroud trousers, a muslin shirt and a short woolen jacket, the type that seamen wore. In fact, he had acquired these garments from members of the *Constellation*'s crew. The hope was that if someone in Charleston spared him more than a glance, he would be taken for a sailor and paid no more attention. Sailors on the streets of a major port like Charleston were ubiquitous and unremarkable.

He double-checked the items in his warbag. His uniform was rolled up tightly in oilcloth in hopes of keeping it dry, and he also carried a pistol and some cartridges. He'd left his saber behind at Fort McHenry, in the care of a fellow officer. That was not the kind of weapon a seaman would carry, and it was too large to secret in the warbag. Once this was done he went up a companionway and out onto the main deck. The frigate's three masts soared to dizzying heights over his head. The sails had been reefed and the *Constellation* lay at anchor with her bow aimed at the shore and into the wind. Gun crews crouched near their cannon on the starboard side. Captain Hawkes and two of his lieutenants were on the quarterdeck, the former with a spyglass to his eye, scanning the dark shape of Bull Island, barely distinguishable from the mainland beyond, and, in Barlow's reckoning, about a half mile off the port bow. Barlow's gaze strayed southward along the coast. Not too many miles in that direction was his ultimate destination—the city of Charleston. But because the state of South Carolina and the federal government were on the verge of war, the *Constellation* couldn't very well sail into the harbor and unload him on the wharves.

A voice from directly behind startled Barlow. "The captain says it's time, sir."

Barlow turned, looked at the frigate's first lieutenant, and nodded. He glanced again towards Bull Island. At first he didn't see anything. Then the small but unmistakable pinprick of light, flickering on and off, on and off. A gang of sailors were lowering a boat away; a rope ladder went over the side, and down went the six oarsmen with the bosun's mate, who would be in charge. Barlow went to the ladder, looked down at the boat bobbing on the sea, and felt his stomach do a slow roll again. He feared that he would not be able to get down the ladder and into the boat without embarrassing himself—by either throwing up or falling into the sea. But he had no recourse but to try it. He handed his warbag to the lieutenant and went over the side, clinging tightly to the ladder. The to-and-fro motion of the frigate as it responded to the ocean's swell caused the ladder to swing away from the hull a few feet and then back into it. Barlow negotiated his way down it slowly, clumsily, his foot slipping off the wooden rungs time and again. He assumed his progress had to be a source of great amusement to the watching sailors—men he had witnessed, in awe, clambering up and down the shrouds with the ease and agility of monkeys during the voyage. At last he reached the end of the ladder; he groped with a foot for the boat below, and strong hands grabbed his legs and hauled him in before he could pitch into the drink. He barely had time to settle himself amidships when the lieutenant up above tossed down the warbag. It came hurtling down at a completely unprepared and befuddled Barlow, and would have struck him, except that a sailor caught it handily. He dropped it at Barlow's feet. Barlow murmured a thank you. The sailor grinned, touched knuckles to forehead and sat down to man an oar. Manning the tiller, the bosun's mate growled at his crew to put their backs into it; the oars bit deeply into the dark sea, and the boat danced over the surface away from the great warship that loomed over them.

The motion of the small boat was far more severe than anything Barlow had experienced aboard the frigate, and when his stomach began to convulse a few minutes later he couldn't refrain from leaning quickly over the side and vomiting. But after three days without food, he couldn't do much more than dry-heave.

"Won't be long now, Cap'n," drawled the Yankee bosun's mate, "and you'll be on solid land again."

"Thank God," gasped Barlow, wiping his mouth with a sleeve and sitting, hunched over, while the burly sailors strained at the oars to carry him closer, ever closer, to Bull Island.

It seemed to take them all night to make the passage—and Barlow was just about at the end of his rope, about to give in to his misery and cry out that he simply could not endure another moment of it, when the bosun's mate called out to his crew, in hushed tones, and the sailors shipped their oars, and the belly of the boat grated against sand in the shallows of a cove. Bull Island was heavily timbered, and the trees rose like black walls on three sides; Barlow could see absolutely nothing beneath them. He could only hope that the person or persons who had worked the signal lantern were, indeed, the Unionists with whom he was supposed to rendezvous. But he'd already reached the point where, if such was not the case, and if in fact he was walking into a secessionist trap, he was quite sure he would not even consider trying to escape back to the *Constellation.* He had been born a landlubber, that was plain for all to see, and he would die one, too.

Two of the sailors got out of the boat and pulled it closer to shore. Barlow couldn't wait to get out; he rose, and promptly fell over the legs of one of the seamen, banging his knee painfully against something. He thought he heard one of the sailors chuckle, but he didn't care. He clambered out of the boat and walked stiffly up onto the sliver of beach and paused a moment to thank the Lord God Almighty. Then he turned—just in time to catch the warbag that was being tossed, without warning, right at him. As the two sailors climbed back into the boat, the bosun's mate bade him farewell and good hunting—and in the next breath barked an order that had the sailors at their oars again. The boat swept away from the shore, and was soon indistinguishable against the blackness of the sea, leaving Barlow alone on the beach.

Or at least he thought he was alone. Turning his back on the sea, he saw a shape moving against the black wall of forest, and his heart skipped a beat. The pistol was in his warbag—he could not get to it in time. All he had was a small knife in a sheath tucked beneath his belt at the small of his back. Instinctively he reached behind him and grasped the knife as the shape separated from the blackness and moved towards him—a man clad in a dark cloak, his features completely concealed by a broad-brimmed hat. Barlow tried to discern whether he was armed, and could not. Thinking it better to be safe than sorry, he drew the knife.

"There's no need for that," said the man curtly. "My name is William Drayton."

Barlow relaxed. It was the one name he had been given. He knew next to nothing about Drayton, except that he was apparently a staunch Unionist, a prominent man in Charleston's affairs, and someone explicitly trusted by the secretary of war, John Eaton.

Drayton stepped closer, and now Barlow could make out his features. The Carolinian had a plump and pleasant face, but there was a glitter of hardness in the dark eyes, and his handshake was firm.

"You have the advantage of me, sir," said Drayton. "I trust you're the one I've come all this way to meet?"

"Captain Timothy Barlow, sir, Thirty-ninth Infantry."

Drayton nodded. "Good. I've heard of you." He smiled at the look of surprise on Barlow's face. "They say you're Jackson's sword. The man he calls upon when he has dangerous work to be done. You served with him against the Seminoles, as I understand."

"That's right." Barlow was eager to shift the conversation away from himself. "Did you come alone, Mr. Drayton?"

"No. Mr. Daniel Huger is with me, and my servant." Drayton turned his head and whistled low and softly. Two more men emerged from the blackness of the trees. One was a tall, broadshouldered man wearing a cloak much like Drayton's. This was the Charleston lawyer, Huger. The other was a very large black man. His head was shaved and his arms were bulging with muscles. He wore a leathern vest and stroud trousers. Drayton introduced him as Napoleon.

"What word do you bring from the president?" asked Huger impatiently as soon as the introductions had been tended to. "Will he honor our request for five thousand rifles and one hundred rounds of ammunition per rifle? Is he sending a fleet of warships?"

"The weapons are aboard a ship that set sail from Baltimore six days ago," said Barlow.

Huger's eyes lit up. "Excellent! Then we will crush these damned nullifiers once and for all!"

"You've got five thousand men?"

"Not yet," confessed Huger. "But in a fortnight we will, and more."

"The only problem," said Drayton wryly, "is that the nullifiers are mustering an army that, conservatively, numbers twenty thousand."

"Twenty thousand!" murmured Barlow, surprised.

Drayton nodded. "I'm afraid so. Most of them have gathered in Columbia, the capital. But there are units drilling in the streets of Charleston these days."

"And when night falls the armed mobs take to the streets," growled Huger. "They threaten every man who doesn't swear he stands for South Carolina over the Union. And sometimes they do more than threaten. Last night they broke into Judge O'Neall's house, terrorized his family, ransacked his belongings, and then put the place to the torch. All because O'Neall ruled against a man who refused to pay the tariff."

"The collector, Mr. Pringle, has abandoned the customs house," said Drayton. "He has moved to the fortress on Pinckney Island."

Barlow nodded. "He was ordered to do so by the treasury secretary. He has been given control of all the revenue schooners along this part of the coast, and he will use them to stop all vessels entering or leaving Charleston harbor. The tariff will be administered on the seas—and if it isn't paid, the cargos will be seized."

Huger looked at Drayton. "When the nullifiers find out about this there will be hell to pay, for certain."

"What of the fleet?" Drayton asked Barlow.

"I arrived aboard the *Constellation*. Believe me, she is sufficient to the task at hand."

"The nullifiers have been talking about establishing batteries on both sides of the harbor," warned Huger. "The only thing that has slowed them down is a shortage of cannon."

"The *Constellation* has thirty-six guns, sir—and a captain and crew that know how to use them. But let us hope it doesn't come to that."

Huger shook his head. "I do not foresee a peaceful solution to this crisis, Captain."

"Come," said Drayton. "We should get going. If we are very late arriving in Charleston we'll attract attention, and it might be the wrong kind. We have a boat on the other side of the island, and horses awaiting us on the mainland."

"Another boat," groaned Barlow.

"You can stay with me," said Drayton. "My servants are fiercely loyal to me. They will not betray you."

"No," said Barlow firmly. "Once we reach town we'll be parting company. I'll know where to find you if I need you. But your sentiments are well known to all hereabouts, Mr. Drayton, and any stranger who emerges from your door will draw immediate suspicion."

"But...where will you stay?"

"You don't need to know that."

"You won't know who to trust."

"No offense, gentlemen, but how do I know if I can trust either one of you?"

Drayton looked offended just the same. "Secretary Cass has vouched for me, has he not?"

"Now William," said Huger. "I suspect that some of the men who have joined our ranks and call themselves Unionists are spies for the nullifiers. The Captain has a point. He doesn't know us. And it's his neck on the chopping block, not that of the secretary of war."

Barlow nodded. "Thank you. Just be aware that any man I identify as a secessionist will have to face the wrath of the president."

"Or the gallows," murmured Huger.

"Let's be on our way," said Drayton.

They plunged into the forest. Napoleon led the way, carrying a lantern blacked out on three sides. He extinguished the light as they neared the other side of the island. Barlow figured the man had to have the eyes of a cat, because he himself could see virtually nothing on this moonless night. But Napoleon led them straight to a dinghy. If anything it was smaller than the craft that had carried Barlow from the *Constellation* to Bull Island, and Barlow looked upon it with a good deal of skepticism. Fortunately, the distance between the island and the mainland was not great, and the passage didn't take long, especially with Napoleon at the oars. The boat fairly skimmed over the waters, and the muscles in the big black man's back bulged as he propelled the craft forward. At the mainland they were met by another of Drayton's servants, holding five saddled horses. Without a word they all mounted up and rode through another stand of timber to a road. This time Drayton led the way, and they galloped south. Barlow thought it likely that anyone they encountered would suspect them of *something*. Fortunately, at this late hour, they had the road to themselves. They rode until they came to the top of a hill and could look down at the lights of the city. Only then did Drayton check his lathered horse, and the others followed suit.

"A mile from here on this very road is a ferry that will take us across the Cooper River," Drayton told Barlow. "As you do not wish to be seen with us, we should part company here."

Drayton still sounded more than a little annoyed at Barlow's evident lack of trust in him, but Barlow didn't let it bother him. He had a job to do. He hadn't come here to make friends. And he wasn't going to take any unnecessary chances just to spare the feelings of a friend of Lewis Cass.

"If I need anything I will get in touch," said Barlow. He pointed at Napoleon. "Is there some place in the city that you could send him every day without arousing suspicion?"

Drayton glanced at the big slave, surprised. "Well, yes, I suppose. I send Napoleon to the docks once or twice a week to take note of the ships that have newly arrived, and the cargos they are unloading. He can read and write, you see. And he's very thorough, not to mention observant. There's one thing, though. He cannot speak. When he was young his tongue was pulled out by its roots."

"Good God," said Barlow. "Why?"

"Napoleon spent the first twenty-five years of his life on a sugar plantation in Cuba. Apparently he offended his master with something he said. His tongue had been removed when I bought him off the auction block down there in Charleston, seven years ago."

"Come to think of it," remarked Huger, "that might make him the perfect man for this job."

Barlow nodded. "Send him every day at noon. If I need to contact you I will find him on the docks."

"Consider it done, Captain. Good luck to you."

"Yes, good luck," seconded Huger. "You're going to need it."

They rode on. Barlow held back, letting them get some distance ahead of him. He did not want to cross the Cooper River ferry with them. So for a while he sat his horse and gazed down at the city, and the harbor beyond. There at the mouth of the Cooper was the island upon which perched Castle Pinckney; he couldn't see it in the darkness, but Barlow imagined that the Stars and Stripes flew proudly over the ramparts of that stronghold. And that, he mused, had to stick in the craw of every good secessionist in Charleston. He was well aware of the fact that he was riding into a hornet's nest. He would not know whom to trust, and so could trust no one. One wrong move might mean his death. The fire-eaters of South Carolina were aching for a fight with the United States government. Barlow could only hope he wouldn't become the first casualty.

When he thought that enough time had passed, he kicked his horse into motion, and rode down the lane toward the ferry and the city beyond.

CHAPTER TEN

Barlow found a place to stay near the docks, a hotel frequented by sailors and wharf workers and run by a man named Slattery, who asked no probing questions—he didn't care where Barlow was from or where he intended to go, so long as he was paid in advance. The rates were reasonable, and Barlow paid for a week in advance. That would not be unusual for a sailor who had just been paid off by his captain at the end of a voyage, and Barlow had decided that, if anyone acted more curious about him than Slattery, he would say that he intended to seek a new ship to sign on to as soon as he'd spent some of the money burning a hole in his pocket. The hotel was located in a disreputable part of Charleston, a part that catered to the whims of sailors, and most of the businesses had something to do with liquor, gambling or women of loose morals—and sometimes with all three. The room itself was about what Barlow had expected; its only furnishings were a narrow bed with a thin mattress and a small table with a rickety chair. Burlap drapes hung over the solitary window, which overlooked an alleyway. Old wallpaper had peeled off the walls in great splotches that revealed bare boards. A single tallow candle in a tin saucer stood on the table—the room's only source of light. Barlow dropped the latch on the door, blew out the candle, opened the window a few inches to let some warm, humid air into the room, and went straight to bed. He was exhausted, having slept fitfully—when he'd been able to sleep—during the voyage aboard the *Constellation*. Tomorrow he would explore the city, get the lay of the land.

He was surprised to find that he could not fall immediately to sleep. He listened to the sounds of the city—the distant clang of ship's bells from the harbor, the clatter of horses' hooves on cobble-stone streets, the rattle of an occasional carriage passing in front of the hotel, several dogs barking, a baby crying, a woman's ribald laughter, the voices of two men quarreling at the mouth of the alley. He thought it likely that they were quarreling about nullification—or possibly secession. Those were the foremost topics of conversation all around the country these days. Barlow sighed. A couple of years ago he had been cautiously optimistic about the republic's chances of remaining intact despite the sectional controversy that had been brewing. Now he wasn't optimistic at all. As far as he was concerned, trouble between North and South was inevitable. And naturally he was right in the middle of it.

He had spent those last few years at Fort Perry in upstate New York, far removed—or so he had thought—from the strife and discord. And he had stayed away from Washington, even though Sarah was there.

She had been shocked to find out that he'd struck a bargain with the secretary of war that had him posted back at Perry. And, ultimately, she had refused to go back with him. That, in turn, had shocked Barlow. It had never occurred to him that Sarah would leave him; he hadn't expected her to jump with joy at the idea of returning to the garrison, but neither had he been prepared for her adamant refusal to return. In effect, she had chosen Marten and his abolitionist firebrands over her husband. She claimed it had to do with her mother—she had finally affected a reconciliation with Mrs. Langford, one which Barlow had always wholeheartedly supported, and she didn't want to abandon her mother again. Besides, Mrs. Langford was old and ailing and needed help running her business. But Barlow knew at once that this was merely an excuse for Sarah to stay. The truth of the matter was that his wife did not want to bid Marten and his antislavery people farewell. Marten—and the cause—had a hold on her that was too strong for Barlow to break.

So he had returned to New York alone, thinking that soon Sarah would come to her senses and rejoin him. But the months passed, and while she felt duty-bound to maintain a regular correspondence with him, she did not show up at his door. He'd spent the Christmas holidays on furlough in Washington with his wife, but it had been a most unpleasant experience. She had seemed withdrawn, reserved, around him. It was as though they had become strangers. He had left with a silent vow never to endure such an ordeal again—and feeling as alone as he had felt in a very long time. The marriage was over. Oh, it still existed on paper, but the love had faded away. He thought he knew where her love had gone. He had never met Marten, but when she spoke of him to her mother, on one occasion in his presence, her face had lit up. That, however, was not a suspicion Barlow had felt compelled to investigate. It wouldn't have changed anything if he had, and might have just made things worse. Washington didn't need another scandal, and a quarrel between an army officer and an abolitionist over the former's wife was fodder for the sensationalist editors of the local newspapers, especially the anti-Jackson ones.

For the next two years Barlow did not see Sarah. They continued to write, though the letters became shorter, more formal, and less frequent. In time he ceased to spend every idle moment trying to figure out what had happened to his marriage. He stopped blaming himself—and Sarah—for the failure. The officers and men of the Fort Perry garrison were his friends, and they spared him any grief with a kind of unspoken pact, implicitly agreed to by all, that the subject of Sarah Barlow would never come up, at least not in his presence. Eventually he even managed to find a certain level of contentment in the daily routine of garrison life.

Meanwhile, events occurred elsewhere in the country that seemed to be leading the republic to disaster. John C. Calhoun had not resigned the vice presidency—something Barlow had expected him to do after their meeting, when Barlow had delivered Jackson's letter to the South Carolinian. Calhoun had stayed on, though everyone agreed that if Old Hickory sought a second term it would not be with Calhoun on the ticket. Instead, there was major cabinet reshuffling. John Eaton resigned, replaced as secretary of war by Lewis Cass. Other cabinet members also turned in their resignations, although they claimed publicly that they had done so under pressure from the president. Van Buren resigned, too, and was promptly made ambassador to the Court of St. James. The conventional wisdom was that Jackson did this to remove the Fox of Kinderhook from the political bloodshed in the capital, so that he could be brought back in 1832 as an unsullied candidate for the vice presidency.

And even while he retained the vice presidency, Calhoun continued to write in defense of the doctrine of nullification. His so-called Fort Hill Address. The individual state conventions, he had said, had created the Constitution, and since this was the case, those bodies had the power to declare acts of Congress unconstitutional and to nullify them. Once nullified, a law would become inoperative within the state. The state, therefore, would have no reason to secede from the Union to protect its citizens or its interests. Nullification, argued Calhoun, was the only way an individual state could protect itself from the tyranny of a central government.

Then, in 1831, radical nullifiers led by the likes of George McDuffie and James Hamilton, both of them South Carolina congressmen, had organized the States' Rights and Free Trade Association. That same year, William Lloyd Garrison had published the first issue of the virulently abolitionist newspaper, *The Liberator,* in Boston. Garrison claimed that slavery was a sin. A sinner did not stop sinning gradually, and slavery could not be ended gradually. It had to be rooted out, by violence if necessary, to save the nation's soul. This was followed by several slave insurrections, and while reasonable men doubted there was any connection, radical Southerners were quick to blame Garrison for inciting slaves to revolt—and never mind that Southern laws prohibited slaves from learning how to read a newspaper. Of the revolts, that led by Nat Turner in Southampton County, Virginia had been the worst, with fifty-seven whites butchered, including women and children; a couple of hundred slaves—most of whom had not participated in the rebellion—were executed. After that the nullifiers won the South Carolina state assembly.

Andrew Jackson reacted predictably. Anticipating an uprising by the nullifiers, he ordered the secretary of war to replace the garrisons in the federal forts around Charleston Harbor with fresh troops, suspecting that the soldiers who had been stationed there for so long might have become "corrupted" by the "traitorous mutterings" of the inhabitants. He placed General Winfield Scott in command of all Union forces there, and assigned a trusted naval officer, Jesse Duncan Elliott, to the naval command at Norfolk with orders to prepare to send a fleet of warships against South Carolina at a moment's notice. The president also began cultivating a network of informants in Charleston, men like Joel Poinsett and William Drayton and Daniel Huger—men whose sentiments in favor of the Union were well known and believed to be genuine. He had sent an agent to Charleston in the guise of a post-office inspector to report on the condition of the federal forts and to uncover any nullifiers that might hold positions in the revenue service.

Then, in 1832, South Carolina held its state elections, and put the radical nullifier James Hamilton into the governor's mansion. Hamilton's first order of business had been to call a special session of the legislature, which promptly enacted a law calling for a state convention to meet in Columbia. The five-day convention produced an ordinance declaring the tariffs of 1828 and 1832 null and void within the borders of the state. The ordinance also stated that it would be illegal for the federal government to try to enforce its revenue laws pertaining to those tariffs in South Carolina after the first of February, 1833. This was a direct challenge to the authority of the federal government; in effect, the state of South Carolina was dictating to the republic what it could and could not do.

It was then that Barlow had received orders from the new secretary of war to report as soon as possible to the War Department.

Barlow had known what that meant. Andrew Jackson was sending for him. Apparently, the president had another dirty and dangerous job that needed doing.

And Barlow had no recourse but to respond to the summons. He was a soldier, after all. He didn't have the luxury of picking the orders he would obey.

His mission, as defined by Lewis Cass, was simple enough—and incredibly complicated at the same time. All he had to do was infiltrate Charleston and determine to the best of his ability the extent of the nullifiers' preparations for armed resistance. As an army officer he was, presumably, qualified to make such assessments. At the same time, he was to assess the ability of the Unionist militia to fight the nullifiers, if it should come to that. If he deemed it unwise to deliver the five thousand rifles that Jackson had promised to the Unionists, he could stop the transfer. Finally, as far as possible, he was to determine the identities of the real ringleaders of the fire-eaters—the men who would probably face charges of treason when it was all over with.

He didn't like it. Not because of the danger involved—if he was found out there would be no shortage of radicals in Charleston who would want to be the hero who did away with Jackson's spy. But because these were fellow Americans. While he understood the necessity of quelling the nullifiers, it didn't mean he had to enjoy the task at hand.

To his credit, Andrew Jackson was handling the crisis with more finesse than many had thought possible. While making it plain that he would brook no rebellion in South Carolina, and no defiance of federal law, he also entreated Congress to amend the tariffs that had so offended the South. In his recent State of the Union address he had called for an end to the "protective system" of tariffs altogether, and for the "moderation and good sense" of all concerned to overcome the situation in South Carolina—a situation that "endangered the integrity of the Union." Old Hickory was showing the way by practicing moderation in his response. But so far, his actions had failed to defuse the crisis. That didn't surprise Barlow. It wasn't really about the tariffs. It was about slavery. It was about the shield of the nullification doctrine, and whether the South would be able to use it to protect the peculiar institution upon which its economy and society were based. And, in a broader sense, it was about whether the United States was going to be able to survive half slave and half free.

He woke to the sound of marching men. Bounding out of bed, he went to the window, pushed aside the burlap, and saw a platoon of men in civilian clothes, being drilled by a man in a uniform Barlow did not recognize. The men were armed with all manner of weapons, from shotguns to percussion rifles to old muskets. The only unifying factor in the group was the blue-and-white cockade that each man wore on his hat. Bringing up the rear was a boy pounding on a drum—he made up with enthusiasm what he lacked in rhythm.

The day had dawned clear and warm, with a humid sea breeze blowing in off the harbor. Now Barlow could see the forest of masts that marked the wharves but a block or two away from the hotel. The streets were bustling with people. It was time to go to work.

He had slept fully dressed, so it was simply a matter of pulling on his shoes and pulling a battered old leathern cap onto his head. He rubbed his bearded chin. He was accustomed to being clean-shaven, and the beard made him itch.

Downstairs, the young man behind the desk paid him no attention whatsoever. Barlow hoped that was a sign of things to come. His life depended on his disguise being sufficient to render him virtually invisible in this port city.

He wandered toward the docks. They were not as busy as he had expected, and he could only assume that this was because some ships' captains, being aware of the trouble brewing, had decided to avoid Charleston, perhaps opting for Savannah to the south or Wilmington to the north. A man dressed like a gentleman in cravat and frock coat was standing on a barrel haranguing a small crowd of seamen and dock workers. Barlow mingled with the crowd and listened for a while. The man was exhorting his audience to join the South Carolina patriots' militia and defend the state against the tyranny of the federal government. As Barlow turned away he was accosted by a man handing out flyers. He took one, moved off a ways and then read it—it was an invitation to attend a series of speeches by Charleston's "leading patriots" at the Meridian Meeting Hall on Palmetto Boulevard. The governor himself, James Hamilton, would be there. Barlow folded the flyer and put it in a pocket. That was an affair he knew he had to attend. By their words he would know how serious these people were about challenging the republic.

While he was still on the docks Barlow was twice approached by men looking for sailors to sign on to vessels about to set sail. One of the recruiters, an old salt with a glass eye and a perpetual snarl on his lips, took Barlow's hand in his and shook it. Then he turned Barlow's hand over and looked at it—before peering suspiciously at its owner.

"You've got the softest hands of any seafarer I ever met," he mumbled.

From that point on, Barlow made sure to keep his hands in his pockets.

By the time the day was done he had covered much of Charleston, acquainting himself with the city and becoming quite footsore in the process. He had dinner and then made his way to Palmetto Boulevard, which he had crossed earlier in the day, and sought out the Meridian Meeting Hall. A crowd had already gathered, and there was some pushing and shoving going on as the common people tried to squeeze into the doors at ground level. The upper class, arriving in their carriages, could walk through a cordon of cadets from the Citadel, climb a curving flight of stone steps, and enter by way of the mezzanine. Barlow had to resort to some pushing and shoving of his own to get into the hall right before a squad of burly men pushed the doors closed, shouting at the disappointed—and very vocal—crowd outside that the hall was filled to capacity.

It was standing room only in the great hall, with the common folk packed in cheek by jowl amongst the columns that held up the mezzanine, where the wealthy were seated in velvet upholstered chairs, the men in the finest broadcloth, their ladies in the newest fashions from Europe. Barlow worked his way around the edge of the room, trying to get closer to the broad dais located at the back of the hall. There was a man at the podium, using a gavel in an attempt to capture the attention of the crowd and quiet it. Four men sat in tall chairs on the dais. Barlow's view of these men was obscured by the placards some of the people on the main floor were holding above their heads. He glanced at a few of them. STATES' RIGHTS OR SECESSION! and GIVE ME LIBERTY OR GIVE ME DEATH. He didn't need to read any further. He was in the enemy's midst, a gathering of nullifiers—of traitors, if one accepted Andrew Jackson's point of view.

The man at the podium was making headway—the crowd gradually quieted. He hammered the podium several more times with the gavel before introducing the "honorable George McDuffie." A roar of approbation rose to a deafening climax in the great hall as one of the four men stood and stepped with much dignity to the podium.

"My fellow citizens," began McDuffie, "I am here tonight to speak to you briefly of the new tariff but recently passed by the Congress of the United States. The president himself, referring to the enactment, has said that the people must now see that their grievances have been removed, and oppression exists only in the distempered brains of disappointed, ambitious men." McDuffie's voice was dripping with sarcasm. "It pains me to say it, but it is the president whose brain must be distempered. It is the president whose ambition has been disappointed—the ambition to become a despot, who would strip away our individual and collective liberties if he could get away with the theft."

The crowd cheered deliriously. McDuffie stood there for a moment, basking in the people's approval, before raising a hand to silence the throng.

"The truth is, the new tariff proves that any hope for a returning sense of justice has finally and forever vanished. The principle of protection has been retained. Rates on iron, cottons, and woolens remain the same. The income derived from protective duties has been increased by one million dollars! Yes, you heard me right, my friends. One million dollars more! The question now is whether the rights and liberties which you received as a precious inheritance from an illustrious ancestry will be tamely surrendered without a struggle, or transmitted untarnished to your posterity. The hope of the country rests now on our gallant little state. Let every Carolinian do his duty!'"

As McDuffie stepped away from the podium, Barlow scanned the other men seated on the dais, wondering idly which one would be the next to speak, and wondering, too, which was the fire-eating governor, James Hamilton.

It was then that he recognized John Claybourne.

The younger Claybourne had changed considerably in the years since they'd last met. Apart from putting on some weight, Claybourne now sported a mustache. All the boyishness was gone from his features. He looked fit and strong and there was a resoluteness in his intent gaze as he watched the crowd, and in the way he sat, with feet firmly planted on the floor, and hands just as firmly planted on his knees.

The master of ceremonies took the podium just long enough to introduce Henry L. Pinckney, the mayor of Charleston.

"I, for one, do not fear federal coercion," said Pinckney haughtily. "I would remind my fellow citizens that the great state of Georgia nullified a decision of the Supreme Court. In the case of *Worcester v. Georgia*, that court denied Georgia's authority over the Cherokee Indians—and, in that particular case, a white man who was with them—who resided within her borders. And when Georgia nullified the court's decision, as enunciated by the chief justice, John Marshall, what did President Jackson do? Nothing! Did he resort to coercive measures to enforce that decision? No. Is not the principle precisely the same with South Carolina? Absolutely. All the president said with reference to Georgia and the Cherokees was to remark that since John Marshall had made his decision, he could try to enforce it."

Half the crowd laughed, while the other half cheered.

"I have heard with my own ears," said Pinckney, shouting to be heard over the din, "unionists say that they have grave doubts about the president, for he seems to be half nullifier himself!"

This elicited an even louder response from the crowd. Pinckney continued, elaborating on why he thought Andrew Jackson was bluffing when he said he would not let South Carolina disobey a federal law. Barlow ceased to listen. He thought that Mr. Pinckney—and anyone else who thought Old Hickory was insincere in his determination to crush the nullifiers and preserve the Union—was in for a rude awakening. But most of all he found himself thinking about Rose Claybourne. If John was in Charleston, might not his sister also be there? He scanned the gallery, searching every high-class woman's face that he could see from his vantage point. No luck. And he knew he would recognize Rose instantly, no matter how much she might have changed in the intervening years.

When Pinckney was done, and resumed his seat to thunderous applause, the master of ceremonies returned once again to the podium, this time to introduce John Claybourne, the man by whose generosity, he said, South Carolina would be prepared to defend herself against the federal tyrant.

Claybourne's arrival at the podium elicited another loud and enthusiastic response from the crowd. Their cheering went on for minutes, until eventually Claybourne had to raise his hands and gesture for quiet. Only when he had it at last did he begin to speak, with an earnest forcefulness that surprised Barlow.

"Much is made of the tariff as the dragon we seek to slay, the monster that threatens our livelihood. But the tariff is not the real cause of the unhappy state of things. This present contest with the federal government is but a battle at the outposts, by which, if we succeed in repulsing the enemy, the citadel would be safe. If we fail, the federal government will feel it has won the right to continue taxing our industry for the benefit of the industries of other sections of the Union, and to appropriate the common treasure to make roads and canals for them, and soon enough it would see fit to erect a standard of servile revolt in the Southern states, by establishing colonization offices here, to give the bounties for emancipation here, and transportation to Liberia afterwards.

"Any course of measures which shall hasten the abolition of slavery by destroying the value of slave labor, will bring upon the Southern states the greatest political and social calamity with which they could imaginably be afflicted. It is this which has animated to raise my warning voice, so that my fellow citizens may foresee, and, foreseeing, avoid the destiny that would otherwise befall them. I believe your eyes are wide open, my friends. That is why we can now boast of twenty thousand men under arms, men who are ready to fight, as their revolutionary ancestors did, for freedom from tyranny. No sacrifice is too great for any one of us in this noble cause. I have emptied my coffers to provide the volunteers with weapons. I am currently seeking to acquire cannon so that, if necessary, we can drive the federal troops from our harbor. But I do not think that I have done enough, and when the pride of South Carolina marches against the foe, I will be there, just another patriot. On that you can rely."

As Claybourne stepped away from the podium the crowd in the meeting hall leaped into a frenzy of approbation. Barlow had to admit to himself that Claybourne's speech had been a stirring one—far and away the best one that night. He had men and women both shouting themselves hoarse, and there were some in the hall who wept, overcome by the emotion of the moment. Barlow's heart sank. There was no question but that the leaders of the nullifiers knew how to rally the people behind their cause. If pushed too hard, the Carolinians would fight. Americans would clash with Americans. It was a most unpleasant prospect.

While the master of ceremonies banged his gavel furiously on the podium, trying in vain to quiet the crowd, Claybourne turned to the one man on the podium who had not yet spoken, shook his hand, and had a few words with him. Barlow assumed the fourth man had to be the governor, James Hamilton. Considering the man's station, it was to be expected that his speech would be saved for last. But what was Claybourne doing? It suddenly became clear to Barlow, as Claybourne discreetly left the dais and disappeared through a curtained doorway in the rear of the great hall.

Barlow began to work his way back along the wall towards the doors by which he had entered the Meridian Meeting Hall. He had to push and shove to make his way, and earned a few ugly looks and a muttered curse or two, but he didn't care. He wanted to see where John Claybourne was going, and he had a hunch he would not be able to follow the man through that curtained doorway.

Once outside he ran to the corner of the meeting hall and ducked into a long, dark, trash-strewn alley. As he neared the far end he slowed, hearing voices, then the clatter of hooves; he pressed himself against the wall as a carriage passed across the mouth of the alley. By the light from a storm lantern on the back side of the meeting hall, above the door through which Claybourne had apparently passed, Barlow could see the man sitting—alone—in the conveyance.

He emerged cautiously from the alley and, as he'd expected, found a man standing guard at the back door to the meeting hall. The man looked at him suspiciously. Barlow turned and walked away—in the direction the carriage had taken. He was relieved to see it turn left at the first intersection. He made his strides as long as he could without breaking into a run—saving that for when he'd turned the corner and was out of sight of the guard at the meeting hall. The carriage was a good two blocks away. At any moment he might lose track of it, especially if he remained on foot.

Luck was with him. Just as he reached the next intersection a carriage came rolling through it. Barlow leaped at the nearest door; clinging to it from the outside, balancing on the metal steps, he reached in and unlatched the door from the inside, managed to swing it open just enough to squeeze inside.

"What in the ...! What is the meaning of this!"

He was an older man, frail-looking, white-haired, with rheumy eyes. He had a walking cane, and he was about to brandish it in self-defense. The driver in the box was slowing the team, aware that he'd gained an unwanted passenger. Barlow had to act quickly.

"I'm trying to learn the identity of a man who just passed by here in a carriage. He left a meeting of unionists a few moments ago."

The old man peered at him—and Barlow caught himself holding his breath. Had he made the wrong guess? Was the man a unionist himself?

The old man grimaced. Then he stuck his head out the carriage window. "Harlin, did you see a carriage just go by?"

"Yes, sir."

"Follow it." The old man pulled his head back into the carriage. "I'd like to know who the scoundrel is, myself."

Barlow started breathing again. He leaned out the nearest window. "Don't follow too close, though, Harlin."

"Of course not, sir," said the driver, sounding somewhat indignant that Barlow had dared question his ability.

CHAPTER ELEVEN

"Who are you, sir, if I may be so bold as to inquire?" asked the old man. "You wear the garb of a sailor, but you don't look like a man who has spent any length of time at sea."

"I am an agent," said Barlow. "A spy, if you will. I work for the governor himself."

"Ah, I see." The old man nodded. "Yes, that sounds like something Hamilton would do. Not that I find anything objectionable about it. Desperate times require desperate measures, don't they? And we must find out who can be relied upon. I knew the republic would never last, young man. I was around to see her created, and I said then that the experiment was doomed to failure. I fought against the redcoats in the War for Independence, you know. We should have learned our lesson then. Yes, we should have learned."

"What lesson, sir?"

"Why, that to centralize power results in tyranny. It is inevitable, made so by the very nature of man. Don't you agree?"

"Yes, of course," lied Barlow.

Fortunately, the carriage ride was a short one. A moment later Harlin was slowing the team, and then he turned the carriage into a side street. Barlow opened the door, leaned out, and looked around. He was on a quiet residential street.

"The carriage we were following pulled up to a house around the corner there," said Harlin.

"Good. Thanks." Barlow got out and was about to move away when the old man called after him.

"Here, young man," said the white-haired gentleman. "Take my card. Be so kind as to inform me of your findings. We should all be made aware of the identities of the traitors in our midst."

"Yes, we should be," said Barlow, looking at the name on the card.

The old man closed the door and tapped on the roof of the carriage with his cane, and Harlin stirred up the team of horses. Barlow watched the carriage move away. He had in his hand the kind of evidence Andrew Jackson had sent him down here to obtain—the name of a man whose neck the president could put a noose around, if an example needed to be set. Barlow thought about it for a moment—then tore the card up and let the pieces fall to the street.

He went to the corner and peered cautiously up the street. He could see the Claybourne carriage; it had pulled under the porte cochere of a handsome three-story residence, having previously passed through an ornate wrought-iron gateway set into a high brick wall. Claybourne waited until a black butler had emerged from the house and come down the steps to open the carriage door. He got out and strode inside. The driver of the carriage whipped up the team and drove on to the back of the house. Though Barlow couldn't see it, he assumed that there would be a carriage house in the back, along with a kitchen and perhaps a few other outbuildings. The houses along here, he thought, belonged to the well-to-do. In some cases they were the town homes of wealthy planters, who required a place to stay while away from their plantations. Of course, in John Claybourne's case, that plantation was hundreds of miles away—on the other side of the Blue Ridge mountains, in Georgia. What was the man doing in Charleston?

And was Rose here, too?

Barlow knew he had no choice. He couldn't simply walk away. He had to find out. Even though by doing so he would be risking everything.

Crossing the street on which Claybourne lived, Barlow proceeded down the intersecting thoroughfare until he came to an alley that ran along the back of the Claybourne house and the rest of the residences in the row. His destination was the third house up on the left. He found himself at the foot of a high brick wall. There was a wooden gate in the wall, but it was bolted from the inside. He had no recourse but to go over the wall. Backing up a few steps, he took a running leap and got his arms over the top of the wall. Then it was simply a matter of pulling himself up with brute strength. He paused for only a few seconds on top of the wall to survey the lay of the land beyond. The carriage house was to his left, the kitchen to his right, and a walkway led from a garden shaded by stately, moss-draped oaks to the wooden gate immediately to his right. He could see lights in some of the windows of the house, beyond the trees. He dropped to the ground and crouched there a moment, straining eyes and ears. Where was the carriage driver? Probably still in the carriage house, tending to the horses. He moved to the rear of the carriage house. There was a row of stable doors, all closed, on one side of the structure. No, he was wrong, one of the doors was slightly ajar. He edged along the wall to this door, peered inside. There was a lantern burning—its light was gleaming off the polished flank of the carriage. A horse whickered softly. There was no other sound from inside the building. Perhaps the driver had already gone into the house.

He took a step—then whirled at a whisper of sound behind him. He caught the merest glimpse of a dark figure and the spanner wrench that came down on his skull, and then he knew nothing else but blackness.

It was the pain that woke him—pain associated with the blows to his face, blows so savage that they snapped his head back. He tried to raise his arms to shield himself, but for some reason he couldn't. Another blow—just the back of a hand, not a fist, but the pain was still intense. What the hell was wrong with his arms? Then he realized that his wrists were bound to the back of the chair he was sitting in. His tried his feet. They weren't tied. The hand struck him again—and in the same instant he lashed out with a kick that connected solidly and sent his tormentor sprawling. He opened his eyes, tried to focus. It was hard to do—his skull was pounding. He remembered why. The man getting up off the floor was a burly character—the driver of Claybourne's carriage—and Barlow had a hunch he was also the man who had very nearly split his head open with the spanner wrench. The driver got to his feet with a snarl of rage on his craggy face and reared back with a fist that he clearly intended to drive straight into Barlow's face. But before he could uncock his arm and swing a sharp voice restrained him.

"That will be quite enough, Henry. He's bleeding all over the rug."

Barlow could taste the blood—his mouth was full of it, and it tasted like copper. His cheeks were still stinging from Henry's blows. He spit the blood out onto the rug at his feet and looked up.

"There's some more," he mumbled defiantly.

Claybourne struggled to control his anger. He smiled coldly at Barlow. Then, without warning, he lashed out. The backhand blow snapped Barlow's head back. More blood sprayed across the expensive carpet in the well-appointed parlor.

"As I recall," said Claybourne, "that isn't the first time I've struck you, Captain. I assume you are still a captain in the United States Army? I must confess, at first I did not recognize you when Henry called me out to see what he'd found lurking around the carriage house. And the first time I struck you, I also warned you that when we met again I would kill you. I have often wondered if I would ever get the chance to carry out that threat. But this proves that all things come to those who wait."

"Your father wouldn't approve," said Barlow.

"My father," said Claybourne, without a touch of remorse, "is dead. He's been dead for over a year now. It's all mine now, you see. The plantation. This house. The river schooner. The cotton gin. And, most importantly, the bank accounts. My father was…very Scottish. Very much the miser. And he made sure, while he was alive, that I never got any of the money. But now I've got it all. I must tell you, Captain, that in large measure I have you to thank for that!"

"Really," said Barlow.

"Yes, really. You see, my father always favored Rose over me. I long suspected that when he died he would will nearly everything to her. And he probably would have—except for you. After you left, Rose spurned all the fine young eligible bachelors who came court-ing. There were several among them that my father would have liked very much for her to marry. But she'd have nothing to do with any of them. She and my father often argued about it. She would tell him that she loved only one man, and she would never give herself to another. Finally, he told her that she would inherit noth-ing unless she married someone of whom he approved. She was not persuaded. So now, I have everything. Naturally, I am duty-bound to provide for her, which I do in a very generous fashion."

"You may still end up with nothing, Claybourne," said Barlow. "You picked the wrong side in this little nullification matter."

"Down to business, eh? Just like a Yankee. Always to the point. No taste for the amenities. Very well. We shall talk business. Yes, I am a nullifier. As soon as South Carolina passed the ordinance of nullification, I came home immediately. I wanted to participate in this noble cause, upon which so much depends. I despise the uniform you ordinarily wear, Captain, and everything it stands for. If I had my way, South Carolina would leave the Union at once. As it is, I am forced to bide my time—and to play whatever role I can in souring relations between my beloved state and the Union which she so rashly joined."

"You're a traitor. And you'll meet a traitor's end."

"I am a patriot," snapped Claybourne, his anger on the rise again. "And you are a spy. Sent, no doubt, by that tyrant Jackson. You know what happens to spies, don't you, Captain?"

Barlow looked at Henry. "I suppose you'll be the one to do it. He doesn't have the guts."

"That's where you're wrong," hissed Claybourne. "We will have that reckoning I promised you years ago. First thing in the morn-ing we shall go to the customary place. I'll allow you to choose the weapon. This is, after all, an affair of honor, and, though you long ago demonstrated that you were without honor, I am not, and I will deal with you in an honorable fashion. It doesn't matter, really. Swords or pistols. Either way, in the morning you will die. I'll have you know I've killed four men on the field of honor in the past two years. Does that surprise you?" Claybourne smiled unpleasantly. "It surprised my father, I can tell you, when he learned of the first affair. I thought he would be proud of me, at last. But he never gave any indication of that. But I do think, near the end, that he was a little afraid of me."

"And that made you feel a lot better, I'm sure," said Barlow dryly.

"It's a shame, though, that you won't be around tomorrow at sundown," said Claybourne. "You'll miss all the fun. The federal troops have pulled back to their island strongholds—with one exception. They still hold the arsenal on Market Street. But after tomorrow, they won't."

"Attack the flag, Claybourne, and you'll have declared war on the United States."

"That is my intention." Claybourne turned to Henry. "Put him somewhere out of sight and watch him until morning." He strode to the doors that opened to the home's main hall. "Jericho! Come here at once!"

Barlow saw the black man enter the room. Jericho looked at him and didn't seem to recognize him. Barlow figured that was because of the beard and all the blood. He wasn't sure if his own mother would recognize him in the condition he was in.

"Jericho, clean up this mess in here," said Claybourne. He turned back to Barlow. "I hope you'll excuse me, Captain, but it has been a long night and I am tired. I will see you in the morning— let's say at dawn?" He grinned—and it wasn't a very pretty sight. Clearly, John Claybourne anticipated with great relish the opportunity to kill him. *Even though his father is gone,* mused Barlow, *he still thinks he has a lot to prove.*

Now Henry had a pistol in one hand and a knife in the other. He used the latter to cut the ropes that bound Barlow to the chair. Barlow rubbed his wrists. He had rubbed them raw straining against the rough hemp. Henry held the pistol on him.

"We're going back out to the carriage house. Mr. Claybourne don't want no stinkin' Yankee in his home. You try anything, I'll shoot you down like the dog you are."

"I'm not going anywhere," said Barlow fiercely. "Not until after I've killed your master."

Henry chuckled. "You don't stand a chance against him."

Barlow wasn't going to debate the point. He got up and walked, with as much dignity as he could muster, out of the parlor and into the main hall. He glanced up the grand staircase as he passed it by, wondering if Rose was up there. Probably not. She was probably back on the plantation in Georgia. It was a shame—he would have liked one more glimpse of her before he died.

Once in the carriage house, Henry found some more rope and made Barlow sit with his back to a stout post before tying his hands behind him—making the bindings as tight as possible. In a matter of minutes Barlow once again had no feeling in his hands. Henry stationed himself on a barrel about twenty feet away, still holding the pistol—the knife was back in its belt sheath. Barlow closed his eyes, rested his head on the post, and tried to sleep. He would need all his strength for the morning. He expected it to be hard, though—most men would find it so, knowing that in all likelihood they were experiencing their last few hours among the living. Barlow had known a condemned man—a private in the Thirty-ninth who had deserted the Fort Perry garrison. He had been captured at the St. Lawrence River and brought back and tried and sentenced to death. Barlow had spent that last night with the man, sitting outside his cell, and watched the private pace, and pray, and sit hunched up in a corner, staring into space—thinking, perhaps, of wrong roads taken and missed opportunities. He had tried to eat, but couldn't keep the food down. He had tried to play a game of cards with Barlow, but couldn't concentrate. And as the dawn approached he had lost control, and broken down. It had been a terrible ordeal—for Barlow, as well. The most difficult—and important—thing a man had to do in life was to die well. The private had failed. Barlow was determined not to.

In spite of the situation he *did* doze off. A sound woke him with a start. Henry lay sprawled face-down on the ground. Barlow stared dumbly for an instant, then looked up to see Rose. She dropped the spanner wrench—was it the same one Henry had used on him earlier that night?—and rushed to him. Kneeling, she gingerly touched his cheek, an expression of horror on her lovely face.

"Oh my God," she breathed. "What have they done to you?"

"It looks worse than it is," he said, trying not to flinch—even her gentle touch hurt him.

She leaned closer and brushed her lips against his.

It was better than any medicine—and Barlow forgot all about the pain he was in.

"Quick," he said. "There's a knife on his belt. Cut me loose."

Rose wasted no time doing as he asked. Barlow flexed his fingers and rubbed his hands together, trying to get the circulation going again.

"Jericho told me you were here, and what was happening," said Rose. "I waited until I was sure John was asleep. I'm sorry it took so long...." She looked close to tears, so severe was the anguish she felt seeing him in this condition. "What are you doing here, Timothy?"

"I'll tell you all about it later. Now's not the time nor the place." Barlow went to the unconscious Henry, rolled the man over. There was the pistol—it had fallen beneath the driver. Barlow picked it up, checked its loads, and stuck it under his belt. He turned back to Rose, having had a few seconds to think it through. "You'd better come with me," he said. "Once your brother finds out what's happened there's no telling what he might do."

"Yes," she breathed, without a second's hesitation. "I will go with you. I will go *anywhere* with you."

Barlow smiled. "The only problem is, I'm not sure where we should go."

She took his hand. "I know a place. Come. Jericho has gone to fetch Hannibal. They should be waiting for us at the corner of the street. There's no time to lose."

"Just one more thing." Barlow used the rope that had once bound him to tie Henry's hands and feet. Then he tore the sleeve of the man's shirt off, wadded it up, and stuffed it in the driver's mouth. The belt came next, pulled tightly around Henry's head to hold the gag in. "There," he said, when done. "That should hold him for a while when he comes to."

"I hit him very hard," said Rose, in a small voice. "But I didn't care. I would kill for you if I had to."

He looked at her—and could tell she was in earnest. It was a simple statement of fact; she wasn't engaging in melodrama.

"He'll be all right," said Barlow. "Let's go."

She led the way out of the carriage house and to the gate in the back wall. She had the key, tied to a string that was looped around her wrist, and in a moment they were through the gate and in the alleyway. They ran hand in hand to the street. Barlow motioned for her to pause at the mouth of the alley and peered cautiously up and down the thoroughfare. There was a carriage waiting at the corner seventy-five yards away. There was a man in the box, and one standing in the street beside the carriage, but it was too dark for Barlow to see who they were. They were the only two people on the street as far as he could tell.

"It's okay," whispered Rose. "That must be Jericho and Hannibal."

Barlow hoped she was right. They left the alley and proceeded down the street. Jericho held the carriage door for them and they wasted no time climbing inside. Barlow caught only a glimpse of the driver, looking back and down at his passengers—a round-faced, portly black man with thick white sideburns and a beat-up old stovepipe hat on his head.

"Tell him to take us to Mrs. Kennedy's place, Jericho," said Rose.

"Mrs. Kennedy's place!" Jericho was shocked. "Miss Rose, are you sure you..."

"Just do it. And tell my brother nothing. *Nothing*, do you understand? No matter what he threatens to do to you, if you care at all about me you'll keep your mouth shut."

"Oh, you don't have to worry none about that, Miss Rose. I ain't gonna tell that man nuttin'. He could skin me alive and I wouldn't make a peep."

He closed the door, spoke briefly to Hannibal—and a heartbeat later they were off, and Barlow allowed himself to relax, a little. Her arm through his, her body nestled against his, Rose put her head on his shoulder. He knew she probably had a thousand burning questions, but she was silent for the duration of the ride, content merely to be with him.

Ten minutes later the carriage came to a stop. Rose looked out, then nodded at him and opened the door. She thanked Hannibal, who simply smiled, touched the brim of his hat, and drove on. They were on a street of row houses—not nearly as magnificent as the Claybourne house. They walked up to the stoop and Rose bade Barlow wait there while she climbed the steps to the door and pulled a rope that set small bells chiming somewhere within. The door opened almost immediately, and Barlow caught a glimpse of a small, frail old woman with a kindly face. She and Rose spoke in hushed tones for a moment. The old woman looked past Rose to peer at him. Then she nodded and stepped aside. Rose turned and motioned for Barlow to join him. This he did without question, and they entered the house. The hallway was dark—there was a single oil lamp on a sideboard. The old woman opened the sideboard, pulled open a drawer, and brandished a key, which she presented to Rose.

"First door on the right at the top of the stairs," said the old woman, whom Barlow assumed was Mrs. Kennedy.

Rose thanked her, and took Barlow by the hand and led him up the stairs. Barlow looked back to see Mrs. Kennedy watching him, a fathomless expression on her wrinkled face. He couldn't tell what she was thinking, but figured she had to wonder about him, considering the condition he was in.

"Are you sure you can trust these people?" asked Barlow, at the top of the stairs. "Jericho, Hannibal, that lady down there?"

"Oh, yes," said Rose, with conviction. "Jericho would die for me. Hannibal is completely trustworthy, and Mrs. Kennedy—well, let's just say she is the soul of discretion. She rather has to be."

Before he could ask why she had to be, Rose was leading him to the first door on the right. She unlatched the door and they entered a small room furnished with a four-poster bed, a small wardrobe, a single armchair and a small table. A thick, oval rug covered the floor. There was a fireplace, but that time of year at that latitude there was no need for a fire. A single window looked out over the street. Barlow checked the street. It was empty, as far as he could tell. He closed the blinds before lighting the oil lamp located on the small table near at hand. The furnishings of the room made it plain that Mrs. Kennedy was not a wealthy person, but neither was she a pauper; this was good, solid English furniture.

Barlow sank into the armchair and winced at the soreness of his muscles. A beating like the one he'd received not too many hours ago affected the whole body—it was akin to falling off a horse a half dozen times. If he sat in the chair for any length of time his body would stiffen, and he would be hard pressed to move again for many hours. He could only hope that the running was over—at least for the time being.

"All right," he said. "Tell me why we're safe here. Who is Mrs. Kennedy?"

"This is a…a place where people meet." Rose looked around the room, and Barlow realized, to his surprise, that she was actually embarrassed. "People who are in love, but who cannot, for whatever reason, demonstrate that love in public. Not very many people know what goes on behind these doors, naturally. I'm almost certain my brother has no idea that this house even exists."

"How did you come to know about it?"

"A good friend of mine, who was married to a man she did not love—it was an arranged marriage, just the sort of marriage my father had hoped for me—met with the man that she was madly in love with."

"I see." Barlow tried to reconcile what he had just learned with the kindly old woman he'd just seen downstairs. Mrs. Kennedy didn't run a brothel; no, nothing quite so blatant. But what she did run here was hardly what you'd expect from a nice old lady, as she seemed to be.

"I know what you're thinking," said Rose. "You are wondering about Mrs. Kennedy, and why she allows her home to be used in that way. As I understand it, it's because of something that happened to her when she was young. My friend told me rumors—that Mrs. Kennedy was seeing someone, the one true love of her life, and her family did not approve, and used threats and violence to drive the man away. But he came back for her, and they were about to run off together when they were caught, and he was killed. She blames the society we live in. The Southern society, I mean. The one that places honor and profit and appearances above the one thing in life that truly matters. Love. She hates the nullifiers, too, I'm sure. I …"

There came a tapping on the door, and Barlow jumped. Rose assured him that it was all right, and boldly opened the door. Mrs. Kennedy stood there with a clean white linen towel draped over her arm and a bowl of water. She murmured something to Rose that Barlow couldn't make out, then handed the towel and bowl to Rose and left, closing the door behind her.

"She thought you might like to clean up a bit," said Rose wryly. Placing the bowl of water on the table near the chair in which Barlow sat, she wet the towel and began to dab, as gently as possible, the blood that was caked to his face. No matter how gentle she tried to be, however, the slightest pressure caused Barlow discomfort. He tried not to show it, though—for her sake. In a way it seemed the cuts and bruises hurt her far more than they hurt him.

"Why did you come?" she asked, as she worked.

"To Charleston? I had a duty to perform."

"No, to the house. I'm assuming you followed John from the meeting at the Meridian. So you already knew that he was a leader of the nullifiers."

Barlow nodded. "That's where I first saw him. I followed him because…well, because I wanted to know if you were in Charleston."

She stopped cleaning his face and looked him, earnestly, in the eye. "You risked your life…for me?"

"Well," he said, embarrassed, and trying to make light of it. "If I'd known I was going to get beat up like this…"

"You would have done the same thing," she said. She bent down and kissed him again, and this time the kiss was longer, more passionate. It had the same effect on him as the other one, though—it seemed to cast the pain right out of his body.

When their lips parted, he said, breathlessly, "I'm…I'm still married, Rose." He wanted to tell her that he and Sarah had not actually been together for years. But that would sound like he was making excuses for himself before the fact. "But, there's no love in the marriage anymore. I…"

"I've got all the love you need," she said. "And if it turns out we can't be together, then I shall never be with another." She said it with matter-of-fact conviction.

"Your brother told me about your father's will. How he wanted you to marry, but you wouldn't."

"Of course I wouldn't. I don't care about that silly plantation, or the money, or anything. I knew it the first time I saw you, Timothy Barlow. I knew you were the man I was destined to love, for better or worse."

"So far it's been for the worse."

"That doesn't matter, though. Don't you see? No matter how much agony it might cause, to be in love is far better than the alternative."

He smiled. "I couldn't have said it better myself. Thank God you're here, Rose."

She smiled back at him, beaming with happiness, so much happiness that she couldn't even speak, and returned to the task of cleaning the blood from his face. He closed his eyes and let her work, made content by her touch, lulled by the faint but heady fragrance of her. His eyes popped open, though, when he felt her fingers at the buttons of his shirt.

"What are you doing?"

She laughed softly. "Don't worry. I won't attack you—though heaven knows I *want* to. You need your rest, and you're going straight to bed."

He glanced out the window. "It's nearly dawn."

"You need sleep. I'll stand guard." She tugged the pistol from his belt and placed it on the table beside the bowl of blood-tinged water. "I'm quite an expert shot, by the way."

She removed his shirt, and gave in to the temptation to run her fingers, just once, through the mat of dark hair on his chest. Then she bade him stand, and undid his belt and trousers. Barlow was embarrassed, but he decided not to make an issue of it for modesty's sake. She pulled back the covers on the bed and ordered him to climb in, and he obeyed. As she tucked him in she bent over and kissed him again, a kiss filled with promise.

"The next time I undress you," she murmured, her lips so close to his that they touched as she spoke, "you're going to make love to me, mister."

"Yes, ma'am," he said.

"Now go to sleep."

"Rose, you must wake me in a few hours. At noon I must meet a man at the waterfront. Your brother plans to start a war tomorrow, and somehow he must be stopped."

"I'll wake you. Now, sleep! That's an order."

She settled down in the chair he had recently vacated, and placed the pistol in her lap. He went to sleep with her warm, loving smile the last thing he remembered.

CHAPTER TWELVE

Thanks to Rose and Mrs. Kennedy, Barlow didn't look at all like the scruffy sailor who had arrived in Charleston in the dead of night less than forty-eight hours earlier. Rose shaved him—and she did a commendable job considering that he winced or flinched at nearly every touch of the razor, and counted himself lucky that she hadn't accidentally cut his throat by the time it was done. And Mrs. Kennedy provided him with a worn but clean suit of broadcloth that fit him remarkably well. There was no hiding the fact that he'd been brutally beaten—his face was swollen and bruised, with cuts here and there. Still, it was the best that could be done, and he could only hope that no one would look too closely. He had to work under the assumption that by now his escape had been discovered. Would John Claybourne raise the alarm? Would the Charleston authorities be searching for him? All Claybourne would have to say was that a spy sent by President Andrew Jackson was on the loose, and the entire city—less the unionists, of course—would be on the hunt for him. He was a marked man, and every nullifier in South Carolina would desire to be the one who could brag about capturing—or killing—him. Still, the soldiers in the arsenal had to be warned. And he was the only one who could do that.

Rose insisted on going with him, but Barlow was adamantly opposed to the idea, and was equally insistent that she remain at Mrs. Kennedy's. There was a part of him that never wanted to let her out of his sight; he'd found her again, after all these years, and he was afraid that if he turned his back on her she would vanish.

That was an irrational fear. What wasn't irrational at all was the fear that if they went to the docks together their discovery would be twice as likely. Barlow had little doubt that John Claybourne would inform the authorities of his sister's complicity in the escape of the spy. He'd gotten the impression that, as far as Claybourne was concerned, Rose was an inconvenience; he took care of her only because society expected him to do so. If he could implicate her in a unionist plot to foil the nullifiers, it would be much to his advantage. She would be spurned by Carolinian society—if not worse. Rose didn't like the idea of Barlow going alone—and he realized, belatedly, that she harbored the same fear as he, that somehow, if she let him walk out that door by himself, she would never see him again. He promised her that he would come back, and, in the end, she relented, for his sake; she was smart enough to know that if she accompanied him it would just magnify the danger.

Barlow reached the docks a quarter of an hour prior to noon, and was relieved when none of the armed patrols that prowled the streets of Charleston accosted him. Apparently, if indeed the word was out on him, his change of appearance was sufficient to throw the hounds off his trail. He could only pray that William Drayton was as good as his word, and that the slave named Napoleon would appear at the noon hour. Everything depended on it.

Being the man he was, Napoleon was easy to spot—especially as the docks were unusually quiet that day. The reason was there for all to see: the frigate *Constellation* had slipped into the harbor under cover of night. She now lay at anchor beyond Pinckney Island, defiantly flying the Stars and Stripes, a defiance backed up with the menace of her guns having been run out. Captain Hawkes was flexing the republic's muscles. The presence of one of the nation's most powerful and celebrated warships made it plain that the republic's patience was not infinite, and that the time available for reconciliation was fast running out. From Barlow's point of view, the *Constellation* represented far more than just his country's resolve and power. The frigate was his refuge. And, even more importantly, it represented safety for Rose.

Once he'd spotted Napoleon, Barlow made straight for the slave, who was standing on the docks gazing out at the warship— doing the same thing that nearly everyone else in Charleston was doing. Walking right behind the big black man, Barlow murmured "Follow me," and walked on. To his credit, Napoleon did not even look around. He remained where he was until Barlow was twenty paces away—so long, in fact, that Barlow began to wonder if the man had understood him—and then turned, very casually, and began to walk in the same direction. Barlow walked to the row of warehouses that lined the wharves and found a likely place to rendezvous behind a stack of cotton bales. Napoleon joined him there.

"Listen carefully," said Barlow. "We haven't much time. I've been found out. And the nullifiers are planning an assault on the federal arsenal at sunset. He must see that this is delivered to Captain Hawkes aboard the *Constellation* as soon as possible." Barlow took a folded piece of paper from under his broadcloth coat and handed it to Napoleon. "Do you understand?"

Napoleon nodded, took the letter. Then he pointed at Barlow and made a guttural sound.

"Me?" said Barlow. "Tell your master not to worry about me. I'll be at the arsenal. But tell him to keep Huber and his unionist militia away. As difficult as it may be for them to stay out of the fight, they won't be helping matters if they interfere. They must leave this to the army—and the navy. I can't stress that enough—the unionists must not get involved! Besides, as Huger said himself, there are nullifiers in their ranks. Is that clear?"

Napoleon nodded. So did Barlow, satisfied that the slave understood perfectly well, and confident that he would relay the message to Drayton.

When Napoleon had left him, Barlow left the docks and made his way as unobtrusively as possible to the nearby hotel run by the man named Slattery. He collected his warbag and went on to Mrs. Kennedy's house without incident.

Rose was so excited to see him that she threw herself into his arms. Barlow kissed her, then held her at arm's length, gazing earnestly into her eyes.

"In a few hours I'm going to the Market Street arsenal," he said. "Your brother and his nullifier friends are planning to attack it at sunset."

"Oh my God," she breathed. "I had no idea. He was careful never to discuss such matters in my presence. That fool is going to try to start a war."

Barlow nodded. "That's why it's of the utmost importance that he fail."

"But why must you ..." She caught herself. "I'm sorry. I shouldn't ask you that. It's your duty as an officer in the United States Army."

He smiled. "Exactly. I want you to promise me that you'll remain here until I come for you. Under no circumstances—no matter what you hear, or what anyone tells you—you must not leave this house. Promise?"

She nodded. "I promise. You're going in a few hours, you say?"

"That's right."

She turned away from him, unfastened the buttons of her bodice—and in a moment the dress she wore fell around her ankles, and she turned to face him, bold in her nakedness.

"I don't care about the past. I don't want to think about the future. We have this time together now. It will never come again. I want you, Timothy. I want you to make love to me."

He went to her.

It was four o' clock in the afternoon when Timothy Barlow approached the federal arsenal on Market Street. Located on a point of land at the southernmost tip of the peninsula upon which stood the city of Charleston, across the mouth of the Ashley River from James Island, the arsenal was a round stone structure, stoutly built, with a cupola on top and earthen breastworks on its harbor side, placed there to protect it from shelling by enemy vessels that might invade the harbor. There were no such defenses on the landward side—it had not occurred to the engineers who'd constructed the place that the arsenal might ever face a threat from that direction. There was a gate in a low stone wall, but no sentry. The building itself had lateral rifle ports in its three-foot-thick walls, and as he approached the heavy, timbered front doors Barlow was aware of the rifle barrels protruding from ports on either side—aimed directly at him. He wasn't surprised that no sentries were posted outside. The small garrison at the arsenal was, in effect, under siege; guards at the front gate would only attract trouble from Charleston nullifiers. There were several small groups of armed civilians located along Market Street in the arsenal's vicinity. Barlow had walked right past them. His uniform was concealed beneath a long black cloak of pilot's cloth—another garment provided by Mrs. Kennedy. But as he approached the arsenal he threw the cloak aside so that the men behind those rifles could see the uniform.

"State your name and your business," came a gruff voice from the other side of the door.

"Captain Timothy Barlow of the Thirty-ninth Infantry. I'm here on President Andrew Jackson's authority. Let me in."

He did not satisfy the urge to turn and look over his shoulder at the armed nullifiers he'd just passed. It would be an easy matter for one of them to shoot him in the back right there and then.

He heard a bolt thrown, a bar removed, and then one of the heavy doors creaked open on its iron hinges and he stepped inside—to find himself surrounded by a half dozen soldiers, all armed, all suspicious. The officer who faced him was a callow young lieutenant, his uniform ill-fitting on a gaunt frame, his eyes sunk in their sockets from lack of sleep. He looked like a man trying very hard not to look scared. Barlow had been educated on the disposition of federal troops in the Charleston area before leaving Washington. He remembered being told that the arsenal and its garrison of eighteen men was Lieutenant Joshua Freehling's first command.

Barlow returned Freehling's salute and extended a hand. "Lieutenant Freehling, isn't it? West Point, Class of '26?"

Freehling flashed a boyish grin; it is always nice to be reminded of the most significant accomplishment in one's young life. "Yes, sir. I've heard of you, Captain. You were at Horseshoe Bend, and in the Seminole Campaign."

Barlow watched one of the soldiers close, bolt and bar the doors. "I see you're prepared for trouble."

"Yes, sir. They've been at us for weeks now. Crowds of men, hurling insults, and other things. Then militia marching up and down the street. I decided to bring everyone in and prepare for the worst."

"Well, Lieutenant, the worst is coming. There's going to be an assault on the arsenal in less than two hours."

Freehling paled. "Are you sure, sir? There are so many rumors floating around this city. ..."

"I'm sure. I have it on very good authority."

"I have only eighteen men, Captain. Did you bring reinforcements?"

Barlow flashed what he hoped was a reassuring smile. "I've arranged for you to have all the help I think you'll need."

"I'm afraid I don't understand."

"I'll explain all to you—later. But first, why don't you show me around?"

As the day came to a close, Barlow and Freehling were up in the cupola, which was accessed by an iron spiral staircase, a vantage point from which they had an excellent view of Market Street and much of the waterfront, as well as the entire harbor. Barlow was watching the activity in the harbor, especially the movements of the USS *Constellation*, which had recently weighed anchor and unfurled her mainsails. Freehling was watching Market Street; they'd both been listening to the distant tattoo of drums, and the lieutenant was expecting the nullifiers to show up at any moment. He was perspiring considerably more than could be explained by the weather conditions. Barlow didn't have to ask Freehling if he had ever been in action before. Though many years had passed, he could still vividly recall his own anxiety when he'd faced a baptism of fire. Perhaps the worst of it was wondering how you would react when the first shots were fired. Would you prove to be as stalwart as you expected yourself to be? Or would you give in to cowardice? No man knew the answer to that all-important question until the time came.

Above Barlow's head the Stars and Stripes, atop a short staff, flapped in the sultry sea breeze. The fact that the *Constellation* was on the move, prowling the harbor, he took as an indication that Napoleon—and William Drayton—had succeeded in getting his message to Captain Hawkes. Barlow steeled himself for what was likely to happen next. Blood would be shed, and at his order. Would it put an end to the nullification crisis, and the threat to the Union? Or would it just beget more bloodshed? Would what he was about to do start a full-scale war between South Carolina and the United States? He didn't think so. But he was making a decision that could affect every man, woman and child in the republic—and he was painfully aware of that fact. Nonetheless, he was pleased with himself to the extent that he had thus far managed to maintain a facade of complete, almost serene, calm.

"Here they come!" breathed Freehling.

Barlow looked down at Market Street. A crowd of men were rounding the corner of an intersecting street and coming down along the waterfront toward the arsenal. Many of them were armed. A few palmetto flags flew above the rabble, and nearly every man wore the cockade on his hat that identified him as a nullifier—or a patriot, depending upon your point of view. A dozen men were carrying a log by means of rope slings; this, presumed Barlow, for the beating down of the arsenal door. Freehling had a spyglass, and was using it. His curiosity getting the better of him, Barlow asked to borrow it. He scanned the men in the front of the mob. As he'd expected, there was John Claybourne himself, waving a saber about, shouting over his shoulder at the others.

"You'd better go down now, Lieutenant," said Barlow. "You must make absolutely sure that your men do not fire first. Whatever happens, whatever is said or done, the nullifiers *must* fire the first shot, and there must not be any doubt on that score."

"Yes, Captain." Freehling went down through the hatch that led to the top of the spiral staircase, leaving Barlow alone in the cupola. Barlow turned his attention back to the harbor. The *Constellation* was turning twenty points to starboard, and heading straight for the point of land upon which the arsenal stood. She was, perhaps, a half mile off. In a matter of minutes she would be close enough for her guns to sweep the waterfront.

The mob had neared the low perimeter wall, and Claybourne stopped them there. He scanned the front of the arsenal, noting the rifle barrels protruding from the gun ports. Then he raised his eyes to the cupola—and saw Barlow for the first time.

"Surrender this building and all of its contents, Captain!" he shouted. "They are now the property of the state of South Carolina."

"You are mistaken, Claybourne. This is the property of the United States—and as long as there's a drop of blood in my veins so it shall remain."

"Surrender now and your men will be spared. Resist, and all of you will die."

"You men!" shouted Barlow, gesturing at the restless, surly mob behind Claybourne. "Return to your homes, before it's too late!"

"Forward, men!" roared Claybourne, brandishing a saber.

The mob rushed forward, led now by the twelve who wielded the battering ram. A shot rang out, then another. Barlow wasn't sure whence these came—until a bullet ricocheted off the retaining wall of the arsenal. He whirled, then, and reached for the flagstaff lanyard, lowered the Stars and Stripes. A triumphant shout rose from some nullifier throats down below—they thought Old Glory was coming down in defeat—but Barlow made short work of that shout by raising the flag once more to the top of the staff. Then he ducked below the retaining wall as a hail of bullets screamed through the air. A couple of them shredded the flag. That made him angry—and pushed aside all second thoughts he'd been having about what he'd just set into motion with the signal made by lowering and raising the flag.

He didn't have long to wait. There was a moment or two of crackling small arms fire—and then the deafening roar that could be only one thing: a broadside fired by the *Constellation*, which had come hard about a few hundred yards offshore. The eighteen-pounders belched smoke and flame, and an instant later the entire stretch of Market Street in front of the arsenal was a scene of incredible carnage.

Barlow peered over the retaining wall. At first he could see very little—a pall of smoke hung over the scene. Gradually, though, the breeze off the sea shredded the smoke, and what met his eyes was worse than he had imagined. The dead and the wounded littered Market Street. Some of the houses facing the street had been severely damaged, and one was on fire. The remnants of the mob were stumbling away in all directions. The attack was over. That single, devastating broadside had seen to that.

Descending the spiral staircase, Barlow checked first to make sure none of the garrison had sustained injuries. No soldier had been harmed. But all of them were stunned, even horrified, by what had just transpired. They looked at him with more fear and awe than respect, and Barlow understood why. He had done this. He alone would get the credit—or the blame. And he reconciled himself to the fact that, for as long as he lived, there would be some people who would always look at him the way these men did now.

Freehling was peering through one of the gun ports. "God Almighty," he muttered. He looked at Barlow and said it again. "God Almighty."

"Open the doors," said Barlow brusquely. His tone of voice demanded instant obedience, and a corporal hastened to move aside the bar and throw back the bolt, putting his shoulder into one of the heavy doors and opening it a crack. Barlow walked outside. The sun, he noticed, was just now setting behind the rooftops of Charleston. The corporal stepped out behind him, but Barlow half turned and motioned him back inside. Drawing his saber, he proceeded to the perimeter wall. Several dead men were draped over the wall, and a cannonball from the *Constellation* had shattered an oak tree that stood no more than fifty yards from the arsenal. The frigate's gun crews had threaded a needle with their shooting.

The log battering ram lay abandoned halfway through the gate. A man was sitting with his back against the wall, his right arm a mangled mess of blood and shattered bone. He was in shock, white as a ghost, but when he saw Barlow approach he managed to raise a pistol in his left hand. Barlow struck it out of his grasp with a flick of the saber that was almost disdainful. The army officer looked out into the harbor. The *Constellation* had come around again, furled her sails and dropped her anchor. Already Captain Hawkes was lowering the boats filled with the frigate's entire contingent of marines. Barlow was glad to see them on their way. He didn't know what would happen now. Either Charleston's nullifiers would rally and seek revenge, or they would crawl back into their holes and lick their wounds. Either way there would be more bloodshed, or the war was over before it had even begun. Barlow prayed that the latter would be the case. Then, at least, there would be some justification for what he had just done.

Aware that there might be more men like the one against the wall—men still able to use a firearm, and still willing to do so when they saw a blue uniform—Barlow surveyed the dead and wounded in the vicinity of the perimeter wall. It was the last place he had seen John Claybourne. He needed to know if he'd slain Rose's brother, and he was willing to take the risk of exposing himself to danger like this to find out. But he found no sign of Claybourne. He was both relieved and a little disappointed as he returned to the arsenal to await the arrival of the marines.

The lieutenant in charge of the marines presented himself to Barlow with a stiff salute; his orders, he said, included making certain that Captain Barlow be transferred safely and as soon as possible to the *Constellation*. One of the longboats that had carried marines ashore was ready to effect that transfer at once.

Barlow shook his head. 'There is a lady in a house about twelve blocks from here. Unless she comes with me I'm not going anywhere, Lieutenant."

"Captain Hawkes was very specific, sir. He said your life is in extreme danger, and will remain so as long as you stay in Charleston."

"My life is of little consequence to me unless ..." Barlow stopped short; the expression on the lieutenant's face made it manifestly clear to him that it would be futile trying to explain why he would just as soon die than leave without Rose Claybourne. "I'm going to bring that lady with me, and that's all there is to it."

The lieutenant grimaced. Barlow felt sorry for him. He had his orders, and Barlow realized that he was just making it more difficult for him to carry out those orders. "Well," said the lieutenant, "I cannot allow you to go alone, Captain." He turned to a sergeant standing watchfully nearby. "Sergeant, take four men and accompany Captain Barlow."

"Yes, sir!" The sergeant barked out four names. Barlow felt a twinge of guilt as he scanned the young faces of the four marines selected for this special—and unorthodox—duty. He was putting their lives in jeopardy. But there was no help for it. He would have preferred trying to reach Mrs. Kennedy's alone—even though he had most certainly stirred up a veritable hornet's nest in Charleston with the bloody dispatch of the nullifier mob—but the lieutenant was not about to let that happen.

Barlow decided to leave at once, thinking it possible that the Charleston nullifiers might yet be reeling from the blow they had just suffered.

The streets were eerily quiet as they marched through the city. The few people they saw took one look at their uniforms and weapons and melted away. Barlow and the marines kept a keen eye on the windows and rooftops along their route, in case of a sniper. They were all more than a little amazed when they arrived at Mrs. Kennedy's house without being shot at. Barlow's knock on the door was answered immediately by the little old lady. She started to smile when she saw Barlow—but the smile froze half born when she noticed the four grim marines on the stoop behind him.

"I'm truly sorry to bring any undue attention to your house, ma'am," said Barlow. "But due to recent events, Miss Claybourne must leave the city under protection, at once."

She looked at him with narrowed eyes and an unreadable expression. "Is her brother, John Claybourne, dead?"

Barlow was startled. "You know of him?"

"I know enough to hope that he's dead," said Mrs. Kennedy forcefully. "And you should, too, if your aim is to steal away his sister."

"He doesn't care about Rose."

"He cares about his reputation. And you'll have made him the laughingstock of South Carolina."

Barlow shook his head. "John Claybourne will soon have far greater things to worry about. He is a traitor."

"A wanted man is all the more dangerous." Mrs. Kennedy stepped aside. 'The lot of you come in. Stand out there too long and you'll be shot."

With the marines waiting just inside the front door, Barlow bounded up the stairs. He had not quite reached the door to their room when Rose came bursting out into the hallway. She flung herself into his arms and covered his face with kisses.

"Thank God you're safe!" she said breathlessly. "I heard the roar of cannon. ..."

"I'm fine. We must leave the city right away."

"Wherever you go, I will go there, too," she said solemnly.

She didn't even ask him where they were going—but that didn't surprise Barlow. On the way out she paused to give Mrs. Kennedy a hug. "God go with you, child," murmured the old lady. "Most of all, be happy."

Rose beamed—a smile that was surprisingly strong, thought Barlow, considering the uncertain future that faced her—and hooked her arm through his. "I *am* happy," she replied. "Truly happy, for the first time in my life."

As they left the house, accompanied by their marine bodyguard, Barlow thought that he, too, was as happy as he had ever been.

CHAPTER THIRTEEN

Barlow and Rose made it safely aboard the USS *Constellation*. Captain Hawkes was surprised to find himself saddled with a woman—and a Carolinian woman, to boot—but he was, beneath that gruff and salty exterior, a gentleman, and he greeted her with the full measure of courtesy due a lady. He offered her the use of his own quarters, but Barlow quickly interjected, and asked that they be taken, as soon as was conveniently possible, to the fortress at Pinckney Island. Hawkes was about to ask Barlow for a reason when he remembered how seasick the army captain had been on their voyage from the Chesapeake. Suppressing a smile, he nodded and assured Barlow that he would see to it. Barlow was vastly relieved. He knew that the *Constellation* would in all likelihood be stationed in or near Charleston harbor until this nullification crisis was finally put to rest, and there was no telling how long that would take. He didn't want to spend a single day, much less weeks, aboard the frigate.

As it turned out, Hawkes was able to transport them by boat to Pinckney Castle that very day. The commander of the garrison there, a Major Stutman, welcomed Barlow with great enthusiasm.

"Captain Hawkes alerted me to your plan, sir. I could not see what transpired from this island, but I've already received word of it from a spy who came across by boat earlier this afternoon. It was a bold stroke, Captain, courageously carried out! My compliments, sir. You have struck what I only hope will prove to be a mortal blow to the designs of those damned nullifiers. The republic owes you a great debt of gratitude."

Barlow was put off by all this praise. "It was a grim and bloody business, sir. They were still Americans, after all."

"Yes, well... of course," said Stutman, suddenly reserved. "No matter how loudly they may cry out for your head on a platter, we won't give it to them!"

He meant it as a joke, and Barlow smiled bleakly—then introduced Rose. "Miss Claybourne is my... companion. She aided me in escaping the nullifiers. She cannot return home at present."

"She is more than welcome, Captain."

It was, of course, impossible for them to share quarters. Rose was given her own room, as far from the barracks as possible, while Barlow found himself housed with a Captain Moore. In the days to follow, the two lovers found it virtually impossible to steal even a few moments to themselves. Castle Pinckney was a stout fortress but not very spacious; Stutman had a full garrison of nearly a hundred men. In addition, most of the federal employees from Charleston, such as those who had previously manned the customs house, had sought refuge here as well. Rose wasn't the only woman in the fortress—several of the garrison's officers were married and had their wives with them. These women treated Rose cordially but with reservations; in a matter of days the rumors were already floating around about him and the pretty Carolinian. Apparently, the word was out that he was married—and not to Rose. Eventually Barlow felt comfortable enough with his roommate to ask how this could be. Captain Moore was reluctant to enter into a discussion of that sort—he was a quiet and intelligent man who preferred to remain above the gossip. But Barlow persisted.

"Several of the officers here were recently posted in and around Washington," explained Moore. "And, um, your wife... well, she has acquired a certain notoriety as one of the most outspoken of the abolitionists. She and that foreigner... what *is* his name?"

"Marten."

"That's the one. They've been ruffling a good many feathers. Southern sympathizers in the capital have made something of the fact that she is the wife of an army officer, as though by doing so they could paint us all with the abolitionist brush."

"I see," said Barlow glumly.

Moore leaned forward. "Your Miss Claybourne is a real beauty, Captain. It's already become apparent to all the hopeful young bachelors around here that she is madly in love with you. You're a lucky man."

"I suppose so," said Barlow. "In that respect, at least."

"On the other hand," said Moore, "you seem to me to be in a situation that I, for one, do not envy."

Barlow nodded. He had a pretty good idea how things would be for him from now on. Not only would he have to deal with the fame—or notoriety—of being the person who had crushed the nullifiers in what the Charleston papers were calling the "Massacre on Market Street," but he was also the husband of an outspoken abolitionist who had abandoned him to pursue the antislavery cause. And now, to complicate matters, he had taken up with a Southern belle who happened to be the sister of one of South Carolina's most zealous nullifiers!

In the report he immediately set about writing, he named John Claybourne as the man who had instigated the attack on the arsenal, and recommended that a federal warrant be issued for his arrest on the charge of treason. Barlow told himself there was nothing personal in that recommendation; Claybourne was, clearly, a threat to the republic. Not to mention a threat, now, to his own sister.

He also made arrangements, through Captain Hawkes, for the delivery of the five thousand muskets to the Union militia. The weapons were carried aboard a merchant brig that waited beyond the harbor, under the protection of two armed sloops. Using the spy network that was already in place, and through which Major Stutman kept apprised of events in the city, he informed Drayton and Huger that they could pick up the armaments on Bull Island— the same location where they had picked him up.

Stutman's informants told him—and Barlow—that the mood in Charleston was mixed: shock and chagrin, some outrage, some resignation. It was hard for anyone to tell what might happen next. There were some, of course, the fire-eaters, who called for a full-scale war with the United States, to defend states' rights, the institution of slavery and the economy of the South, and to avenge the deaths of the twenty-eight brave men who had perished under the mighty guns of the USS *Constellation*. According to the most rabid pro-nullification newspaper, those twenty-eight citizens had been brutally butchered by the tyrannical federal government—as though they'd merely been taking an innocent stroll down Market Street when the frigate opened up on them for no good reason. But there were other voices, voices of caution and reason, suggesting that the debacle at the arsenal be taken as a warning against rash and precipitous action. This was the message Barlow had hoped to convey.

There was not much more for Barlow to do but wait. If the crisis ended, he could go back to Fort Perry. If it worsened, his services would in all likelihood be required at Castle Pinckney. He tried not to think of the fortress as a prison, but as time went on he felt more and more constrained and restless. And he worried about Rose. Though she did not complain, and seemed perfectly happy just being with him, he was concerned about the hardships such living conditions, so foreign to a high-born lady accustomed to luxury, might cause her. She had sworn that such things mattered not to her as long as they were together, and he had no reason to doubt her sincerity on that score. On the other hand, he couldn't help but wonder if, in time, she might change her mind, might have second thoughts, might wonder, herself, if this was the sort of life that she was destined to lead now that she had hitched her fate to his.

Less than a fortnight after the attack on the arsenal, a copy of the president's Nullification Proclamation arrived at Pinckney Island. Barlow was pleased with its message. Andrew Jackson was issuing a stern warning to the nullifiers. He ridiculed their belief in the nullification doctrine, and pointed out that it would set a dangerous precedent. If tariff collection could be stopped at South Carolina's whim, it could be stopped in every port. The Union had existed before the states were even formed; during the colonial period, there had been efforts to present a unified resistance to the unfair taxes and regulations levied by King George III. There had been the Albany Congress, the Continental Congress, the Committees of Correspondence. The people had ratified the Constitution. They, not the individual states, were represented in the presidency. The Constitution had formed a government, not a league. The nullifiers insisted on the existence of an undivided state sovereignty; Jackson insisted that the states had "surrendered many of their essential parts of sovereignty" to the federal government. He might have elaborated, Barlow thought, by pointing out that the people had elected to give some of the rights they had endowed in their state governments to the federal government. They had established direct relations between themselves and the central government, and those relations should not be trifled with by the states. It was the right of the people, after all, to determine what powers, if any, their governments would hold, and for how long, and to what extent. Jackson closed the proclamation by calling upon the people of South Carolina to turn away from treason and "show that the descendants of the Pinckneys, the Sumpters, the Rutledges ... will not abandon that Union to support which so many of them fought and bled and died."

A few uneventful weeks later, word arrived at Pinckney Island that the Congress had passed a tariff reduction. The bill had been authored by Barlow's old acquaintance, Henry Clay of Kentucky; they had been fellow boarders at the Langford House nearly twenty years earlier. Clay proposed lowering the rates, which averaged 33 percent, with annual reductions until the year 1842, when they would be dropped sharply to 20 percent. Manufacturers in the North—those most protected by the tariffs—supported the measure because it made the reductions happen quite gradually; their whole argument for tariffs had been based on the complaint that all they needed was a few years to be able to compete with foreign goods. They couldn't very well turn around now and say they needed protection in perpetuity. And the nullifiers in the South were more than willing to accept the bill; it gave them a face-saving way to get out of the crisis. They could actually say they had won the war (even while they might have lost the battle on Market Street), as a lower tariff was what they'd wanted all along, and their resistance to it had forced the federal government to back down. The bill was made into law, and Andrew Jackson signed it. Almost immediately, the South Carolina assembly voted overwhelmingly to recall the statute that had declared the previous tariff null and void. The militias were disbanded on both sides. Both sides claimed victory. Barlow was vastly relieved.

There was only one other matter to attend to. As per his request, a federal warrant had been issued for the arrest of John Claybourne. For Rose's sake, Barlow strove to stay out of the search for her brother. A pair of U.S. marshals—a pair of Tench Ringgold's no-nonsense, tough-as-nails men—arrived in Charleston to arrest him. But John Claybourne was nowhere to be found, and the marshals found few of the city's inhabitants willing to cooperate with them in their search. It was thought that perhaps he had sought refuge on his Georgia plantation. But he was not there, either. He remained a fugitive at large, and a hero to many in the South—and Barlow deemed it quite possible that he would never be apprehended. As long as he remained free, he also remained a threat to Rose. Barlow saw no recourse but to take her back to Washington with him. He was to report personally to the president. And in Washington he could find help in the legal transfer of the Claybourne holdings to Rose. Barlow wanted that, not for himself, but for her. As a traitor to his country, John Claybourne had forfeited his rights, including the right to private property. Rose was ambivalent; she did not care whether she inherited her father's plantation and townhome and slaves and bank accounts—she had what she wanted—Captain Timothy Barlow—but neither did she want everything her father had worked so hard to build falling into her brother's hands.

The voyage back was just as difficult for Barlow as the one before, and after the first twenty-four hours aboard the *Constellation* while she was under sail on rough seas he no longer cared that his seasickness left him without a shred of dignity. Rose seemed completely unaffected by sea travel, and did her best to ease his travail. Barlow, meanwhile, tried to figure out what he was going to do about her—and Sarah—once he arrived at Fort McHenry. Assuming, of course, he survived the voyage. Rose had nothing but the clothes on her back; it was up to him to provide for her. But as long as he was married to Sarah that meant Rose was, in effect, his mistress, a kept woman—and she would be treated as such by other women who learned of her circumstances. Barlow hoped that he could arrive without fanfare, without drawing a lot of attention to himself—and to Rose. Yet that seemed hardly likely, as word of his exploits in Charleston had probably preceded him. He suggested to Rose that she remain temporarily at Fort McHenry while he went on to Washington to take care of business, both professional and personal. She was not amenable to that idea, and Barlow didn't press it; it was hardly right for him to secret her away at an army outpost, and the last thing he wanted her to think was that he was ashamed of her. No matter how he looked at it, it was a bloody mess.

He decided that the only recourse open to him was to seek the help of the president.

Barlow felt that Andrew Jackson owed him.

He hadn't seen Old Hickory for over three years; his instructions prior to departing for Charleston had come entirely from the secretary of war, Lewis Cass, who spoke for the president. When Major Donelson ushered Barlow into Jackson's private study upstairs at the White House, the latter was shocked by the president's appearance. He seemed to have aged twenty years. He was pale, gaunt, his deeply lined face reflecting the constant physical pain in which he lived. Quite apart from the usual ailments of the elderly, Jackson suffered greatly from not one but two bullets which he carried as mementos from past duels. One had been the gift of Thomas Hart Benton, now a respected senator from the great state of Missouri. Where once the two men had been mortal enemies, they were now staunch political allies. Such was the irony of politics—it made for strange bedfellows. The other bullet, which rested dangerously close to Jackson's heart, was the consequence of an earlier duel with Charles Dickinson over a bet made on a horse race. A notorious duelist, Dickinson was expected to kill Jackson, and demonstrated his expertise on the morning on which the affair of honor was scheduled to take place by putting a bullet into Jackson's chest—a bullet, it was learned later, that shattered two ribs and lodged within an inch of the heart. But that heart did not fail Andrew Jackson. Teeth clenched, Jackson stayed standing. Dickinson was forced to stand at his mark while his adversary raised his pistol and took careful aim. Jackson's bullet struck Dickinson directly below the ribs, passing cleanly through his body. Dickinson soon bled to death.

Now, though, Andrew Jackson hardly looked like the kind of man who could have performed such heroics. He sat slumped in his chair behind a map cluttered with correspondence, his chin on his shoulder, and for a moment Barlow thought that perhaps the president had dozed off. But when Major Donelson loudly cleared his throat Jackson started, raised his head, and pushed his spectacles further up his nose so that he could identify the two men standing across the desk from him. An expression of pure delight danced across his features as he recognized Barlow. He got up and, leaning for support against the desk, extended a hand. Barlow was honored, and took the hand.

"Captain Barlow!" exclaimed Jackson. "The hero of the hour! By the Eternal, I *knew* sending you down there was the right decision from the very start. You showed those damned nullifiers the error of their ways! Major, some brandy for our guest. Or perhaps you'd prefer bourbon?"

Barlow needed a drink, and opted for bourbon. Donelson went to a side table and poured him a glass. Jackson bade him take a seat, and Barlow complied. He was in full dress uniform, and every brass button shone. He was as impeccable as he'd ever been, thanks to the efforts of Rose Claybourne, whom he had left in her room at Gadsby's Hotel. Thinking about her—as he usually did when in a conscious state—he became anxious to get past the business of his meeting with the president so that he could move on to the favor he wanted to ask.

Jackson wanted to hear all the details of his adventures in South Carolina, though, and he asked many questions, preventing Barlow from delivering a concise report. In fact, the process took more than an hour. At the end of it, Jackson nodded and pursed his lips. This Barlow was surprised to see, for he knew it to be a sign of disapproval.

"I am disappointed in one respect, Captain," said the president. "And that is that you failed to provide me with the evidence I would require before I might get away with hanging that scoundrel, Calhoun."

Barlow was startled. He'd thought the personal quarrel between Jackson and Calhoun had gone by the wayside, so many were the more pressing issues of state that weighed heavily upon the president. But apparently Old Hickory was still not one to forgive a perceived slight.

"I wasn't aware that was part of my mission, Mr. President."

"Of course it was. You were to provide me with the names of the ringleaders. Those damned South Carolina fire-eaters who want nothing more than to tear our republic asunder! We've shut them up for a while, I'll grant you. But they won't stay quiet forever. Mark my words, they'll make more trouble in the future. The whole lot of them ought to be hanged. And John C. Calhoun is the Great Nullifier himself."

"John C. Calhoun must have been at Fort Hill," said Barlow, speaking of the South Carolina statesman's home. "He was nowhere near Charleston and, as far as I know, had nothing whatsoever to do with the events that took place there."

"Oh, he's too sly for that. He's a cunning devil, that one. Always working behind the scenes. Letting others take the risks, or do his dirty work for him."

Barlow had to wonder how much of this contempt harbored by the president for Calhoun stemmed from the Peggy Eaton affair of a few years earlier. Then, Jackson had been convinced that Calhoun was masterminding a scheme to embarrass his administration.

"Well, sir," said Barlow, "if you *want* to start a war with the Southern states, then put Mr. Calhoun's feet upon the scaffold. I guarantee that would get the job done."

Jackson peered at Barlow for a moment, and the latter had no idea what was coming next. An explosion of anger? A sharp reprimand? Instead, Old Hickory slowly smiled.

"Still not afraid to speak your mind, I see, Captain."

"You once told me that you preferred it that way."

"You and I don't see eye to eye on many matters. Makes me wonder why it is that in a crisis you are always willing to serve me."

"I serve the republic, sir."

Barlow was aware of the look Major Donelson fired at him—a look of amazement as well as amusement. Evidently, the major was unaccustomed to people speaking to Old Hickory so bluntly.

"I *am* the republic, Captain, as long as I hold this office."

"No, sir. That's the kind of thing a tyrant would say. And you're not a tyrant, Mr. President, even though your political enemies call you King Andrew."

Jackson threw back his head and laughed, a dry, raspy sound that reminded Barlow, for some reason, of corn husks. "Keep talking like that, Captain, and I may reconsider giving you a promotion."

"A promotion, sir?" Now Barlow was truly shocked.

"Yes. To major, unless you object. I've requested that Secretary Cass begin the process."

"Thank you, sir. I could use the increase in pay."

Jackson leaned forward, planting an elbow on the desk, and pitching his voice to a conspiratorial level. "Might that need for money have something to do with the pretty Southern belle you've brought back with you?"

Barlow was taken aback. "I had no idea it was common knowledge."

"It isn't—yet. But I've been aware of it almost since you stepped off the *Constellation*. Who is she?"

"Her name is Miss Rose Claybourne."

"Claybourne? Any relation to that black-hearted rascal, John Claybourne?"

"He is her brother."

"And what is she to you?"

"She is ... everything."

"Everything," muttered Jackson, and leaned back in his chair to stare balefully at Barlow. "An odd thing for a married man to say about a woman other than his wife."

"My wife and I have been ... estranged for several years now." Barlow winced as he spoke the words—it sounded entirely too much as if he was making excuses for wrongdoing, and he did not want to leave the impression that he felt any sort of guilt where his relationship with Rose was concerned.

"I've heard she's been active in a group of abolitionists in the city," said Jackson. "An organization founded and run by a rather mysterious foreigner named Marten."

Barlow nodded. "When I was ordered back to Fort Perry she refused to go with me."

"And what are your intentions now?"

Barlow looked the stern old man squarely in the eye. "I intend to petition for a divorce."

Jackson pursed his lips. Barlow had a fairly good idea that Old Hickory disapproved of his plans. The old man was a stickler when it came to personal matters. He believed in the sanctity of marriage. This, despite the fact that he had fallen in love with—some said he'd run away with—Rachel when she'd been married to another man.

"It seems to me," said the president, after a moment, "that you should escort Miss Claybourne home to Georgia."

"Excuse me, sir?" At first Barlow thought the president was advising him to rid himself of Rose. And that was one thing he would never do.

"Her brother has, so far, eluded capture. As a fugitive from justice and a traitor to his country he has no right to the property bequeathed to him by his father's will. Confer with Judge Tolliver on that matter."

"Judge Tolliver will not be inclined to help me, Mr. President."

Jackson chuckled. "A man with principles makes many enemies. I will write a letter, requesting that he do so. The judge will comply with my wishes, I assure you."

"And then what, sir? I still won't have resolved my problem."

"Given time, some problems will resolve themselves. Besides, you're going to Georgia anyway. Might as well kill two birds with one stone."

"What else am I going to Georgia for, sir?"

"The Cherokees have agreed to sign a treaty that requires their removal to new lands west of Mississippi."

"What?" Barlow could scarcely believe his ears.

Jackson nodded. "They have come to their senses. Realized that this is their only recourse to avoid certain annihilation. I want you to be on hand at the treaty's signing. The Cherokees respect you, perhaps above any other white man, and certainly more than any other member of the government, or officer in the army. And once the treaty is signed, I want you to take charge of making the arrangements necessary to facilitate their removal from Georgia before the year is out."

"Before the year is out!" The immensity of the task Andrew Jackson was setting for him left Barlow stunned. "That's hardly enough time to adequately arrange for the movement of thousands of people, sir!"

"It must be done, as quickly as possible. I've given you some difficult jobs before, Major. I'm confident you will be able to carry this one out, as well."

Barlow thought about it. He couldn't deny that it would be better for Rose if she were home in Georgia, rather than stuck in a hotel room in Washington, the target of the disapproving clique of Washington women who had caused Peggy Eaton so much grief several years ago. And he felt a certain responsibility toward his friends, the Cherokees. If they were going to move westward, he owed it to them to be there and to facilitate that move to the best of his ability. Of course, it did nothing to resolve his problem of being a married man in love with another woman. But perhaps Andrew Jackson was right—the unpleasantness of acquiring a divorce, a long and taxing process that included petitioning the state assembly and bringing forth evidence to demonstrate that he had just cause for making the request—could be postponed for later. The damage was done—he was already living in sin with Rose Claybourne.

Barlow nodded. "I'll do my best, sir. When do I leave?"

"At once. You will carry the treaty back to Judge Tolliver—he is once again acting as commissioner in these negotiations—with my signature on it."

"Rose … Miss Claybourne and I will leave tomorrow, then."

Jackson nodded, well satisfied. "Good, good. This town is no place for young lovers. If you lingered here, both of you would surely be destroyed."

CHAPTER FOURTEEN

The Claybourne plantation looked just the way Barlow remembered it, with the only differences being that the forest had been pushed back farther and that more acreage was under cultivation. At the midsummer mark, the cotton and tobacco were faring well—in a matter of weeks it would be time to start harvesting. There seemed to be more slaves, as well. Of those Barlow knew, he was most pleased to see Jericho. He knew that Rose had written a letter from Pinckney Castle and had it carried by a Unionist informant to the Claybourne house in Charleston—a letter telling Jericho to take her belongings back to the plantation and await further word from her. Jericho was beside himself with joy at seeing his beloved mistress again, after so many months. The other slaves shared his delight. There was one person, though, who did not seem at all pleased by her arrival—Richman, the overseer.

Of course, everyone at the plantation—indeed, in all the country by this time—was aware of the fact that John Claybourne was a wanted man, a fugitive from the federal government, with a bounty on his head. Richman and Jericho swore to Barlow that they had not seen Claybourne, nor heard anything of his whereabouts, and while he would have been suspicious of the overseer's assurances on this score, they were substantiated by Jericho, and Barlow believed that the slave would tell him the truth. Though sometimes, for his own purposes, Jericho might play the fool, he wasn't one; he understood all too well that John Claybourne now posed a direct threat to Rose's well-being, and he cared for nothing in the world more than his mistress. Rose explained that she and Jericho had been raised together; he had been designated her childhood companion, and they had become the fastest of friends. Jericho would die for her, if need be, or so she declared—and Barlow was inclined to believe her.

The journey from Washington had been nothing short of idyllic for them. They had taken their time, enjoying the majesty of the Smoky Mountains, spending their nights in inns along the way, and had been able to pass themselves off, tacitly, as husband and wife, for they met only strangers, and no one had to be the wiser. No one asked them any questions—they took one look at the couple and could tell they were madly in love with one another, and merely assumed the rest. It was a journey that Barlow didn't want to end, even though he knew that Rose was excited about going home again. She understood full well the massive responsibilities that awaited her as the mistress of Claybourne Plantation, the person who would have to make all the decisions to keep the concern that her father had built going. She knew, too, that there would be people who'd doubt her ability to do so, if for no other reason than that she was a woman. But she was supremely confident in her ability to manage the affairs of the plantation. Unlike her brother, she had paid close attention to her father's efforts in that regard, and she would emulate him. She knew, as well, that some people would scorn her for having anything to do with Barlow. Bad enough that he was an officer in the United States Army, and wore the blue uniform that so many in the South now viewed with suspicion. But he was also the man responsible for what had become known throughout the region as the Massacre on Market Street, and consorting with that man would be an unforgiveable sin on her part where numerous Southerners were concerned.

None of this fazed Rose Claybourne, however. She was willing to fight to keep her father's legacy and the man she loved. She condemned her brother for his willingness to bankrupt the entire Claybourne empire in order to fund the rebellion he'd longed for. As she told Barlow, it was her intention to protect the plantation from her brother, even if she had to kill him with her own hands to do so. As for Barlow, she would not give him up, no matter what. People could say and do what they liked. She had in her possession the only man she would ever love and nothing would separate them now.

And, indeed, she had full possession of Barlow, of his heart and his mind, his senses, every fiber of his being. She was the most remarkable person he had ever met, with profound courage and compassion, an intelligent woman and a sensuous one. She was everything a man could hope for in a woman, and then some. On top of that, she was, he thought, becoming more beautiful every day.

On their first evening at the plantation, Rose had a couple of the house servants fill a clawfooted iron tub with water so that Barlow could bathe. The tub was placed behind a curtain in a corner of a bedroom that Barlow assumed would be his for the duration of his stay. He had not questioned her about the sleeping arrangements. This was her house, and her people, and while he was away dealing with the Cherokee situation she would have to live in it, with them, and if she wanted to maintain some sort of fiction that required that they sleep in separate chambers he was willing, reluctantly, to comply. Once the servants had filled the tub with steaming hot water, carried all the way up from the big fireplace in the kitchen, Barlow stripped down and sank with a sigh of pleasure into the bath. The warmth of the water soothed his trail-sore body. He lay his head back on the rim of the tub and began to drift off to sleep—only to jerk awake as he heard the rustle of the curtain. He thought it might be one of the house servants, and he was prepared to be modest in his nakedness—but it was Rose. She was wearing a chiffon robe, and her raven-black hair hung loose around her shoulders.

"How does it feel?" she asked, smiling at him in a way that captured his heart every time she used it on him.

"It's heaven," he said.

She pouted. "Oh, surely not—it's heaven, without me?"

She let the robe drop, and he gazed at her body. He knew every inch of it, and yet the sight of her never ceased to awe him—the slender legs, the flare of the hips, the narrow waist, the full, firm breasts, the swan-like neck, the heart-shaped face framed by luxuriant hair. She stepped into the water and slid down into it, sitting so that she could face him.

"*Now* it's heaven, I should think," she murmured.

"I should go into Athens tomorrow, deliver the treaty to Tolliver," he said, without much enthusiasm.

"No," she moaned. "Just stay here with me for a few days. What will a few more days hurt? When you take the treaty to the judge then you will both be off to New Echota or some other faraway place, and I won't see you for days, maybe weeks."

Barlow grinned. "We've been together every day for months, Rose. You're not tired of me yet?"

She brushed the side of her foot down the inside of his thigh. "I'll never be tired of you, Timothy Barlow."

He reached down and grabbed her foot before it could reach its intended destination. "You're ... incorrigible."

"I know. And you love that about me."

"I love everything about you, actually."

"Then do what I ask, and stay a few days. And promise me you won't go west with your Cherokee friends. I know that's what you've been thinking about."

"My task is only to make the necessary preparations for their move. To secure wagons, sufficient provisions, a military escort. Things like that. I wasn't ordered to see them across the Mississippi."

"No, but you've been thinking that perhaps you should go with them. Haven't you?"

Barlow sighed. She had this knack for knowing his most secret thoughts. This was something he had never discussed with her, and yet she was right, he *had* been contemplating the possibility that he owed the Cherokees that much, at least.

"I've thought about it," he confessed.

"So will you promise?"

He looked at her for a moment, struggling with his desire to please her, to make her happy, to be with her—and a feeling, almost a foreboding, that his sense of responsibility towards the Cherokees rendered such a promise a dangerous one to make.

Seeing that he hesitated, Rose smiled salaciously. She slowly slid down lower in the tub, placing her feet on his shoulders and running her big toe from his right ear down his cheek to his chin.

"If you promise, I'll make it worth your while," she said.

He grabbed her by the knees and pulled her closer; her head went under water. When he let go she came up spluttering, and he was on top of her, looming over her. Laughing, she gave him a playful punch on the chest, payment for pulling her under—but then, as their bodies joined and became one, she gasped, threw her arms and legs around him, and clung tightly to him. The rhythm of their lovemaking quickened; water sloshed over the rim of the tub, but she didn't mind and neither did he. All that mattered was the two of them.

Three days later, Barlow rode into Athens, Georgia, and delivered to Judge Tolliver the treaty signed by President Andrew Jackson. The judge hadn't changed in the years since last Barlow had seen him, and neither had his house. But the rest of Athens had changed significantly. It was a much larger and busier town than Barlow remembered, the major crossroads of northern Georgia.

Tolliver was still a study in officious dignity, with a faint whiff of condescension. He stood by the window in his sitting room and examined the treaty with meticulous attention to detail, leaving Barlow to wait. Then he placed the treaty on a table and read the letter from the president.

"I remember," said Tolliver finally, "that you brought a letter from the president when you came here the first time. That one, like this one, requests that I give you as much assistance as possible. It seems to me that you accomplished nothing, Captain—pardon me, Major—except to give the Cherokees some hope that they might remain in Georgia."

"And, as I recall, I didn't get any help from you," said Barlow tersely. "I trust this time will be a different story."

Tolliver peered at him coldly. "I've heard, of course, about your exploits in Charleston," he said sarcastically.

"I put down a rebellion. As a federally-appointed judge, sworn to uphold the Constitution and the laws of the republic, I have no doubt you'd have done the same," replied Barlow, with every bit as much sarcasm as Tolliver had injected into his comment.

Tolliver smiled faintly. There was no warmth to it. "I will help you, as the president requests. After all, *this* time you will be engaged in the removal of the Cherokees. What is it that you want of me?"

"I want you to put the word out that it would be in everyone's best interest if they cooperated with me. I will need wagons, provisions, blankets and other supplies—and I expect I will get much the same reception everywhere else I go as I received here under your roof, Judge."

"You're not the same man that I met several years ago, Major," mused Tolliver, looking him over. "You have a...harder edge to you."

"A lot has happened since then. Can I depend on you?"

"I'll do as you ask. But first we must have the Cherokee chieftains sign this treaty. If they don't, then I imagine your orders will change. I have the assurances of the government that if they do not go of their own free will the army will remove them by force."

"They've given their word. That will suffice."

"For you, perhaps." Tolliver returned Jackson's letter to Barlow, but kept the treaty, "I will be ready to leave for New Echota in the morning. I trust you will be, also."

"I'll be ready." Barlow started for the door. He liked Tolliver even less now than he had the first time they'd met, and he wasn't inclined to abide by the rules of Southern etiquette—to beg his host's forgiveness for having to leave. He was ready to go, and he was sure Tolliver was equally ready for his departure.

"A word of caution, Major," said Tolliver, stopping Barlow at the door to the hallway. "The last time you were here, someone tried to kill you. You say your attackers were white men—men who, if indeed you were correct, evidently disliked your affinity for the

Cherokees. Though much time has passed since then, there will still be those who consider you a friend to the Indian, and that means you're no friend of theirs. Add to that your recent activities in South Carolina, and I think it's safe to say you've made plenty of enemies in this part of the country. So I encourage you to have a care. And watch your back."

Barlow wasn't sure if Tolliver was issuing a warning—or a threat. He nodded and left the judge's residence.

Upon arrival in New Echota, Barlow was reunited with his old friend Mondegah. In contrast to Judge Tolliver, the the Cherokee chief had not been treated kindly by the years. He looked careworn and fatigued. There were streaks of gray in his hair. His face was more deeply lined. He was flawlessly cordial to the judge, arranging for Tolliver to stay in his house, and moving himself and his family into another for the interim. But when he and Barlow parted company with Tolliver, and took a walk through the town, Mondegah let his guard down.

"That man's presence at the treaty-signing is a slap in the face of all Cherokees," he said fiercely. "Tolliver has done more than any other man to take away our homeland."

He told Barlow of the case of the Cherokee brave named Corn Tassel, who had killed another Cherokee and should have been punished according to tribal law. But the state of Georgia had taken him into custody and put him on trial, sentenced him to death, and hanged him—even though the United States Supreme Court had issued a writ of error to the state court and had subpoenaed the state to appear before it. Georgia had ignored the writ and the subpoena, and Mondegah claimed that Tolliver, while officially acting on behalf of the federal government, had privately counseled state officials on how to handle the matter without giving up Corn Tassel.

"Sharp Knife did not help matters any," said Mondegah bitterly, using the Cherokee name for Andrew Jackson. "He issued a statement to your Congress, saying that the federal government could not prevent the states from extending their jurisdiction over Indian lands. And then, the year after that, they took Sam Worcester away."

Barlow remembered well the fiery, somewhat odd-looking missionary-turned-crusading-newspaperman he had met in New Echota on his previous visit. "I'd heard he was put on trial and convicted for violating a state law that required all white persons living among the Indians to have a state license."

Mondegah nodded. "Our friends in the north employed the services of two highly respected men, William Wirt and John Sergeant, to take Samuel's case before the Supreme Court. The Chief Justice himself said that the Cherokee Nation was a distinct community, occupying its own territory, and that only the federal government had jurisdiction within it. Not the state. Justice Marshall even issued a special mandate to the Georgia court, requiring that Samuel's conviction be overturned. Judge Tolliver delivered that mandate—and then wrote an open letter to a newspaper claiming that Marshall's edict was a violation of Georgia's sovereign rights. Of course, he used a pseudonym, but everyone knew who had written that letter."

Barlow shook his head. As they walked he studied the faces of the inhabitants of New Echota. Riding in he had noticed that their fields had been neglected. The faces revealed why. The Cherokees had lost hope. They no longer cared to contemplate the future. It was too bleak. Too full of uncertainty.

"When I was here several years ago," he told Mondegah, "it seemed that most of the people were determined to stay. Even to fight, if necessary. What happened?"

Mondegah heaved a sigh. "Many things—all of them bad. The gold seekers came, and though I and other chiefs tried our best to prevent violence, there were … incidents. Several of our people were murdered, but we found no justice in the Georgia courts. Then the Congress passed a law that allotted 320 acres to each Cherokee family. They said it was to give clear title to the Cherokees, so that no one could challenge our right to the land. We were foolish enough to believe them. The truth of the matter is, the reserves were just the first step in a scheme to steal away our land. Some men were made drunk with cheap whiskey and tricked into signing over their land to white speculators. Others were forced to sign; their families were threatened, or their fields were burned and livestock stolen. Still others had their land stolen from them by fraud. The land speculators would use another Indian, sometimes not even a Cherokee, to swear that he owned a piece of land in exchange for a payment of money. It was not his land, but the land agent would certify the conveyance of title to the land speculator, who would then sell the land to a settler. The settler would show up on the allotment and drive the rightful owner out of his house. And if the owner resisted, the law would be brought down upon him. Look about you, my friend. Many of the people you see no longer have a home. They depend now on the generosity of friends or family. I do not know how much land has been stolen from us in this way, but a lot of it has been."

Barlow stopped walking, turned earnestly to Mondegah. "You've done everything you could do. Best of all, you prevented your young braves from going on the warpath. I'm pretty sure some of the Georgians were just waiting for that. Perhaps praying for it to happen. Then they would have crushed you. But you didn't give them the excuse they were looking for. You've held out for as long as you could. And you have held onto your honor. Now it's time to leave. The Cherokees are a great people. They will prosper again in their new home, far removed from whites."

"And for how long?" asked Mondegah bleakly. "They say we will be given land that the whites will never want. Do you believe that to be true?"

Barlow grimaced. "I have to believe that the government will defend your right to the land they have set aside for you."

Mondegah looked into Barlow's eyes—and shook his head. "You have doubts, as do I. Your people will always want more than they have. We are not the first tribe this has happened to. Ever since whites came to this land they have driven out or destroyed the tribes that stood in their way." The old warrior placed a hand on Barlow's shoulder. "I am not angry at you, my brother, and I do not say this to burden you with guilt. The strong take from the weak. It has always been that way. Your tribe is stronger than mine. So be it. We must leave our homes. We know this now. But you cannot expect us to hold out much hope for the future. It will just be a matter of time before we will have to give up our new homes, too."

Barlow shook his head again. He refused to accept such defeatism. "Maybe not, Mondegah. The Indians have friends, mostly in the North. Not every white person is pleased with what has been done to the Cherokees. They will insist that the government keep its promise to you, as well as to the Chocktaws, Creeks and Chickasaws who have gone before you."

"We shall see," murmured Mondegah. "We shall see." He didn't sound convinced.

"Your people must prepare for the journey ahead," said Barlow briskly. "You should harvest what you can from the fields. And you need to tell me exactly what every family will need to make the trip. Whatever is needed, my job is to get it. But we don't have much time. As soon as the treaty is signed, the whites will expect you to go. If you linger too long I'm afraid there will be more trouble— and more people may get hurt."

The treaty signing was a solemn affair Barlow had expected the assembled Cherokee leaders to speak long and eloquently before putting their marks on the paper. It was the Indian way. But the Cherokees were strangely silent, and what Barlow had assumed would be an all-day affair took but an hour. Judge Tolliver made a perfunctory oration that focused on the sanctity with which the federal government viewed this agreement and said something about how the Great White Father in Washington, who had the best interests of his red-skinned children at heart, hoped that he could always rely on the friendship of the Cherokee Nation. Barlow hardly listened. He knew it was all nonsense, and that Tolliver wasn't sincere. The chiefs seemed to know this, too.

Not all the towns were represented. Barlow was aware that a large number of Cherokees had refused to participate in the treaty signing. Led by John Ross, they continued to adamantly oppose removal. The treaty gave all Cherokees a deadline for removal, and Tolliver had told Barlow he was confident that when that day came the United States Army would be called upon to remove the recalcitrant Cherokees at the point of a bayonet. It was Barlow's opinion that if such a thing transpired it would be a dark day indeed—not just for the Cherokees, but for the republic as well. But he kept his opinion to himself.

When the treaty-signing ceremony was concluded, Tolliver repaired to his temporary quarters in Mondegah's house. He was very well satisfied with the way things had turned out; Barlow could take one look at him and see the elation on his face. But that elation faded when the judge perused the list Barlow handed him.

"This is ... preposterous," decided Tolliver, at last. "A hundred wagons, with oxen teams? Six hundred mules? Five thousand blankets? Five *thousand*? And enough flour, beans, rice and potatoes to feed an army of ten thousand in the field for three months?" The judge tossed the list down on a table. "You can't be serious, Major. At best, a couple of thousand Cherokees are going to be making the journey westward. They must use whatever conveyances and provisions they possess. Because it will be impossible to acquire all of these things. Absolutely impossible."

"I've been authorized to pay for everything with government scrip. I would have thought you and your fellow Georgians would be more than happy to contribute to the departure of the Cherokees. After all, it's what you've all wanted for years.

Tolliver eased his bulk into a chair and snorted. "And I thought the Cherokees were supposed to be a prosperous people. The most prosperous of the five civilized tribes. I'm sure they have all they need."

"Maybe they *used* to be prosperous," said Barlow curtly. "But fields and homes have been put to the torch. Hundreds of Cherokees have been hounded or tricked or swindled out of their land. Many of them have almost nothing left to call their own. They would not survive the trip."

Tolliver shrugged. "Frankly, that's not my problem—or Georgia's."

"You're saying you don't care if they make it to their new homes."

"As long as they leave the state, I personally don't care what happens to them. I'm glad this business is over. I wish to wash my hands of it."

Barlow kept a tight rein on his temper. "I call to your attention, sir, what happened to the Choctaws. Hundreds of them perished along the way due to lack of food or exposure to the elements. Many more lost everything on the trek. I do not intend to see that happen to the Cherokees."

Tolliver looked at him coldly, without a glimmer of sympathy in his eyes. "I have done as you asked. Encouraged everyone I know to cooperate with you. But I can't snap my fingers and make a hundred wagons and five thousand blankets appear. I know of no one who can help you—or who would want to. Yes, we want the Cherokees to go. But you will be hard pressed to find anyone around here who will assist them."

Barlow nodded. "Then I'll have to look somewhere else," he said.

CHAPTER FIFTEEN

The study at the Claybourne plantation was a room on the northeast corner of the ground floor, behind the formal sitting room; it was here that Rose's father had written his correspondence, tended to his business ledgers, and, if he'd had any leisure time, taken one of the books down from the shelves that lined the walls and read for a while. After his death Rose had insisted that the room be kept exactly as it had been on the last day of his life. Her brother didn't mind—he had no use for the books that his father had spent a lifetime collecting. The room, then, was a shrine of sorts, and for that reason Barlow had resisted when Rose urged him to use it for his office. She had insisted, though, and—as was usually the case when Rose Claybourne had made up her mind about something—she carried the day.

Upon returning from the treaty signing at New Echota, Barlow immediately fell to work writing letters. In addition to the president and the secretary of war, he wrote to the commandant of the army garrison at Fort Gaines, three days ride to the south. He wrote, also, to Henry Clay, the speaker of the House of Representatives, to the American Board of Missionaries—and to his wife in Washington, care of the Langford boardinghouse on Pennsylvania Avenue.

As he explained to Rose, the last three addressees would, he hoped, be able to help him acquire the things needed by the Cherokees. All three, he thought, would know of the private organizations that had sprung up in the North to send aid to the Indians. In the letter to his wife, he made no mention of personal matters;

he expressed only the hope that she was in good health and happy, and he made no attempt to explain about Rose. Considering how swiftly gossip traveled in Washington, he assumed that by now Sarah had heard about him and Rose; he could not even venture a guess as to what her reaction might be. The Sarah he had once known and loved would have been crushed, of course. But the old Sarah no longer existed.

While he worked, Rose sat in a high-backed chair across the room, near the cold stone fireplace, reading a book by the light of a lamp—the curtains were drawn on the windows and the paneling of the room was dark. Now and then she would glance up at Barlow and smile contentedly.

It was a pleasantly domestic, idyllic scene thought Barlow—and one rudely disturbed by the arrival of the overseer, Richman, shouting at someone in the hallway. Barlow looked up, surprised, at Rose, then rose and went to the door, opening it to find the burly Richman grappling with a man Barlow had never seen before.

"What's going on here?" he asked.

The grappling ceased; Richman had the man by the arms and was trying to restrain him. The man wore the homespun garb of a poor farmer. He was gaunt, dirty and weathered.

"Rawley here insists on seem' Miss Rose," said Richman. "I told him to wait outside but he wouldn't do it."

"See me about what?" asked Rose, coming up behind Barlow. "It's all right, Mr. Richman. You can let Mr. Rawley go."

Richman released the farmer, who, at sight of Rose, swept the battered hat off his head. "Sorry to bust in like this, Miss Rose, but it's Mary. She's awful sick. She's burning up with fever."

She stepped forward and put a comforting hand on his arm. "Don't worry, Mr. Rawley. I'll come right along. You get back to your wife now."

Rawley's head bobbed. "Thank you, Miss Rose. Thank you!" He turned and, with a sullen look at Richman, left the house.

Richman shook his head. "You ought not waste your time on that trash, ma'am," he muttered.

"Thank you, Mr. Richman," said Rose icily. "I'm sure you have plenty of things to do today."

Richman went stomping down the hall and outside. Rose turned to one of the house servants, who stood nearby. "Fetch the medicine kit, Lizzie."

"I don't understand," said Barlow, watching Lizzie hurry away. "Athens isn't that far away. Why doesn't Mr. Rawley go there for a doctor if his wife is so sick?"

"These people can't afford a town doctor—even if they could find one who would consent to ride out to their place. This is the way of things down here. If one of the farmers needs help he comes to the big house. They could always count on my father, and they'll always be able to count on me, too."

"What if it's a contagion?" asked Barlow, worried for her well-being.

"I'll be fine," she said.

"I'm going with you."

The Rawley place consisted of a ramshackle dogtrot house in a hollow about eight miles west of the plantation. There were about sixty acres under cultivation, most of them corn with a little tobacco thrown in. The Rawleys used the corn to feed themselves and their livestock, which consisted of some pigs, some chickens, a plow mare and a milk cow. They used the tobacco to make a little money for luxuries like coffee, sugar and perhaps, once in a blue moon, a bolt of calico. All of the furniture in the house—save a much-scarred bureau—had been homemade. There was a common room on one side of the dogtrot and a bedroom on the other; Mary Rawley lay in the latter, and in a glance Barlow could tell she was in a bad way. There was no color in her cheeks. Her eyes were sunk deep in their sockets. She was perspiring heavily. Rose took one look at her and ordered Rawley to fetch as much cold water as he was able. Rawley and his oldest son, a scrawny boy of about thirteen or fourteen, hastened down to a nearby pond and returned a few minutes later with four buckets of water. Meanwhile, Rawley's young daughters had fetched Rose some clean linens. Once the water arrived, Rose announced that she was going to bathe Mary Rawley in it and try to bring the fever down—and that meant everyone would have to leave. The Rawleys repaired to the dogtrot. Barlow joined them. Rawley was too worried to talk, and Barlow didn't figure there was too much he could say that would make the man feel better. The Rawley boy couldn't sit still and took a walk, while the two girls played in a subdued way with some puppies that ventured out from beneath the sagging porch of the dogtrot.

More than two hours later, Rose emerged from the bedroom. She looked tired, leaning against a wall and brushing a stray tendril of hair from her eyes with the back of her hand. "Her fever has gone down," she told Rawley. "I believe she has the influenza. I gave her a touch of laudanum to ease the pain; she was complaining that her whole body ached terribly. She must have as much tea and broth as she can keep down. But I think she'll be fine."

Barlow glanced at Rawley. The man looked as if he were about to cry with relief. "I don't know how to thank you, Miss Rose. I—I don't know what I'd do without Mary."

Rose smiled. "Well, you won't have to worry about that for a very long time, I'm sure, Mr. Rawley. I'm going to go back and sit with her for a while longer," she told Barlow. "Just to make sure the fever stays down."

When she had gone back inside, Rawley took a corncob pipe from a pocket of his stroud trousers and packed it with tobacco. As he worked he shook his head and said, "That's a fine lady." He gave Barlow a sidelong glance. "You gonna marry her?"

The question caught Barlow off guard. Rawley didn't give him time to think of an answer.

"You ought to," said the farmer. "You'd never regret it. Same with me and Mary. First time I laid eyes on her I knew. You know what I mean? It was clear as mother's milk to me that she was the woman for me."

Barlow nodded. "I know that feeling."

Rawley lighted the pipe and puffed on it for a moment, looking around carefully—and Barlow got the sense that something was deeply troubling him. "Reckon I ought not to talk to you, what with you wearing that uniform and all," he said. "But you're a friend of Miss Rose, and I'll be telling you this for her sake."

"Telling me what?" asked Barlow, intrigued.

"John Claybourne. He's here."

"What?"

"He's here. Well, around here. Someplace. Not sure where. But I seen him. Not three days ago. He come to my door. Asked for some food. Said he was camped nearby. Said I weren't to tell no one that I seen him."

Now it was Barlow's turn to take a long look around. He felt a chill crawling up his spine. Suddenly, he felt like a target. His worst fear had been realized. It made sense that Claybourne had left South Carolina and returned to Georgia. There were still plenty of wild places in the foothills of the Smoky Mountains for a fugitive to hide.

"Did he say why he was here?"

Rawley shook his head. "He didn't say nothing else. I give him some venison and biscuits and he went on his way without telling me nothing more." Rawley glanced over his shoulder at the door to the bedroom. "But I reckon he knows now that Miss Rose has taken his place. That won't sit well with him. I know John Claybourne pretty well, mister. He has a short fuse, and a mean streak a mile wide."

Recalling the beating he'd received in Charleston at Claybourne's hand, Barlow smiled ruefully. "Yes, I know."

Rawley puffed on his corncob pipe a while longer, then said, "He'd kill her if he had to. I'd hate to see that happen. Like I said, Miss Rose is a good lady."

Barlow didn't say anything.

"I don't know exactly where his camp is," continued Rawley. "But if he told me the truth—that it's somewhere close by—I'd guess he was down along Killhorse Creek. It's mighty rough country, and nobody goes down in it unless they have to."

"Thank you, Mr. Rawley."

Rawley nodded. "One good turn deserves another, I always say."

Barlow debated whether to tell Rose the news about her brother. He thought it likely that Rawley was telling him the truth. Claybourne was lurking nearby, and it was a certainty that he was up to no good. But the wisest course seemed to be to wait until he knew more about Claybourne's whereabouts and intentions before alarming her.

It was late when they arrived back at the plantation. Rose was exhausted. She ate a quick dinner and announced she was going to bed—and tried to seduce Barlow into going with her. He created the fiction that he had one more important letter to write, and that he would be up soon. Disappointed, she went upstairs without him. Barlow waited ten minutes before slipping out of the house.

The overseer's cabin was located near the row of slave quarters—a small clapboard structure with a porch across the front. Lamplight poured from a window in front. Down in the quarters, the Claybourne slaves had built a bonfire, and many had gathered around it to sing spirituals, accompanied by a fiddler and harmonica player. Barlow slipped unseen around to the back of the building. There was a door—he tried the latch as quietly as possible, and the door swung open on a squeaking hinge. He stopped, listened with bated breath. No sound came from within. He eased the door open wider. He was in the back room of a two-room shotgun house—the door to the front room was closed, and there was no light there. He could dimly make out a narrow bed, and a chair and a trunk. He crossed the room, cat-footed, but despite all his care a loose board groaned beneath his weight. He stopped and listened again. Still no sound. He began to think that perhaps Richman wasn't in the house. He was a little less careful as he opened the door to the adjoining room. This one was illuminated—a lamp on a table across the room was lighted. There was no one in the room. Barlow crossed the threshold—and then realized his mistake, too late.

The door was shoved into him and he lost his balance, falling back against the jamb. Richman had been hidden behind the door, and now he tried to use it to batter Barlow into unconsciousness. Barlow twisted, put his shoulder into the door, and pushed back with all his strength. Richman stumbled backwards, giving Barlow time to get through the door. Richman cast about for a weapon, grabbed an axe that was leaning in a corner of the room, and swung it with one hand. Barlow ducked under the swing; the blade of the axe bit deep into the door, partially shattering the planking. It caught momentarily in the debris, giving Barlow the opening he needed. He lowered his shoulder and plowed into his assailant, driving Richman back against a wall. He drove a knee into the man's groin. Richman let out a growl of pain and rage and drove his forehead into Barlow's. Barlow reeled away, stunned. Richman stumbled forward and grabbed Barlow by the back of his coatee and hurled him across a table. Barlow hit the floor hard enough to knock the wind out of him. Gasping for breath, he rolled, fetching up against a fireplace, knocking an iron poker. Groping for this, he lashed out as Richman closed in on him. He was more lucky than accurate; the poker caught Richman squarely in the jaw and he fell. Barlow got uncertainly to his feet, still dazed by the blow to the head, and slammed the poker against Richman's skull as the overseer tried to get up. Richman went down again—and stayed down. He was out cold.

Barlow sat down with his back to the wall and caught his breath, waiting for the pain to subside and for his vision to clear. By the time he could see, and stand up without the world tilting, Richman was beginning to stir. The overseer was as strong as an ox. Barlow figured the last blow he had landed with the poker might have killed a lesser man. He hadn't come here to kill Richman, but by that time he'd been fighting for his life. And he didn't want to have to do that twice in one night. He went to Richman, removed his belt, and tied the man's hands behind his back. He did it just in time. As Barlow stood up and backed away, Richman came to, rolled over, discovered that he was bound, and snarled a string of epithets, spitting blood all the while. Barlow just waited for him to run out of wind, and every time Richman tried to get to his feet, he pushed him back down with the poker. Richman finally got tired of trying and just lay there, glaring at the army officer.

"What the hell do you want?" he rasped.

"John Claybourne."

Richman's eyes were hooded. The look on his face told Barlow part of what he wanted to know. It confirmed what Rawley had told him. Claybourne was there—and Richman knew it. Knew, also, that this was why Barlow had paid him a call.

"What about him?" asked the overseer.

"You've seen him lately. He's hiding nearby. I want to know where he is, and what he intends."

Richman grinned. It wasn't a pretty sight. "By God, you're scared, aren't you, soldier boy? Well, you damn sure ought to be. John's going to kill you, that's certain."

"You're his friend. You conspired with him once, years ago, when you lied about finding moccasin tracks and the sign of unshod ponies at the place where those two men from town ambushed me. My guess is you're conspiring with him again."

"I don't know what you're talking about," said the overseer truculently. "But even if I did know there's nothing you could say or do that'd make me tell you anything."

"Okay. That's fine. You don't need to tell me what I already know. But just remember to tell Claybourne, when you see him, that I'm here, with his sister, in his house. I'm sitting in his father's chair—and I'm no more impressed by him than his father was."

Richman stared at him. "You're asking for more trouble than you'll know what to do with."

"John Claybourne isn't trouble. He's just an annoyance. Like a mosquito."

"You better get out while you can, Yankee. You don't belong here."

Barlow shook his head. "No, it's you who'll be getting out. If you're still on this property when the sun comes up I'm going to finish what I started here tonight."

"You can't send me packing," sneered Richman. "Only Miss Claybourne can fire me and she..."

"She'll do anything I ask," said Barlow, smiling. "So get out. You're fired."

Still wielding the poker, he rolled Richman over on his belly and untied his hands. The overseer got up, rubbing his wrists and glaring at Barlow. But he didn't make a move against him. Barlow backed to the front door, opened it and disappeared into the night, carrying the poker with him and disposing of it only after arriving at the big house.

He stopped off at the library to help himself to some of Claybourne's brandy before going upstairs. One of the house servants came in, saw the condition he was in, and went right back out. She returned a few minutes later with a bowl of water and a towel. Barlow thanked her. She asked no questions—said nothing at all; simply nodded, smiled, and left the room. Barlow cleaned himself up as best he could, then went up. Rose was asleep. He undressed and slid his pistol under the pillow before slipping into bed as quietly as possible, hoping not to wake her. She mumbled something in her sleep, rolled over, and threw an arm over him. He placed his hand lightly over hers and closed his eyes and tried to go to sleep. That wasn't an easy thing to do, and by the time he did doze off he'd come to the conclusion that it wouldn't be an easy thing ever again unless and until John Claybourne was behind bars—or dead.

CHAPTER SIXTEEN

O ut of sensitivity for Rose Claybourne's standing in the community, Barlow arranged for the detachment from Fort Gaines to meet him on the outskirts of Athens. Not that he didn't understand the damage already done by his presence there. But a contingent of blue-coated soldiers bivouacked on her plantation would just add to her troubles. As per his request, the commander of the contingent, who turned out to be a Lieutenant Armstrong, sent a rider ahead to inform Barlow of his imminent arrival. Barlow returned with the rider to the column—and was dismayed when he saw it. There were only sixteen men in the detachment, including the young lieutenant.

"This is the best your commanding officer could do?" asked Barlow, after he and Armstrong had introduced themselves.

"Well, there's a war about to break out down south, Major," said Armstrong. "With the Seminoles. You knew about that, didn't you?"

"I've heard about it."

Barlow didn't mention that he had fought the Seminoles with Andrew Jackson over a dozen years earlier. He was aware that since then, in 1823, the Seminoles had signed a land-cession treaty at Fort Moultrie. Or, at least, a few of the more pliant Seminole chieftains had agreed to sign, in exchange for bribes. They had signed away all the tribal land in Florida save for reservations located in the northern panhandle along the Apalachicola River. In return, the Seminoles were restricted to the northern panhandle or to an area in the central part of the state north of Lake Okeechobee. The vast majority of this land was swamp. Most of the Seminoles refused to abide by this treaty. In 1832, another treaty was negotiated, this one for removal. A severe drought and constant conflict with encroaching whites had taken their toll. Many Seminole towns were starving. They were persuaded that if they agreed to move west and live among the Creeks they would receive generous government annuities, on one condition—that a delegation sent west approved of the lands that would be their new home. The delegation did more than approve; they were bribed into confirming the treaty. The Seminoles back in Florida protested, but in vain. The United States insisted that they move within three years. The Seminoles were equally firm in their insistence that they would stay put. And so the stage was set for another war in Florida.

"Most of my regiment has been transferred down there," continued Armstrong, "and the garrison at Fort Gaines has been stripped to the bare minimum. Just the unlucky ones remain."

"I take it you're hoping for orders dispatching you to Florida, Lieutenant."

"Yes, sir," said Armstrong fervently. "If there's going to be a war, I want to be a part of it."

Barlow nodded, allowed himself a faint smile. "I thought that way myself—once."

"Did you get your wish, sir?"

"Yes, I did. And much more than I'd bargained for, as well."

"Is there any hope of action around here, Major?"

"Your job, Lieutenant, is to keep the peace between the Cherokees and the Georgians, until such time as the former can be ... removed."

"Then you're anticipating trouble," said Armstrong hopefully.

"In this situation, anything is possible." Barlow went on to inform the lieutenant that he was to choose a likely site somewhere between Athens and New Echota for his encampment. He also warned Armstrong to keep on the lookout for John Claybourne, and explained to him that Claybourne was wanted for treason, and why. Barlow didn't mention his personal reasons for wanting to see Claybourne captured, figuring Armstrong was probably one of the few people left in the vicinity who didn't already know about his clash with the fugitive in Charleston, and his romance with Claybourne's sister.

He got back to the plantation in time for supper. After they'd eaten, Rose asked him to walk with her in the garden. The garden, especially bathed in moonlight, evoked strong memories for Barlow—memories of his first night at the plantation, when he and Rose had walked here, and she'd flirted with him, and he'd struggled against the desire for her that stirred inside him. Much had happened since that night. Much had changed. One thing that hadn't changed was the desire—Barlow marveled at the fact that, if anything, he wanted her more now than he had then.

She had something on her mind—he'd sensed this at the dining room table—but Barlow waited for her to broach the subject. He thought it might have to do with Richman; of course, she had noticed that her overseer was missing—and the morning after Barlow's fight with the man she hadn't failed to notice, too, the bruises on Barlow's face. She'd put two and two together, and hadn't even mentioned Richman. But he knew she was curious as to why he had driven the man off, and that she was smart enough to surmise that it could have something to do with her brother. So he had been expecting her to bring it up at some time, and debated with himself whether to tell her the whole truth.

He was, therefore, caught utterly by surprise when she finally said what was on her mind.

"I know you love me, Timothy, as I love you—with all my heart and soul. We were meant to be together, forever. Ours is the kind of love that most people only dream about. And I know you would marry me, if you were … free to do so."

"Rose, I …"

She stopped, turned into his arms, and touched his lips with a fingertip. "No, darling. You don't have to explain it to me. I understand. It's not an easy thing, getting a divorce. And you've scarcely had the time to pursue it. I would never, ever, put any pressure on you about it. Except that … well, now there's someone else involved."

Barlow was shocked. "Someone else?"

She smiled at the expression on his face. "Not another man, silly. Well, it might be another man. In about, oh, eighteen or twenty years from now…"

"I don't…"

She watched his eyes, and smiled, nodding, as the recognition came into them.

"Yes, it's true," she whispered. "I'm carrying your child."

Barlow's heart skipped a beat. "Are you certain?" he gasped.

She nodded again. "Yes, quite certain. Are you… happy?"

He framed her face with his big, scarred hands and kissed her passionately, breathlessly, on the lips. Then he wrapped her in his strong arms and held her tightly. He was stunned. And he sensed that his whole world had changed. Been added to. Made more complete.

"I've never been happier," he whispered, his voice husky with emotion.

Then he realized what she'd been saying—and a chilling horror gripped him.

"My God," he said, breaking the embrace. "We've got to… I mean, I have to…" He made an effort to compose himself. "I must go to Washington at once and, um, settle my affairs there, at once."

"But you have a job to do down here. Won't you get into trouble with your superiors if you drop everything to attend to a personal matter?"

"That can't be helped," said Barlow sternly. She was right. There would probably be hell to pay if he returned to Washington before completing his mission in Georgia. But he couldn't help that.

Then he remembered John Claybourne. He took her by the shoulders and looked at her earnestly.

"There's nothing else to be done. I must go. And I'll be gone for six weeks, perhaps two months, at a minimum. I don't want to be away from you that long, Rose. Don't want to leave you alone that long. Especially now—now that your brother is back."

Her features became a stoic mask. "John … is here in Georgia?" She turned that over in her mind. "Is that why you sent Richman away?"

"Yes. I'm sorry, I should have told you about it. But I didn't want to alarm you. Now I have no choice. You need to know. If I'm gone he may show up here."

Her chin rose a defiant inch. "I'm not afraid of him."

"I know you aren't. You're not afraid of anything."

"Except losing you."

"But I'm afraid. Afraid of what he might do."

"He won't touch a hair on my head."

"I'm not so sure. He's an angry and violent man. And he has some peculiar ideas about honor. Having taken up with me, you'll have betrayed him. The whole South, to his way of thinking. And if he finds out you're bearing my child…" Barlow shook his head. He didn't even want to think about what Claybourne might do then.

"You take care of your business in Washington," she said firmly, "and don't worry about me. I can fend for myself. I won't let John do anything to me. Or the baby."

Barlow gazed at her bleakly. He was in a difficult spot. Of course he would worry. He would worry terribly. But what choice did he have? He had to go. He had to end his marriage to Sarah Langford, and he had to make Rose Claybourne his bride. He was not going to sire an illegitimate child. Rose was giving him something Sarah had never been able to give, something he had wanted, and which, at one point, he had reconciled himself to never having. He'd created a bad situation for all concerned, and he had to set things right. Now he had a deadline; it couldn't be put off any longer.

"I'll leave first thing in the morning," he said.

She pressed her body against his. "Then let's go to bed, and you can give me a memory that will keep me warm all the nights that you're not beside me."

It was a cold, gray, rainy day, a preface to the coming winter, when Barlow reached Washington. He'd had two weeks to mull over his course of action upon arrival, and had decided that since time was of the essence he would have to try the straightforward approach—no matter how much trouble it was. With that in mind, he headed straight for the Langford boardinghouse. He braced himself before going in, uncertain as to what reaction he would get from Mrs. Langford when she saw him. And then there was always the possibility that Sarah would be home, too, though he doubted that he'd have that kind of luck.

Mrs. Langford, thin, bent and gray, was in the kitchen, making bread, when he showed up. He paused at the threshold and watched her for a moment; she had her back to him and was unaware of his presence. He was struck by a wave of nostalgia—those days when he had been a boarder here, and had first met Sarah, and was in the process of falling in love with her, seemed to be from a much simpler time. Regret followed hard upon the heels of those memories. He regretted that things hadn't worked out between himself and Sarah, even while he was glad that he had met and fallen in love with Rose Claybourne. It didn't make much sense to be glad of something and to regret it at the same time, and he was confused by the conflicting emotions.

Some belated instinct warned her that she was not alone, and Mrs. Langford turned and saw him. Her hands and lower arms and apron were covered with dough. She just stood there for a moment, staring at him. Then, quite composed, she motioned to the chairs at the small wooden table in a corner of the kitchen.

"Rest yourself, Timothy. You look weary."

"Thank you, but I can't stay, Mrs. Langford. How have you been?"

She pushed a tendril of iron-gray hair from her face with the back of her hand. "I have my good days and my bad days. And how do you fare?" She glanced at his travel-worn uniform. "I heard you'd been promoted to major. Congratulations. You always said the army was the only career for you. I suppose now no one can deny you've made the best of it."

Barlow wondered what else she had heard. Did she know, for instance, about Rose?

"I'm looking for Sarah, ma'am," he said. "Do you know where she might be?"

A look of infinite sadness fluttered across Mrs. Langford's face. She half turned away from him and began to wipe the dough off her hands, using her apron.

"I don't see much of her. She rarely comes by. She spends all her time with that man."

"Marten?"

Mrs. Langford nodded. "He ... he has some sort of hold on her, Timothy. I'm afraid for her. She isn't herself. She isn't the Sarah I once knew." She looked earnestly at him, and Barlow was surprised, and discomfited, by the tears that were welling up in her eyes. "You must save her from him. I know you can do it. I don't know who else to turn to."

Barlow sighed. "I'll see what I can do. But you should know ... I've come here to ..."

"I understand," she said sadly. "I don't blame you. I blame myself, partly."

"No. You had nothing to do with what happened to us."

"Yes, I did. She should have gone back to Fort Perry with you, as any dutiful wife would have. But she stayed. And she used me for an excuse. I made it easy for her to do so. I was selfish. I had missed her all those years that she was gone, and I wanted her to stay. I was thinking only of myself. And now ... now she is trapped in that man's web. I met him once, you know."

"No, I didn't know that."

"He is a strange fellow. Cold shivers ran up and down my spine when he looked at me. He has the most mesmerizing eyes. He has the devil in him. He has this terrible power over her. She'll do whatever he wants her to do, without question. I think she might even be so far gone that if he asked her to jump off a bridge and drown herself in the Potomac she would do it."

"Do you know where I can find Sarah?"

"She's with him. At one point I thought I would go to his home and take her out of there, whether she wanted to go or not. But then I realized I was too old, too weak, to force anyone to do anything against their will. I did ask around, though, and was told he has a house on Seventh near H Street. It's not hard to find. There is usually an angry group of Southerners in the street outside, and men with weapons at the door."

Barlow nodded. "That figures. Don't worry, Mrs. Langford, I'll make sure no harm comes to Sarah."

He felt a little guilty giving such an assurance, as he wasn't at all sure he could fulfill the promise. But Mrs. Langford needed reassuring.

He needed a place to stay, but under the circumstances he didn't think it would be fitting for him to stay at the Langford boarding-house, so he took a room at Gadsby's Hotel. He changed into his one suit of civilian clothes, a suit of broadcloth, ill-fitting compared to his uniform, and wrinkled from two weeks in the single valise he'd brought with him. But the uniform would draw too much attention.

After eating a late dinner he walked to Seventh Street and turned up it to H. As Mrs. Langford had said, there was a group of a half dozen men in the streets beyond the retaining wall and closed gate to a three-story red brick house. Two men with pistols in their belts patrolled the veranda of the house, keeping an eye on the troublemakers in the street. There was no shouting—the Southerners were merely standing there, talking to one another, and watching the house. Barlow found a spot behind the trunk of a large black oak tree at the corner of Seventh and H Streets and watched from its shade. He had but an hour to wait for sundown. Perhaps then the Southerners would disperse. The scenario resembled what he had seen at the Claybourne house in Charleston, and he did not want a repeat of that evening. There would be no sneaking in over the back wall; he intended to go straight through the front door—assuming he could get past the guards and Marten.

As it got darker the Southerners in the street did begin to wander away, so that, as Barlow had hoped, they were gone by dark. He was about to make his move when a man walking briskly down H Street turned the corner, then crossed Seventh to the gate of the Marten house. There was only one guard on the porch now, and he went down to the gate and spoke to the visitor for a moment and then opened the gate to allow him entry. Barlow uttered a silent curse—and decided to wait until the visitor had departed.

He didn't have long to wait. Ten minutes later the front door opened, spilling a rectangle of lamplight, and the visitor emerged. He was escorted out by a very tall, cadaverous man with a full head of unruly dark hair and long sideburns that reached down to the line of his jaw. They shook hands, and then the visitor exited through the gate. This time he turned up Seventh Street and hurried away with purposeful stride. The tall man went back inside and closed the door.

Barlow was again about to leave his vantage point and approach the house when he heard a sound behind him—and whirled.

There was a young woman approaching him. She was wearing a dark dress, a black shawl over her shoulders to ward off the dampness of the night, and a bonnet. In the darkness he could not make out much of her features, except large, glistening eyes that she raised to fasten upon him.

"I know you," she said. "You're Captain Barlow, aren't you?"

"Have we met?" Barlow was wary—and quite sure he'd never seen this woman before in his life.

"No, we haven't. But I know who you are. I once watched you for an entire day."

"What?"

"Charles told me to."

"Charles? Charles Marten?"

She nodded. "I used to be his...I used to belong to his association."

"He told you to watch me? What for? When was this?"

"Several years ago. You had just returned from down South, I believe. And your wife had just joined the association. It was because of your wife that Marten was having you watched. He was suspicious, at first. I think he wondered if she was genuine. At the same time I think he desired her."

Barlow's features tightened with anger. "Does Charles Marten make a habit of desiring the wives of other men?"

She looked away, and her voice had a wistful quality. "He desired me, once. I was married. I was against slavery. But he made me an ardent abolitionist. He also made me his mistress. I was his...until your wife took my place. I became...jealous. I caused a scene—and he threw me out. Out of his bed, out of his house, out of the association."

"So what are you doing here?" Barlow had to wonder if this woman posed a threat of any kind to Sarah.

"I've been watching him now," she said, fiercely. "I'm going to ruin his life, just the way he ruined mine."

There was no doubt that she meant every word of it—Barlow could tell as much by the tone of her voice. There was nothing more terrible—or dangerous—than a woman scorned.

"For instance, did you see the man who just left?" she continued. "His name is Lawrence. He's a simpleminded man who has also fallen under Charles Marten's sway. He is going to kill the president."

Barlow's blood ran cold. "What? What did you say?"

"You heard me." She smiled slyly. "Oh, yes, it's true. The plan has been in the works for quite some time. Ever since Andrew Jackson became president, in fact. It was Charles' brainchild."

Barlow recalled how he had been dragooned into providing Jackson protection on the day of the inauguration. Maybe there *had* been something to the rumors of an attempt on Old Hickory's life, after all. Maybe Major Donelson and the others had gotten a whiff, somehow, of the scheme this woman was telling him about.

"When is the attack on the president supposed to take place?" asked Barlow.

She shook her head. "I don't know. It doesn't really matter. What matters is that Charles Marten is connected with the crime.

And now you are a witness to it. You've seen them together with your own eyes."

"Where can I find Lawrence?"

"I don't know."

Barlow turned to leave her. "Then I must follow him."

She grabbed his arm. "What are you doing here? Have you come to take your woman back?"

Barlow realized that, in her fevered mind, she thought it possible that he would remove Sarah from the picture, creating a void that she could fill. She wanted to destroy Marten—or get him back. And the life of President Andrew Jackson wasn't important to her; Old Hickory was just a pawn in the game she was playing.

He wrenched his arm free. "Meet me back here tomorrow night, same time," he said, and ran up H Street.

Several blocks away he caught sight of the man again. His stride was unmistakable. Lawrence turned abruptly on Thirteenth Street and headed south. It occurred to Barlow then that he could be heading for the Executive Mansion. When Lawrence turned again, this time west on E Street, Barlow was sure of it. E Street took Lawrence directly in front of the White House. Barlow had been hanging back, for fear that Lawrence would look back and spot him. But Lawrence hadn't looked back once since H Street, so now Barlow closed the distance between them. It would be possible for the man to walk right up to the president's house and knock on the door. He would not be allowed entrance at this hour without proof of pressing business, but once the door was open he might conceivably force his way past the butler. Barlow wanted to be near enough to prevent him from even getting inside.

But Lawrence didn't try to go inside. Instead he stopped and looked across the grounds at the White House. Barlow was too close now to stop without drawing attention to himself. He kept walking, passing Lawrence, and, in that instant, making a bold decision. Instead of continuing on by, he stopped right alongside the man he had just followed halfway across Washington.

"Magnificent building, don't you agree?" he asked and, with an amiable smile, took his first close look at the man who, if the woman he'd spoken to earlier was right, was the would-be assassin of Andrew Jackson.

Lawrence looked at him suspiciously. He was a slender young man with blond hair. "I suppose so," he mumbled.

"It was a great day for the republic when we put Andrew Jackson into that house."

"We're all entitled to our opinions," replied Lawrence.

Barlow smiled apologetically. "I take it you don't concur. Well, that's why we have elections, I guess, as we don't all agree on such things."

"The people are easily led, and easily fooled," said Lawrence, with fervor. "And much damage can be done to the country in the four years between elections."

"Still, our system is preferable to the alternatives. We wouldn't want to live under a dictator, or under the threat of a coup every year."

Lawrence gave him a long look, then touched the brim of his beaver hat. "I must be on my way," he said, and with that continued westward on E Street.

Barlow realized that meeting the man face to face might have been a mistake—he'd learned little from the conversation, and he had to continue to follow Lawrence until the latter settled some-where, hopefully at his own abode. Only then could Barlow go to Major Donelson or Marshal Tench Ringgold and tell them what he knew. Where the would-be assassin could be found was an essential piece of information. If he let Lawrence go, there was no guarantee he would be seen again—until, perhaps, it was too late.

Lawrence glanced over his shoulder at Barlow several times as he walked briskly away from the White House. Barlow stayed where he was as long as he dared, letting Lawrence get a block away. Then he crossed to the other side of E Street and proceeded west-ward. He tried to stay at least one block back while never allowing his prey to extend his lead by more than two blocks. He tried to stay in the shadows as well. Fortunately, there were no street lamps, so the shadows were plentiful; it was light spilling from windows that Barlow had to watch out for. Lawrence looked back a few times more, but he hadn't seen Barlow cross the street, so he scanned his side of the thoroughfare and, failing to see Barlow, remained oblivious to the fact that he was being followed.

When Lawrence reached the intersection of E, Twenty-first and Virginia Avenue, he turned north on Twenty-first, heading for the upper end of Pennsylvania Avenue. This was a busy intersection, and Barlow was wary, thinking that Lawrence might opt for one of the carriages for hire that sat empty at the street corners. But the man continued walking. He didn't go much further, though. On the second block up on Twenty-first Street he went up the stoop of a three-story house and stepped inside.

Barlow went up to the stoop and saw the sign indicating that this was the Granger Boardinghouse. He stepped back into the street and watched the windows. Most of them were dark. Then lamplight poured through an upstairs window. The silhouette of a man appeared briefly—and then Lawrence—Barlow assumed it was he—closed the drapes.

Barlow whirled and quickly retraced his steps, making for the White House to warn Andrew Jackson.

Chapter Seventeen

He was back on Twenty-first Street at the crack of dawn the following morning, but this time he wasn't alone. Tench Ringgold and two city constables were with him. A light drizzle fell from the leaden sky.

After leaving the Granger Boardinghouse the night before, Barlow had hastened to the White House. He was met there by Major Donelson, who reminded him of the lateness of the hour, and that the president had retired early and couldn't be disturbed. But when Barlow told him that he had met a man who intended to assassinate the president, Donelson debated whether to awaken Old Hickory. He took Barlow into a downstairs parlor and poured two brandies, keeping one for himself and handing Barlow the other. He sat down and asked Barlow to tell him everything.

Barlow did just that, mentioning the fact that Lawrence had met with the abolitionist leader Charles Marten and that, according to one disaffected member of Marten's group, there was a plot afoot to murder Jackson.

"Are you sure Marten is the mastermind?" asked Donelson. "Who is this informant of yours? Can you rely on him?"

"It's a woman. And I only met her tonight. I don't even know her name. But if you ask me whether I believe what she told me is true, I'd say absolutely."

Donelson knocked back his brandy, gasped, and slumped back in the chair. "Lawrence," he muttered, then shook his head. "I don't think I know anyone by that name. Is he an abolitionist, too? Why would Marten want to kill the president? What could he, or his cause, possibly gain from the commission of such a crime?"

"Who knows? Maybe we should ask him."

Donelson looked at Barlow for a moment, thinking it over. "We have to be careful. We must be sure of our facts, and have overwhelming evidence. If we had Charles Marten arrested, many in the North would cry foul. They would say the charges were trumped up, that it was all a ploy to discredit one of the leading lights of the antislavery movement. Politically, it is dangerous ground."

"I'm not worried about the politics. It's the general's life that concerns me."

Donelson took offense to the implication behind Barlow's comment. "No one is more devoted to the welfare of the president than I am," he said tersely.

"At least have Lawrence apprehended. Maybe he will give evidence to damn Charles Marten."

Donelson nodded. "I agree. Lawrence must be taken into custody. I will send for Marshal Ringgold at once. You'll stay here tonight, of course. Ringgold will need you to take him to Lawrence."

Barlow agreed. One of the servants showed him to a nicely appointed room upstairs. He stretched out on the big four-poster bed fully clothed—and fell fast asleep.

He was awakened by Ringgold, shaking him roughly. A disoriented glance at the window revealed to Barlow that it was still dark outside.

"Wake up, Major," said the burly, broad-shouldered marshal curtly. "It's time to go."

Barlow sat up, ran a hand over his face, and looked at Ringgold. The man carried a brace of pistols under his belt and wore a grim look on his face. There was no need to ask if the U.S. marshal took Barlow's information seriously.

There had been a carriage and two constables, also armed, waiting at the east entrance to the White House. A journey through the still-sleeping streets of the capital had taken them to Twenty-first Street. Barlow pointed out the window to Lawrence's room.

Ringgold sent the two constables around back. He and Barlow climbed the stoop to the front door. The sun was just peeking over the rooftops. Ringgold didn't knock—he went straight in, and Barlow followed. The smell of breakfast came from the end of the hall. They moved quietly past the staircase to the last door on the left, which gave access to a kitchen. A stout, middle-aged woman was humming as she prodded a fire burning in the hearth, making the flames lick the blackened bottom of a Dutch oven. Something made her look up—and she straightened, gasping, at the sight of the two men in the doorway. Ringgold put a finger to his lips and pulled open his coat so that she could see the badge on his shirt.

"Are you the landlady?" asked Ringgold.

"Y-yes, I'm Mrs. Granger. And you are …?"

"Tench Ringgold, United States Marshal. This is Major Timothy Barlow of the United States Army. We're here to see Mr. Lawrence."

"Richard Lawrence? What on earth for?"

"Is he here?"

"He should be. Third floor, the room on the southwest corner. But why…"

Ringgold interrupted her. "You stay put, ma'am, until we're gone." It was not a request.

He led the way up the stairs to the third floor. When they reached the door to Lawrence's room, Barlow crossed to the other side. Ringgold glanced at him, nodded—then stepped back and prepared to launch himself at the door. But Barlow put up a hand to stop him. Ringgold hesitated, scowling. Barlow tried the knob. The door was unlocked. He swung the door open and looked inside.

The room was empty.

Ringgold bulled his way past Barlow. There was a wardrobe against one wall—the marshal drew a pistol and threw the doors open. No Lawrence. He checked under the bed. No luck. Then he muttered a curse, and turned to see Barlow taking a cherry-wood box out of the bottom of the wardrobe. Barlow put the box on the bed and opened the hinged lid. There was a pair of matching dueling pistols within. He looked up at Ringgold.

"So where is he?" growled the marshal.

Barlow shook his head, wondering if he'd been wrong, wondering if Lawrence was aware that he'd been followed all the way home last night, and whether the would-be assassin had flown the coop sometime during the night.

"I'll leave the constables here, in case he comes back for those," said Ringgold.

"I have an idea," said Barlow. "Let's leave the constables in hiding outside, where they can watch the house without being seen. If Lawrence comes back, they can report back to you. And we can go from there."

"What's the point in that?"

"It would be better to catch him in the commission of the crime."

"Are you mad? You'd put the president's life at risk to catch this man red-handed?"

Barlow smiled coldly. "Not at all. There's a way to fix it so that President Jackson won't be in danger at all."

"Oh? And how is that accomplished?"

Barlow picked up one of the pistols. "I'll show you."

That night Barlow was back at the black oak tree located on the corner of Seventh and H Streets. It was still overcast, but the streets were dry; a cold, blustery wind came out of the north and thrashed the limbs over his head. As had been the case the night before, there was a guard on the veranda of the Marten house. And, again just as on the previous night, the woman came up Seventh Street, clad as before in dark dress and bonnet and shawl so that she blended well with the nocturnal shadows.

"Did you get him?" she asked. "Did you get Lawrence?"

"That's been taken care of."

"And what of Marten?"

"It remains to be seen."

She gave him a long look, and he expected her to ask him what he meant by that, but she didn't. "And what about your wife?" she asked.

"Who are you? What's your name?"

"Who I am is not important."

"It's important to me."

She shook her head, looking past him at the Marten house with what he took to be wistful longing mixed with barely contained rage, and he began to wonder if this mysterious woman was entirely sane. Barlow waited a moment, then accepted the fact that she wasn't going to give him the information he wanted.

"It doesn't matter," he said. "Mr. Lawrence will hang himself. But without your testimony, we won't be able to convict Charles Marten of conspiring with Lawrence to kill the president. Maybe you don't really want him to pay for his crimes. I don't particularly care, myself. All I care about is getting my wife away from him."

"She won't come with you freely," warned the woman. "You'll have to take her out by force."

"I'll do whatever I have to do," he said grimly.

"Have a care. Marten is dangerous. So are some of the men he employs to protect himself from the slavepower."

"Thanks for your help," he said, and turned away, angling across the intersection.

Even before he reached Marten's gate the guard on the veranda spotted him, and watched his approach from that point on. He didn't draw the pistol in his belt, but his hand never strayed far from it. Barlow didn't pause at the gate. It wasn't chained or padlocked, so he opened it, passed through, and went up to the veranda steps. He didn't hesitate there, either, walking toward the front door as though he owned the place. The guard had to move quickly to place himself between Barlow and the door.

"What do you think you're doing?" asked the guard in a surly tone. He was a brawny man, with a scar over an eyebrow and a nose that had been broken at least once—a brawler by the looks of him, someone accustomed to violence, no doubt able to do a lot of damage in a fight, and able to sustain a lot of damage, too, by the looks of it.

"I've come to see my wife. I'm Major Timothy Barlow, Thirty-ninth Infantry. Who are you?"

He spoke assertively, without fear, and the guard was put off balance. Barlow presumed the man was accustomed to intimidating people. It was one of his chief weapons, and he'd come to rely on it a bit too much. Now he was faced by a man who didn't appear to be the least bit intimidated, and he experienced a moment of self-doubt, uncertain what to do next.

"I work for Mr. Marten," he said, defensively.

"Good for you. I want to see him. And my wife. Her name is Sarah. I know she's here."

"You wait here," said the man. "I'll see if Mr. Marten wants to see you."

"Go ahead. But he doesn't really have a choice."

The guard gave him one last wary look, then turned and went inside, closing the door behind him. Barlow decided he wouldn't wait long. He didn't want to have to enter the house by force, without invitation, but he would do so if necessary. It turned out not to be necessary. The guard was back in a couple of minutes.

"Mr. Marten says he's been expecting you," he said, looking surprised. "Follow me."

He led Barlow into a tastefully appointed main hallway, and from there into a parlor. There was dark red damask on the walls, velveteen upholstery on the furniture, all imported from Europe, vases and figurines of Oriental origin on highly polished tables and on the mantel above the fireplace. It was very continental, not at all in the prevailing American style of furnishing a house.

Marten came in immediately. He was even taller than Barlow had expected, with a leonine head topped by thick, silver-streaked black hair, a sallow complexion, gaunt cheeks, thin lips, a hawkish nose and eyes so dark blue that they appeared almost black. His gaze was keen, disconcerting in its directness. He wore a crimson swallowtail coat over a gold vest, a snowy-white linen shirt with lace at the cuffs, and doeskin trousers tucked into black boots polished to a high sheen.

"Major Barlow," he said, and smiled warmly, then crossed the room to extend a hand in greeting. He had a thick accent, though

Barlow couldn't quite place it, yet his English was flawless. "We meet, at last."

Barlow ignored the proffered hand. "I've come to see Sarah, sir. If you'd be good enough to…"

Marten raised a hand. "Say no more. She is on her way." He turned toward the door just as Sarah entered, and Barlow wondered how he had known she was just about to cross the threshold, for she moved without making a sound, and nothing had forewarned them of her imminent arrival. "Ah," said Marten, delighted, "there she is. Your lovely wife."

"I've come to take her home."

"Have you now. Sarah, be a dear and pour us both a drink. What is your preference, Major?"

Sarah stopped staring at Barlow, and mutely crossed the room to the sideboard. She was clad in a taffeta gown that Barlow didn't recognize—and could not have afforded to buy. He assumed Marten had bought it for her.

"Nothing for me," said Barlow.

"Then I'll forego the pleasure as well. I don't like to drink alone. Sarah, have a seat, please."

Sarah did as she was told. She continued to gaze at Barlow. She seemed alert, inquisitive, perfectly aware of everything that was going on around her. Barlow had half expected, from everything he'd heard about Marten, to find her in some sort of hypnotic trance.

Marten went to the chair beside hers and sat down. There was something possessive about that, and a clear challenge in the way he looked at Barlow. He had control of her, somehow, and he was defying Barlow to take that control away.

"So, Major," said Marten coolly, "you wish to take Sarah *home*. I think, if you were to ask her, you would find that she feels that she is at home right here. Three years ago you went off to some dreary army outpost and left her behind. Why do you want her back now?"

"That's not exactly how it happened," said Barlow—and then caught himself, recognizing that Marten was trying to put him on the defensive. "I don't want her back." He switched his gaze to Sarah. "As a matter of fact, I intend to seek a divorce. What I want is for her to be free of your influence."

Marten laughed softly, glanced at Sarah to judge her reaction to the news Barlow had just imparted. For her part, Sarah looked down at her hands, folded neatly in her lap; she was unwilling to meet Barlow's gaze, and trying not to display any emotion.

"Again, I suggest you ask her whether she wishes to be free of my influence."

"I don't need to ask her. I already know the answer."

"Then you have in mind taking her away from here against her will?" Marten raised an eyebrow.

Barlow was careful with his response. His first impulse was to mention Lawrence—and the fact that Lawrence's plans had been found out, not to mention, too, that there was a known connection between Lawrence and Marten. This might rattle Marten, and give him something more important to worry about than Sarah. But to do that would be to risk alerting Lawrence. The woman at the Granger Boardinghouse had been sworn to secrecy by Tench Ringgold, and Barlow was confident she would say nothing to her mysterious boarder about the marshal's visit. If he wanted to catch Lawrence red-handed, Barlow realized he would have to forego the pleasure of telling Marten that his role in the assassination conspiracy was no longer a secret. Barlow realized, too, that if he tried forcing Sarah to make a choice between him and Marten he would lose. It was a realization that didn't do his male ego much good, but this was hardly the time to let ego come to the fore. No, he had to outmaneuver Marten. He had to use the one thing that might matter more to Sarah than her attachment to this man.

"I won't have to take her against her will," replied Barlow. "I think she'll come willingly, once she learns that her mother is in desperate need."

Sarah looked up at him sharply. "What's happened to my mother?" she asked.

Marten looked at her disapprovingly. Was that a glimmer of worry on his face, wondered Barlow?

"She's very ill," said Barlow. "She can't handle all the work at the boardinghouse any longer. She needs you, Sarah. More now than she did three years ago."

Sarah nodded slowly. She understood—Barlow was reminding her that her stated reason for not returning to Fort Perry with him three years ago had been her concern for her mother, and her feeling that she needed to stay and help Mrs. Langford.

"Well, that can easily be remedied," said Marten. "If Sarah's mother needs help, I can see to it that she receives it."

Sarah looked at him. "You would hire help for her?"

"If that is what you wished, yes, my dear."

Sarah was silent for a moment. Both men watched her.

"No," she said in a small voice. "My place is with her."

Marten's hand lashed out—clamping down on her arm. "Your place is here with me," he said, his voice like silk, but with steel right below the surface.

"So is she free to come and go as she wishes?" asked Barlow. "Or is she your slave?"

Marten looked at him with hooded eyes—and removed his hand from her arm. "You are hardly in a position to accuse someone of being a slave owner, Major. After all, rumor has it that you are consorting with a slaveholder yourself. Miss Rose Claybourne, isn't that her name? How many slaves does she own?"

"I never counted them. A good many."

"And if you marry her—and I suspect, from what I've heard, that this is your intent—then you yourself will be a slaveholder."

Barlow looked at Sarah. Her eyes were filled with pain. No woman, regardless of the circumstances, liked to be replaced in a man's heart by another woman, even if that man was someone she no longer loved.

"That's none of your concern," said Barlow, sensing that he was losing the upper hand.

"Oh, but it is," said Marten, with a barely contained ferocity. "I concern myself with every single human being held in bondage. Slavery is a sin, an affront to God, the most heinous crime on the face of the earth. It is the duty and obligation of every civilized, God-fearing man to do his utmost to rid the earth of that scourge. In England there is a strong movement to abolish slavery throughout the British empire. It will succeed, of that I have no doubt. Now we must move to abolish slavery here. By tolerating that peculiar and brutal institution, we make a mockery of everything this republic stands for."

"So do the ends justify the means?" asked Barlow. "Is there anything you would *not* do in your crusade to free the slaves?"

Marten smiled. "I would not, of course, commit a crime. Two wrongs do not make a right."

"Would you give up your life for the cause? Or the lives of your followers?"

"There have been more than a few of our colleagues who have already given their lives for the cause. To die for what is right, for what you believe in—that is no crime, Major."

Barlow nodded. "He'll make a martyr of you yet, Sarah."

She shook her head. "If I must choose between the cause I believe in and the woman who gave me life, I will choose the latter." She stood up, quite suddenly, determination in her every fiber. With fear—and resolve—she forced herself to look Marten squarely in the eye. "I must go to my mother."

"You actually believe him?" asked Marten, incredulously.

"Timothy would not lie, especially about such a thing as my mother's health."

Barlow watched Marten closely. Would the man resort to violence to keep from losing Sarah? Barlow was convinced that Marten didn't love her; for him it was all about possession, dominance, control—things that were far more important than love to such a man. Here was someone who did not like to lose, and would go to almost any length to achieve his ends. How far would he go to keep Sarah? He was not a weak or placid man by any means—violence seethed behind that genteel facade.

But Marten surprised him by backing down. He smiled wanly at Sarah, and shrugged, a very continental gesture. "You are making a mistake, my dear."

"I've made many mistakes," she said.

"This man doesn't love you."

"That's my fault." She looked solemnly at Barlow. "He *did* love me, once. Timothy, just give me a few minutes to collect some things."

Barlow nodded. "I'll wait outside. I don't think Mr. Marten and I have anything more to discuss."

She left the room. Barlow bowed curtly to Marten and did likewise. But Marten followed him, all the way to the front door.

"It's difficult to be sure where you stand, Major, on the great moral issue that confronts us all. You went down to South Carolina, into the belly of the beast, as it were, and struck a blow for freedom. Nullification had to be crushed, or the slavepower would have used it as a shield to protect its institutions. You crushed it. Yet, at the same time, you play an important role in removing the Cherokees from Georgia. Surely you realize that this will only solidify the hold that the slavepower has over the nation."

"How is that?"

"Georgia challenged the federal government in the matter of which had jurisdiction over the Indians. It's clear to all that the government has backed down."

"I'm given orders and I obey them."

"And what do you do with your conscience if an order runs contrary to your beliefs?"

"Are you really all that worried about my conscience?"

Marten smiled coldly. "Not at all. I'm just curious to know how you live with yourself. Actually, you're a perfect representative of the present administration. You threaten the South like it was a recalcitrant child—and then you give in to its whims."

"You'd prefer a government filled with abolitionists, I presume," said Barlow caustically. "And then you would have a nation split into two parts. Maybe that's what you're really after, Marten."

They were interrupted by Sarah, coming down the stairs behind Marten, a single valise in her hand. Marten glanced at her, then turned back to Barlow and pitched his voice low.

"I'll have her back, you know. You won't be around—you'll have returned to your Southern, slaveholding woman. You won't be able to *protect* her from me."

"You might be surprised," said Barlow, then brushed by Marten to take the valise from Sarah and offer her his free arm.

Marten stood aside to let them pass. He bowed slightly, smirking, as Sarah passed him and went outside. The guard was back on the veranda; he glowered at Barlow, but the latter ignored him.

Once they were through the gate and out into the street, Barlow couldn't help but glance down at the intersection of Seventh and H, to the big black oak. He couldn't see the woman there, the one in the dark dress and shawl. He wondered if she was out there, though, watching, and what she would be thinking when she saw him leave Marten's house with her rival for the abolitionist leader's affections. He led Sarah in the opposite direction, north up Seventh, towards Mount Vernon Square, knowing he could find a carriage for hire there.

They went two blocks without a word passing between them. Finally Barlow stopped, turning her around to face him.

"I'm sorry, Sarah."

Once again she did not care to meet his gaze, taking an unusually keen interest in the darkened houses across the street. "Sorry? Whatever for?"

"That you had to find out about…about Rose Claybourne that way."

"I just hope you'll be happy." She said it without rancor. "You deserve to be. And I hope she can…she can give you children. I know that's something you've always wanted. Something I could not give you."

Barlow thought it would be unwise to mention Rose's pregnancy. "I'm sorry, too, for the way things turned out, just in general."

She touched his face, and smiled. "I should have listened to my mother. She warned me that men were trouble."

Barlow had to laugh—and, much to his delight, she laughed, too.

"But then," she added, and stopped laughing, "I never would have gotten to know you, Timothy. And I'd have been the poorer for it."

Barlow turned serious, too. "You must stay away from Marten. He's a dangerous man. He's part of a conspiracy to kill the president."

She stared at him. "I know he despises Jackson. He thinks the president is a pawn of the slavepower. After all, he's a slaveholder himself."

"Trust me, Sarah. Andrew Jackson is nobody's pawn."

"I *do* trust you, Timothy. I knew before you came tonight that I wasn't where I belonged. I knew I ought to be with my mother, helping her. But when you're in Marten's presence, well…" She sighed. "It is difficult to do something he doesn't want you to do."

"I can understand that."

"Now that I'm… *away* from him, well…You'll have to trust me, too."

"I will."

"And I'll do whatever you need me to do where the… divorce is concerned, Timothy."

He nodded, uncertain how to respond, but deeply grateful.

"She's very lucky," murmured Sarah, walking on with a shudder as the cold wind cut through her. "Rose, I mean."

They walked the rest of the way in silence.

CHAPTER EIGHTEEN

On the following day, President Andrew Jackson attended the funeral of Representative Warren R. Davis of South Carolina. The ceremony was conducted in the House chamber, and members of both houses of congress, as well as the president, his cabinet and other dignitaries, were present and accounted for. So were U.S. Marshal Tench Ringgold and Timothy Barlow. The former had appeared at the latter's hotel room door early that morning to inform him of the president's plans to venture out into the public. "I advised him against it," said Ringgold grimly. "I confess I don't have much faith in your scheme to trap Lawrence. It could too easily backfire—and if it does, we'll have a dead chief executive on our hands."

"Trying to get Andrew Jackson to hide indoors because of some perceived danger was a waste of time, Marshal. You should be well enough acquainted with him by now to realize that."

Ringgold nodded ruefully. "At any rate, I thought you would want to come along. You're the only one who actually knows what this lunatic looks like."

"Absolutely."

And so there he was, in the House chamber, trying to remain discreetly out of the way, and yet never more than a few strides away from the president. The chaplain gave an excruciatingly long-winded eulogy. Barlow doubted that Lawrence would try anything in the chamber, but he didn't let down his guard, and kept an eye on all the aisles providing access to the president, who sat just in front of him, surrounded by his cabinet. When at last the rites had been concluded, the deceased's colleagues, the members of the House, filed solemnly past the bier upon which rested the casket, paying their last respects. They were followed by the senators, then by the cabinet and lastly, the president.

Jackson left the House chamber and headed for the east portico. Many of the senators and representatives were tarrying in the marbled hallway. A man in a long cloak of pilot cloth, his face obscured by a thick black beard, came from behind one of the columns. Barlow glanced at him, then continued to scan the crowd. This, he thought, was the most dangerous time, when the president was most exposed—between the door and his carriage, waiting at the foot of the steps. But then something about the bearded man drew his attention again. He swung his head that way again—just as Richard Lawrence drew a pistol from beneath his cloak and aimed it at Jackson's chest at a range of no more than six feet. On the other side of Jackson, Tench Ringgold shouted a warning. As he saw the pistol, Jackson reacted. His reaction was not what one might have expected from a person with a pistol aimed at his heart. The president started towards Lawrence, raising his walking cane to strike at his assailant. Barlow was instinctively moving to place himself between Jackson and Lawrence, but the president's counterattack foiled that endeavor, and Lawrence had a clear shot in the instant that it took him to pull the trigger.

There was a loud popping sound, and Barlow's heart lodged in his throat—had he made a terrible mistake? Had the president been shot? But no, Jackson was unharmed; the pistol had misfired. Realizing this, Lawrence shrunk back in the face of Jackson's relentless onslaught and dropped the first pistol, only to brandish a second from beneath the cloak. Tench Ringgold caught the president and restrained him, placing his bulk between Jackson and the would-be assassin. Seeing that the president was sheltered, Barlow altered the direction of his lunge and reached Lawrence just in time to knock the man's gun arm up. The second pistol's hammer fell. It, too, misfired. Barlow shoved Lawrence down and reached to draw his sword. But before he could clear the blade from its scabbard, several men had leaped upon Lawrence to restrain him, and none too gently. Barlow turned to confirm that Jackson was unscathed. Ringgold was staring at him.

"My God, Barlow," was all the marshal could say. Then he and several constables hurried the president down the hallway and out to the waiting carriage.

Barlow noticed that the first pistol lay at his feet. He picked it up, examined it—and drew a long, calming breath.

The cap had discharged properly, but it had not ignited the powder in the barrel. It had not done so because, on that morning in Lawrence's room at the Granger Boardinghouse, Barlow had plugged the vent-hole with some shoeblack he had found in the wardrobe. The shoeblack had hardened quickly, rendering the pistols useless. The sabotage had been undetected by Lawrence. Barlow had noticed that the pistols had already been cleaned and loaded; Lawrence would have had no reason to unload and clean them again.

Barlow handed the pistol to one of the constables that had swarmed into the hallway. Several of them, assisted by civilians, were escorting the subdued Lawrence away. Barlow noticed that the man's false beard had come partially detached from his face. Shaking his head, Barlow left the Capitol by another route.

He went to the White House to make sure that Andrew Jackson had suffered no ill effects from the events that had just transpired. He was welcomed effusively by Major Donelson, who hailed him as a hero.

"Tench Ringgold told me what you did," said Donelson. "He also told me that he objected, on the grounds that it was too risky. But the men he left at the boardinghouse to watch for Lawrence never spotted the man, so, as it turns out, your plan was the correct one. We're left to wonder how it is that he acquired the pistols that remained in his room. Clearly you were right—he was part of a conspiracy against the president's life. Now the question is, how do we acquire sufficient evidence to put Charles Marten behind bars?"

Barlow hesitated. They had only the mystery woman's word for it, and even though he knew assassination was something Charles Marten was fully capable of, and he felt it would be an injustice to convict a man based on the testimony of a woman who was probably not entirely sane, and who, at the very least, was motivated by jealousy. He told Donelson as much.

He had a personal reason, too, for discouraging Donelson from pursuing an investigation into Marten's part in the assassination attempt. Sarah. He wasn't sure if she was in love with the abolitionist leader—in fact, he doubted that she was really sure about her feelings for the man. But there could be no denying that those feelings were strong. Barlow was of the opinion that he had done enough to hurt her—after all, putting aside the question of whether she had abandoned him, or vice versa, three years ago, he had fallen in love with another woman. He had broken his wedding vows, and whether Sarah had broken hers as well did not mitigate that. So he decided not to broach the subject of Charles Marten.

"But you said you saw Lawrence and Marten talking together just a couple of nights ago," said Donelson, clearly disappointed by Barlow's ambivalence.

"I did, but I didn't hear anything that passed between them. They might have been talking about the weather, for all I know."

"Well, perhaps Lawrence himself will tell us of Marten's involvement. At any rate, the president wants to see you."

Barlow was escorted into Jackson's inner office. The old man was pacing the floor behind his desk. Tench Ringgold was there, and they were sharing a glass of good Kentucky bourbon. The president looked more vital than he had when last Barlow had seen him. There was color in his cheeks, vitality in his frame, a light in his eyes. Barlow smiled. There was nothing like personal danger to invigorate Old Hickory.

"Ah, Major," boomed Jackson, when he saw Barlow. "Tench has told me all about the trick you played on that scoundrel, Lawrence. I should count my lucky stars that you were in Washington. Even though you should be in Georgia, attending to the business that I sent you down there to see to."

"I had urgent personal business here," said Barlow, without a trace of apology in his voice. "I am meeting with some difficulty in acquiring sufficient supplies for the Cherokees to make their move. Things are going slowly, Mr. President, on that front."

"But not in your own affairs, I take it." Jackson nodded. "Yes, I knew it would be a difficult task that I set for you, Major. But that's why I chose you. And the Cherokees must be removed as quickly as possible."

"The Georgians agree with you, sir," replied Barlow wryly. "They're just not willing to help speed matters along."

"You make the mistake of painting all Georgians with the same brush," rasped Jackson. "But that's of no consequence. I'm doing this for the Union. The Cherokees must be moved, and the crisis averted. The republic cannot withstand another strain like the one we suffered over South Carolina and those damned nullifiers."

"So the Cherokees are to be sacrificed on the altar of unity," said Barlow.

"Really, Major," said Donelson, disapprovingly. "That kind of comment reeks of insubordination."

Jackson laughed. "Oh, didn't you know?" he asked Donelson. "This fellow has always been insubordinate with me. I'd have had him broken to private, or drummed out of the army altogether, long before now—except that he gets difficult jobs done."

"Aren't you going to tell him about the attack, Mr. President?" asked Donelson.

"What attack?" asked Barlow.

"A dispatch from General Gaines arrived at the War Department," said Donelson. "Gaines received a report from a Lieutenant Armstrong claiming that a band of armed civilians attacked a party of about three hundred Cherokees who had left one of the Upper Towns on their journey west. About a dozen Indians were killed. Many of their wagons were burned, and a lot of their livestock slaughtered or stolen."

"Good God," muttered Barlow.

"Apparently Armstrong has no idea who the civilians were."

"No?" asked Barlow coldly. "I have a pretty good idea who's behind the attack, though. Good citizens of Georgia like Judge Tolliver."

Jackson looked at Donelson and Ringgold. "Would you gentlemen excuse us? I would like some words alone with Major Barlow."

Once Donelson and the marshal had gone, Jackson eased his stiff frame into the chair behind the desk. Elbows on the chair's arms, he steepled his bony fingers together and rested his chin on the tips of them, peering at Barlow.

"Personally," said Jackson, "I wouldn't be surprised if Tolliver *was* behind the attack. But he's not the kind of man who would lead it. I know there are men in Georgia who wish to sabotage the removal of the Cherokees. The longer the Indians remain the more likely it is that the federal government and the state of Georgia will come to blows over who has jurisdiction in their case."

"Exactly, sir," said Barlow. "Furthermore, the Georgians are envious of the prosperity the Cherokees have enjoyed through their hard work and diligence. That's why they don't want to help the removal."

Jackson nodded morosely. "How will the Cherokees react to this outrage?"

Barlow thought it over. "Some will clamor for war—the same ones who have always advocated staying put and fighting it out to the bitter end. But as long as men like Mondegah are alive there won't be a war. Not a full-scale one, anyway. No, what this will do will be to dissuade many other Cherokees from making the move until the last possible moment. You need to send a full regiment down there, Mr. President, to guarantee the safety of the Indians."

"I don't have a full regiment to spare," said Jackson. "We have a war brewing in Florida with the Seminoles. And the militia of the western states cannot be expected to defend Indians, for God's sake—they've been waging war against the redskins for generations."

Barlow leaned on the desk. "It's not too late to reverse the course of events, Mr. President. You once employed the Cherokees to help you fight the Seminoles. You can do that again—and in return give them the right to stay on their land."

Jackson shook his head. "Your affinity for the Cherokees blinds you to the political realities, Major. I *cannot* save the Cherokees *and* the republic, too. If the Cherokees don't go, the nullifiers will have another cause, one even more potent than the tariff." He looked balefully at Barlow. "You must get back down there as soon as you can, and *fix* this situation—somehow."

Barlow sighed, and straightened, standing stiffly, almost at attention. "I must respectfully ask to be relieved from duty, then, Mr. President. The situation requires immediate attention, but … but I can't leave Washington right now."

Jackson leaned back in his chair, his keen gaze fixed on Barlow. "Yes, you can," he said sternly.

"No, sir. And I would prefer not to go into the details."

"You don't have to." Jackson jerked open a desk drawer, removed a document and handed it to Barlow. It bore the seal of the Maryland state assembly. "This is your divorce, Major. Now you can put aside your personal affairs for the time being and go attend to the people's business."

Barlow stared at the document in his hand. "But … how?"

"I called in some markers," said Jackson gruffly. "Damn it, Major, I need you in Georgia, not moping around in some assembly house, bending the ear or twisting the arm of any representative that might be inclined to listen to your pleas. Your divorce has been granted. Your marriage is dissolved. I hope you've made the right decision."

"I take it you don't approve, sir."

Jackson shrugged. "Whether I approve or not won't change your mind, I know you well enough to be certain of that!"

"Thank you, Mr. President."

Jackson waved his gratitude away with an impatient gesture. "No. I should thank you. Not for my life, because my life matters not to me. I've been ready to meet my Maker for many years now.

Ready to join my dear Rachel once more." Jackson heaved a deep sigh and looked across the room at…nothing. Ghosts, perhaps, mused Barlow, struck by the fact that he was being allowed a rare glimpse of the old man's emotions. Jackson usually maintained a stoic facade, but now that was gone—and he saw a deeply grieving and profoundly weary man. "Life is a long misery to me now," continued the president, his voice a gravelly whisper. "Every day is one of continual pain. Not just physical pain, though there is plenty of that to keep me occupied. But the pain of…loneliness. And that, my friend, is a far greater agony than could result from any physical ailment. No, were I not president I would have welcomed the bullets that Mr. Lawrence was unable to fire, thanks to you. But had he killed the president, war might well have broken out between North and South. A war the republic cannot survive in its present state."

"I almost started a war for you in Charleston."

"No, you prevented one. The bloodshed was regrettable, but necessary. And I know it must have been difficult for you, firing upon your fellow Americans. Still, you did what was necessary. The nullifiers were defying the flag. They were attacking a federal arsenal. You were well within your rights to stop them."

"Not everyone sees it that way."

Jackson shrugged. "Some say a war is inevitable. They may be right. But if it is, I pray only that we may delay it long enough so that right is strong enough to prevail over evil."

"So you think slavery is evil, sir?"

"Of course it is."

"But…you own slaves."

"That I do," said Jackson curtly. "I also have two bullets in me. I would rather have neither bullets nor slaves, yet I have both, and cannot help that I have them. And what about you, Major? If you marry that Southern girl you've been seen with, you'll be a slaveholder yourself. What will you do about that?"

Barlow shook his head. "I honestly don't know, sir. All I know is that I *am* going to marry Rose Claybourne. And I'm going to be a father."

Jackson stared at him a moment—then leaped to his feet with more agility than Barlow had seen him exhibit in a decade. He came around the desk and wrung Barlow's hand.

"By the Eternal!" exclaimed Old Hickory. "That's splendid news, Major, splendid news indeed! My most heartfelt congratulations, sir! One of my biggest regrets is that Rachel and I could never have children of our own. That's why we adopted Lincoyer."

Barlow nodded. He knew of the Creek Indian child that Jackson had adopted in the wake of the Red Stick uprising.

"All the more reason, then, for you to hasten back to Georgia," said Jackson. "Marry that girl—and prevent any more violence being done to the Cherokees. I would think those are two orders you could obey without giving me any grief!"

"Yes, sir." Barlow grinned. "I'll try not to give you any more grief, Mr. President."

Jackson clapped him on the shoulder. "I appreciate the sentiment. But I won't bet on it."

CHAPTER NINETEEN

When he arrived in the vicinity of Athens, Georgia, Barlow's first impulse was to stop first at the Claybourne plantation to see Rose, to make sure she was all right, and to give her the good news about being a free man. But he felt duty-bound to go first to the military encampment established by Lieutenant Armstrong between Athens and the Cherokee Upper Towns.

Armstrong was there, with five other soldiers—all the rest, he informed Barlow, were out on patrol. He expected more trouble, and didn't have enough men to cover all the territory that he felt needed covering. Barlow commiserated, and told him that they would have to do the best they could with the resources on hand, because more troops were not forthcoming. Armstrong didn't seem nearly as eager for action as he'd been when first Barlow had met him; the reality of the situation had caught up with him on the day he'd visited the site of the attack on the Cherokee caravan.

"Whoever did this caused a lot of damage," said Armstrong. "Wagons burned, livestock slaughtered—and people killed. Women and children, for God's sake." The young lieutenant shook his head. "I understand that there's plenty of hard feelings between the Indians and the settlers around here. But to make war on innocents? I'd like to get my hands on the bastards who did that."

"Maybe you will. How many were there, do you think?"

"Sergeant Conley can read sign as good as any Indian. He told me he counted twenty-two horses among the raiders. All shod, by the way."

"Why do you say that?"

"Because some of the folks around here are saying no white men would do such a thing, sir. They're blaming the Indians themselves. Saying that it was probably some Cherokee troublemakers. You know, part of that group that refuses to move west. That they wanted to make an example of the ones who were willing to relocate, in order to discourage any others from trying it."

Barlow nodded. "Pretty smart. Any trouble from the Cherokees?"

"Not yet, Major. But I think you better go talk to any friends you might have in the villages."

"I will," said Barlow. "Because I have a plan to capture the men who attacked that wagon train. But we're going to need bait."

"What kind of bait, sir?"

"Another caravan of Cherokees."

"What if we can't protect them? Then more women and children could get killed."

"Then we'll just have to make sure that we *do* protect them, won't we, Lieutenant?"

"Yes, sir," said Armstrong, dubiously.

Barlow rode next to New Echota to see Mondegah. When he arrived in the Cherokee town he could feel the animosity directed at him by many of the inhabitants who gathered to observe his arrival in mostly sullen silence. Fortunately, Mondegah was there, and took him into his house for a private talk. Barlow remarked on the coldness of the greeting he had received.

"The people are angry and confused," said the old chieftain. "Can you blame them? The whites do not want them to stay, and now it seems the whites do not want them to leave, either. So what are we to do? I must confess, my friend, I am beginning to lose hope. More and more of the young men clamor for war. It is better, they say, to die with honor, like men, then to live like the white man's dogs."

"Don't lose hope yet," said Barlow. "I want to catch the men who attacked that caravan. If I can, then it will show that the army is serious about protecting the Cherokees, and others will think twice about doing anything of that sort again."

"How will you catch them?"

"Well, I need to draw them out." And Barlow proceeded to explain his plan to Mondegah.

When he was done, the old chief shook his head. "Some of the warriors would take part in your plan. But I know of no one who would risk their families. There can be no women and children involved."

"There must be," insisted Barlow. "It must look completely normal. Or the men we're after will recognize it for a trap."

Mondegah sighed. "I will speak to my people. But do not expect miracles."

Barlow smiled. "Now, come on, old friend, I saw you pull off a miracle or two against the Creeks and the Seminoles. How about one more for old time's sake?"

Mondegah promised he would do his best.

When he arrived at the Claybourne plantation, Barlow didn't even get all the way up the road before Rose burst out of the big house and came running out to greet him. As she neared he bent down and curled an arm around her slender waist and lifted her up to him and kissed her with all the pent-up longing of the six weeks he had been away. When finally their lips parted Rose laughed, gasping for air. He set her back down on the ground and swung out of the saddle and took a long look around.

"Everything seems to be going well here," he observed.

"We've had no trouble," she assured him. "And the baby is just fine."

He touched her belly, and could feel but a slight swelling. "You're not showing."

"Of course not," she said, in mock indignation. Then she smiled. "Well, I am a little. You'll see—tonight. Oh, darling, I missed you so much! I'd swear you'd been away for an entire year!"

Barlow nodded. "It seemed at least that long to me. But I didn't come back empty-handed."

"You brought me a present?" she asked coyly.

He laughed. "I brought you not one, but two presents." He unbuttoned his coatee and produced the sealed document that Andrew Jackson had given him. "I'm free to marry you now, Rose. If you'll have me."

"I'll have no other man, ever," she vowed.

"And then there's this." He turned to his horse, opened one of the panniers strapped to the back of his saddle, and extracted a small wooden box. He opened the box and showed her the contents.

"A ring," she whispered, delighted.

"It isn't much," he apologized, "but it was all I could afford."

"It's the most precious thing I've ever seen," she breathed, and threw her arms around his neck to kiss him again. "I love you, Major Barlow."

"And I love you, Miss Claybourne. Soon to be Mrs. Barlow."

She laughed and hugged him tightly, and they stood there for a few minutes, in the warm sunlight on the dusty lane that ran straight as an arrow between the fields of cotton. The slave crews working in the fields stopped what they were doing and stood there and watched them, and smiled.

"And when shall we be wed, sir?" she whispered in his ear.

"How about today?"

"Don't be silly. I have arrangements to make. I don't even have a dress. ..."

He gently broke free of her embrace and held her at arm's length, suddenly very serious.

"I'm not sure about a big wedding, Rose. I don't know that very many people would respond to an invitation."

"I don't care—as long as you're there."

"It's because of me that you've been ostracized."

"That is of no consequence to me," she insisted.

"And it may get even worse," he added. "You heard about the attack on the Cherokees?"

"Yes, of course. A terrible thing."

"I'm going to set a trap for the men who did it. Once that happens I might be the least popular man in the state of Georgia."

"Don't be silly. You already are the least popular man. Except where I'm concerned."

"I'm serious, Rose."

She nodded, and tried to look serious, too. But looking serious wasn't easy because she was deliriously happy.

"So what do you suggest?" She looked about her. "I don't want to leave this place, Timothy. But if you insist on living elsewhere, I'll go with you. I'll be at your side, no matter where you want to go."

It was an alternative Barlow had already contemplated—and, reluctantly, rejected. He knew how much the plantation meant to Rose. It was her home, the only home she had ever really known. The Charleston town house didn't count. She'd grown up here, and had rarely spent any time in Charleston while her father lived. Barlow was not going to take this place away from her.

"No, this is where you want to be, and this is where we'll stay," said Barlow. "All I'm saying is, I think we should have a small wedding."

"A very small wedding," said Rose—and laughed.

"Yes, probably." Barlow couldn't help it—he started laughing, too. Because it really didn't matter if the whole world was against them. As long as they had one another they had all they would ever need.

Late that night, when he was certain that Rose was asleep, Barlow slipped out of bed, sliding reluctantly out from under the bare arm and leg that she'd draped over him. Sleeping with Rose, her body tucked against his the way she liked to sleep, had been something he'd dreamed about every night for the past six weeks. But there was something he had to find out.

He dressed quietly, and sneaked out of the room without awakening her. He left the big house and headed for the slave quarters. He noticed that the overseer's cottage was dark; Rose had told him that she'd hired a replacement for Richman, a man named Clark who had a good reputation as a man who knew how to handle large numbers of slaves without resorting to brutality. Barlow bypassed the cottage and moved on to the shanty where he knew Jericho lived with his family. A dog barked at him from on down the row of huts. He tapped lightly on the door.

"Jericho. It's me, Major Barlow."

The door opened just a crack, and he could see Jericho's angular face, adorned with an expression of sleepy alarm.

"Sorry to come calling so late, Jericho, but I need to talk to you."

Jericho glanced back inside, then slipped out through the door, closing it very quietly behind him. He checked the stars automatically to gauge the time, then glanced around the quarters.

"Somethin' wrong, suh?"

"That's what I've come to find out from you."

"I don't follow, suh."

"In the time that I was gone, did you see any sign of John Claybourne?"

A veil of caution descended over Jericho's normally expressive face. "What did the missus tell you, suh?"

"She told me nothing had happened. But even if it had she might not tell me, now would she?"

"Why wouldn't she, suh?"

"Because she wouldn't want me to worry. Should I be worried, Jericho? Tell me the truth."

Jericho hesitated and looked around again, this time like a man hoping for someone or something to come along and save him from an unpleasant task. Finally he sighed, and nodded.

"Mebbe you should, suh. Mebbe you should. I seen a man. Don' know if it war Mastuh John or not. Whoever it was, he was just a-sittin' on a horse back up in the woods over yonder." He pointed to the north. "Way 'cross the new field we been clearin'. I didn't get a good look at him cuz he was so far away, but he sat there for the longest time, so's finally I goes up to the big house and tells Miss Rose, but when she come out to see who it war, the man had just vanished like a ghost."

"You have no idea who it was."

Jericho emphatically shook his head. "No, suh, I sure don'. Coulda been Mastuh John. I know it warn't Mr. Richman, now. I knows that for sure. I'd know that man if he was a-comin' from a mile away."

Barlow nodded. "Anything else happen?"

"Well, one night, about a week ago, I was in the stables late, and I could've swore I heard someone a-walkin' around out in the dark. I went out to look but didn't see nobody. Nex' mornin', though, I went back to look and seen the tracks of a man wearin' boots. I ask Mr. Clark if he was the one I'd heard, and he said no, and I showed him the tracks and he went up to the big house and tol' Miss Rose, and I believe she told him to keep an eye out the next night. He did, too, but ain't nothin' happened."

Barlow nodded. He had a hunch the tracks were John Claybourne's. He wondered what the man was after. Even if something happened to Rose, he could not take over the place as long as he was burdened with the label of traitor. Still, Barlow was worried. John Claybourne was not the kind of man who would let logic stand in the way of exacting revenge. And he shuddered to think what the man might do if he found out that his sister was pregnant with Barlow's child.

"Reckon Miss Rose jis' didn't tell you, suh, so as not to worry you," said Jericho. "But I's worried."

Barlow put a hand on the slave's shoulder. "Don't worry too much. I'll take care of Mr. Claybourne."

"You be careful, suh. That Mastuh John is a mean one. I'd purely hate to see anything happen to you. It would likely jis' kill Miss Rose."

Barlow told Jericho to go back to bed, and returned to the big house. He managed to undress and slip under the covers without waking Rose. She murmured contentedly and draped an arm and leg over him again. Barlow tried to sleep, but couldn't. Every sound in the house caught his notice, and he'd listen hard, wondering if it was just the house—or something more.

Early the next morning he took a ride, alone. Rose wanted to go with him, but he convinced her that she was too far along to be doing much riding anymore. She said that was nonsense, but she wasn't going to do anything that might jeopardize the baby, and she let him go without her. Barlow thoroughly searched the woods where Jericho had said he'd seen the mysterious rider. It was a fruitless search, and a frustrating one for Barlow. He decided that if he was ever going to get a moment's peace he would have to locate John Claybourne and deal with him.

Right after the noonday meal, a messenger from Armstrong arrived to inform Barlow that the lieutenant needed to see him as soon as possible. Barlow warned Rose that he might be gone for a few days. She tried to conceal her concern for his safety.

"By the time you get back I'll have a dress made," she said. "And then we'll go to the justice of the peace."

He kissed her, a long and passionate kiss. "I miss you already," he confessed.

"Then hurry back," she whispered.

He promised.

When he and the messenger reached the encampment night had fallen, and they came close to being shot by a nervous sentry. Barlow was soon to learn the source of the sentry's nerves—there were Indians in the camp. Cherokee Indians, true, but as far as the soldier was concerned, no wise man was careless with his scalp when redskins were in the vicinity.

Mondegah was there, along with nearly a score of other warriors, all of them of middle age, and some of whom Barlow recognized from the Seminole campaign. Upon Barlow's arrival, all congregated in front of Lieutenant Armstrong's tent.

"These men have agreed to risk their families and their belongings so that you can catch those who murdered our people," said Mondegah gravely. "I, too, will go. We do this because we trust you, White Warrior."

Barlow scanned the somber faces of the Cherokees—and nearly faltered in his resolve. If his plan didn't work, if some of these men and their families came to harm, it would be entirely on his head. It was a grave burden to carry. He had to remind himself that if he didn't succeed the Cherokee removal might never take place—and then there would almost certainly be war. Not only between the Cherokees and the whites who coveted their land, but possibly even between the state of Georgia and the republic.

He nodded, and tried his best to look more confident than he felt. "Good. It will be a small group, so we must make certain it isn't overlooked." He turned to Armstrong. "Lieutenant, send two men into town. Tell them to have some drinks at a couple of taverns. Tell them to talk about the caravan of Cherokees going out tomorrow. And be sure they mention, if asked, that there will not be an army escort."

"No escort, sir?"

"That's right. Oh, you'll be there, Lieutenant, never fear. But hopefully you'll remain unseen until the trap is sprung."

"Yes, sir!"

Barlow turned then to Mondegah. "When will you be ready to go?"

"We are ready now."

"In the morning, then. I'll be with you. Lieutenant Armstrong and his men will remain out of sight but, hopefully, not so far away that they cannot hear a gunshot."

"Are we allowed to defend ourselves?" asked Mondegah. "And if so, what will happen if we kill white men?"

Barlow assured them that there would be no consequences. "The men we're after are outlaws."

"They're still white," said Mondegah.

"You'll just have to trust me, my friend."

Mondegah nodded gravely. "We do. That is why we are here."

CHAPTER TWENTY

M ost of the twenty men from New Echota who had agreed to go with Mondegah and Barlow had sons, and most of those sons had families and were determined to go with their fathers and mothers regardless of the risks. In the end there were about fifty families in the caravan. All had their own wagons, filled with personal belongings and provisions, for it had been decided that they would not return to New Echota unless they were forced to do so; Barlow figured this was because, aside from all the work involved in preparing for a trek, it was too emotionally wrenching to leave twice the home you love. The caravan was accompanied by a small herd of horses, cows and even some pigs; usually the children were charged with monitoring the livestock on the trail.

It was a good day for travel—cool and sunny—and the ground was dry, for several days had passed since the last rain, so there was little chance that the overloaded wagons would get bogged down. The night before, though, had been chilly, and they knew that winter was just around the corner. Barlow knew that if these people continued on to the Arkansas they would probably not arrive before the first snow. Barlow had made what arrangements he could by letter—the Cherokees would proceed to Vicksburg and cross the Mississippi by ferry there. On the other side of the river they would find a cache of provisions, secured by an association in Massachusetts which had been recruited by some of Samuel Worcester's friends at the American Board of Missions. There was a fairly good road that followed the river northward about seventy miles, and they would take that, at the end of which would be another cache of provisions—this one, like the last, paid for and transported under the aegis of a benevolent society in the North. The Cherokees would then strike out due westward, and they'd face tough going, because all the reports Barlow had received indicated that they would have to cross numerous rivers and many miles of swampland before reaching the hills where the Indians who had gone before them had established their new homes. Barlow wished he could be with them, to share the ordeal, to help in any way he could to pave their way. But he had even greater responsibilities— Rose and the baby, and John Claybourne. He could not leave Rose again until Claybourne was taken care of.

He traveled in Mondegah's wagon, keeping out of sight. His uniform had been exchanged for stroud trousers and a buckskin tunic. His horse was tied to the back of the wagon with Mondegah's best pony, and he had removed the saddle and army-issue saddle blanket from its back. If anyone was watching, he did not want them to know that an army officer was traveling with the Cherokees, for fear that this might discourage an attack. He kept by his side his pistol and saber, and a rifle that Lieutenant Armstrong had supplied him. There wasn't much room in the wagon, and before the first day was done his backbone was complaining even though they spent the day traveling one of the good roads that connected the Upper Towns. By the end of it he was praying that the attack would come, if for no other reason than it would mean he wouldn't have to spend another day crammed between sacks of corn and a large wooden trunk.

But there was no attack. They made, by Mondegah's reckoning, seventeen miles that day. Barlow could have sworn it had been more like a hundred. Camp was made in a clearing nestled between wooded slopes, with a nearby creek to provide fresh water, and plenty of graze for the livestock.

Barlow ventured out of the wagon after night fell. He was hoping that, should anyone be watching the caravan, they would not be able to distinguish him from the Cherokees in the darkness. Most of the Cherokees had long ago adopted the white man's dress, and many had cut their hair short. But though they looked like whites, Barlow knew that the fierce heart of the warrior still beat in their chests. To a man they were hoping, like him, for an attack, a chance to avenge all the injustices visited upon them by the whites.

That night the group with which Barlow associated sat around a campfire and waxed nostalgic about the old days. They spoke of the battles they had fought together against the Red Stick Creeks and the Seminoles. No one raised the subject of their new home out west—it was an uncertain future, at best, and one they did not care to dwell on. Sitting there listening to them, sharing their food and their fire, Barlow felt deep shame for his own kind and the way they had treated these noble people—a people who had consistently been friends to the Americans.

Mondegah and his family slept underneath their wagon. Barlow couldn't sleep, so he spent the night sitting with his back against a wagon wheel and the rifle across his legs. Several other Cherokees remained on guard as well, and the livestock were closely watched over. Barlow wondered how Lieutenant Armstrong and the twelve soldiers with him were faring. Hopefully they were nearby, in a cold camp, as Barlow had advised the lieutenant to build no fires, lest they give their presence away. If the attack was to occur, Barlow had assumed it would happen within the first few days, as he doubted that the raiders would be inclined to travel too far from home.

Morning came, cold and misty and overcast. The fires were restored, and breakfast was made. The oxen were yoked and the few animals that had strayed into the trees returned to the fold. It was a quiet time, a scene of serenity, and for a moment Barlow let down his guard and began to contemplate, without relish, another day of being bounced and joggled in the suffocating confines of an overloaded wagon.

And that's when the attack came.

They came out of the east, with the just-risen sun behind them, shouting and shooting aboard galloping horses, surging down out of the timbered slope and plunging into the encampment. Barlow whirled and lunged for the rifle he had negligently left propped up against the wagon wheel. Several bullets kicked up dirt at his feet, prompting him to dive under the wagon and then reach out to retrieve the rifle. Several Cherokees were falling, victims of the first fusillade. One of those who fell was a woman. The rest were scattering for cover. Barlow picked for his first target a raider who was trying to run down a young girl of about ten. The horseman grabbed the girl by the back of her dress and began to pull her, kicking and screaming, up over his saddle. Barlow wondered if he should hold off on the shot for fear of hitting the girl—but took it anyway. If he didn't kill the man the girl was as good as dead; as soon as she was draped across his saddle the man raised his pistol, gripping its barrel, and prepared to crush her skull. Barlow's bullet entered his side below the upraised arm and hurled the man out of the saddle. The girl slipped off the horse, fell, got up, and ran for the nearest wagon. A Cherokee warrior ran out to meet her, but was shot down. Barlow muttered a curse and went out to get her, pistol in one hand, saber in the other. Unnerved by the buzzing of hot lead around her, the girl faltered, then knelt down and covered her ears. Barlow was nearly to her when, out of the corner of an eye, he saw a rider coming through the powder smoke and mist. He turned and fired, not having the time to draw a bead. His bullet missed the rider but killed the horse outright. As the pony went down the rider leaped clear, rolled, came up, and yanked a pistol from his belt. He fired at Barlow from a distance of twenty feet—and somehow missed. Shouting incoherently, he hurled the pistol away and charged Barlow, brandishing a big knife. But Barlow's blade was bigger. He stepped into the charge, parried the man's knife-thrust with ease, and ran him through. The impetus of the man's forward motion carried right up onto the blade, to the hilt. Face to face with Barlow, he looked shocked. Then the light went out of his eyes. Barlow had to brace a foot against the man's body to pull the saber free. Turning, he grabbed the little girl by the arm and returned at a run to the wagon, half-dragging her with him.

Once he had the girl safely tucked away under the wagon, Barlow reloaded his pistol, using a percussion cap and paper cartridge from the pouch slung over his shoulder. There was a constant din of gunfire now, the thunder of horses at the gallop, the shouts and cries of men, and sometimes women—the noise of battle, coming from every direction. The Cherokees had recovered from their surprise, and were fighting back. *But where was Lieutenant Armstrong?*

Propped up on one elbow beneath the wagon, Barlow saw a horse go galloping past. He rolled out from under the wagon, stopping on his belly, both elbows planted, and took aim at the back of the raider who had just gone by. He squeezed the trigger, and the impact of the bullet knocked the man forward; he slid sideways out of the saddle, dead. Barlow rolled back under the wagon, just in time, as another raider rode up and took a shot at him. Feeling the burn of the bullet, Barlow checked his sleeve. It was just a graze. But the raider wasn't done. He dismounted and knelt to peer under the wagon, and there was a pistol in his other hand that Barlow had to assume was loaded. Lashing out with a foot as the man squeezed the trigger, Barlow spoiled the raider's aim; the bullet plowed into the underside of the wagon bed. The Cherokee girl cringed against a wheel, covering her ears, her mouth open in a silent scream of terror. Barlow picked up his saber and struck at the bearded face of the raider, but the man fell back, avoiding the blade. Pressing his advantage, Barlow scrambled out from beneath the wagon again and raised the saber to strike. The man swung an empty pistol in a desperate attempt to parry the blow. He was lucky, and accomplished his aim. He kicked at Barlow's groin and caught the upper thigh instead, but the blow was enough to throw Barlow back against the wagon. That gave the man time to run away. Barlow started to give chase, then saw another rider looming out of the smoke.

It was John Claybourne.

Claybourne recognized Barlow in the same instant, and checked his horse. He was caught completely by surprise. But only for a moment. Then, his face a mask of hate, he drew a saber from the scabbard at his side. Barlow just had time to wonder if it was the same blade Claybourne had been brandishing on Market Street when he'd led the ill-fated nullifiers' assault on the federal arsenal.

Then Claybourne was urging his horse forward, waving the saber overhead and shouting like a Cossack.

Barlow braced himself. At the last minute he stepped quickly to his left and brought his saber up to parry Claybourne's downward stroke. Steel clanged against steel, and the impact nearly jarred the weapon out of Barlow's grasp. But he deflected the blow, letting Claybourne's blade slide off his and over his head. And as Claybourne's horse swept by, Barlow whirled to his right and slashed at the rider's leg. The blade bit deeply into Claybourne's thigh, a few inches above the knee. But Claybourne wasn't deterred. He checked his horse so sharply that it nearly sat down on its haunches. Turning the horse, he made a second charge. But an instant before he reached Barlow he suddenly veered sharply away. Barlow looked over his shoulder. Lieutenant Armstrong and his soldiers were leaping into the fray. The crackling of their rifles added to the din of battle. Disconcerted by the sudden appearance of the bluecoats, the raiders disengaged and headed back into the timber. Armstrong urged his men to pursue. He checked his horse briefly at Barlow's side.

"You've been hit, sir," he said.

Barlow looked at his arm. The sleeve of the buckskin hunting shirt was black with the stain of blood.

"It's just a nick," he said. "The traitor John Claybourne was with them. Leading them, probably. Catch him, if you can, Lieutenant."

"Yes, sir!" Armstrong spurred his horse forward.

Barlow looked bleakly around at the carnage. The fight had lasted but a few minutes, yet it had been his experience that great damage could be done in a short time. From where he stood he could see a dozen men lying dead or wounded on the ground. A grimmer sight than that was the Cherokee mother and child who had died embracing one another—the husband and father knelt beside their bodies, head bent in silent grief, while his brothers gathered around him. Barlow was relieved to see Mondegah coming through the mist and powder smoke. The old chieftain seemed to have shed a dozen years. His stride was purposeful, his shoulders squared. He was directing the gathering-up of the wounded raiders. There were three of these. They were quickly bound together and directed to sit on the ground beside a wagon. Barlow went to them.

"I recognize you," he told one of them. "You were in the tavern in Athens, three years ago, trying to start a fight with me."

The man leered at him. "I remember you. Yankee Indian-lover. Figures, you being here to fight against your own kind."

"Was it John Claybourne who put you up to this?"

"Ain't nobody had to put me up to it. But at least Claybourne knows what color his skin is."

Barlow felt the rage building inside of him. He pointed at the dead woman and child. "You're a filthy coward, making war on innocents."

"Nits make lice," sneered the man.

"I'll see you hanged."

"Not in this state you won't."

Barlow walked away and went to Mondegah. "What are your losses?"

"Five dead," replied the Cherokee chief gravely. "But we killed seven of them." He listened for a moment—occasional gunshots were echoing down from the wooded slope up which Armstrong and his men had gone in pursuit of the raiders. "Perhaps we will get lucky, and more will die."

"I don't think they'll try this again," said Barlow. "So what will you do now? Go back to New Echota?"

"Yes, but only long enough to bury our dead in the land of their ancestors. Then we will continue to our new homes. Perhaps now more will come with us."

"I hope so," said Barlow.

"Me, too," said Mondegah, looking bleakly at the trio of captives. "Personally, I am sick and tired of being around these people."

Barlow smiled. "They're not all bad. But there are enough rotten apples in the barrel to sour the whole lot."

Mondegah nodded. "I think we have fought our last battle together, my friend."

❧   ❧   ❧

Armstrong and his men returned a couple of hours later with four more prisoners. According to the lieutenant they had killed two more raiders, without suffering any casualties themselves. The few who were left had gotten away. Including, Armstrong was sorry to say, John Claybourne.

The dead raiders were buried on the spot, while the dead and wounded Cherokees were loaded into one of the wagons. It took a while for the livestock, some of which had scattered during the fight, to be rounded up. But by midafternoon the entire caravan was on its way back to New Echota, the prisoners in tow behind one of the wagons, securely bound at the end of long ropes. Barlow waited until they were on their way. Then he said his farewells. The Cherokees, he knew, would be in good hands with Lieutenant Armstrong around. He rode ahead, pushing his horse as hard as he dared, keeping in mind that the plantation was a two-day ride away.

He had a feeling that John Claybourne would go home now. And he wanted to get there first.

Two mornings later, Barlow was sitting in a chair, staring at the road, when Rose Claybourne stepped out onto the veranda of the big house. His travel-worn horse stood, head hanging low, at the foot of the veranda steps.

"Darling!" She rushed to him, threw her arms around his neck, kissed him—and belatedly saw the bloodstained sleeve of his hunting shirt, and gasped. "Dear God, you've been wounded! What happened? No, tell me later. Come inside and I'll see to your arm."

"My arm is fine," he said. "I'm staying out here for a while. But you should go inside."

"What do you mean? What's wrong, Timothy?"

He looked at her bleakly. "I think your brother is on his way here. We met up two days west of here. He was with the raiders. Leading them, I think. He's wounded, but escaped. But he and I have some unfinished business."

She looked at the pistol in his hand. He was covered with the dirt and grime of the trail. And the dried black blood from his wound caked his hand. He was haggard, weary beyond words. But there was a resolve in his eyes and in the set of his jaw that she knew well.

Nodding, she straightened, maintaining her composure, and went back inside without saying a word.

An hour later Jericho emerged from the house, bringing coffee, which Barlow gulped down gratefully. The young slave took Barlow's horse off to the stables, only to return three quarters of an hour later to sit on the edge of the veranda, leaning against a column, glancing sidelong at Barlow as though he half expected to be sent away. But Barlow didn't mind the company, and after a while, he spoke.

"Jericho, what would you do if you were a free man?"

"A free man?" It was as though the thought had never occurred to him. He pondered the question for a full minute. "I reckon I'd stay right here, suh. This is my home. 'Sides, Miss Rose, she needs me."

Barlow smiled. "She would truly hate to see you go, I know that much."

"I ain't got nowhere to go."

Barlow gazed out at the fields. The crews were already at work in the cotton. "And what about the others? If they were freed?"

"Reckon some would go. But some would stay. 'Specially now that Mastuh John is gone, and Miss Rose is runnin' things. They're sayin' that right soon the state won't let a mastuh free his slaves. That it'll be against the law. But if they was freed, most of 'em would stay. 'Cause they'd only be free here, and everywhere else they'd still be slaves."

Barlow nodded. They lapsed into silence again. The minutes passed, accumulating into hours. The sun rose to its zenith and began to slip down the western sky. Barlow never left the chair. Once or twice he dozed off, knowing that Jericho would remain alertly on watch, and would wake him if anyone came up the road.

Without asking, he knew that the slave was aware of the reason for his vigil.

By mid-afternoon Barlow was wondering if he'd been wrong about Claybourne. He was so tired he thought he'd be able to sleep for a week, and thought with longing of the big four-poster bed upstairs, the one he shared with Rose. But he reminded himself that if he slept at all it would be a troubled sleep, as long as John Claybourne remained at large. And if he didn't come, Barlow would have to go looking for him, and *keep* looking for as long as it took.

"Rider comin', suh," said Jericho, quickly getting to his feet to peer down the road.

Barlow got up stiffly and stood alongside the slave at the edge of the veranda, peering down the road at the lone horseman. He was holding his horse to a walk, and was slumped in the saddle, head down, his face concealed by the brim of his hat. But Barlow was certain of the man's identity, even at this distance.

"Go inside, Jericho. If he gets past me, it'll be up to you to protect Rose."

Jericho looked at him, and Barlow could see his doubts reflected in his expression. But the slave did not give voice to them. He just nodded, gulped, and went into the house.

Barlow stepped down off the veranda and began walking down the road.

When he was less than a hundred yards from the rider, Barlow saw Claybourne slowly raise his head. Then he stopped the horse. He sat in the saddle for a moment, watching Barlow, who kept walking. Then Claybourne glanced around him, at the workers in the fields, all of whom had stopped what they were doing and were standing there, watching. He dismounted, slowly, stiffly, and, leaving his horse behind, walked towards Barlow. He was limping badly, and as he drew closer Barlow could see that the leg of his trousers was black with blood. *We make quite a pair,* mused Barlow.

When they were twenty paces apart, Claybourne stopped—and Barlow did likewise. He saw Claybourne bring his right hand from behind his back. He was holding a pistol. But Barlow had already assumed that to be the case. He noticed that Claybourne looked very pale—his eyes sunk deep in their sockets, his cheeks hollow. He'd lost a lot of blood.

"This is my home, Barlow," he said, his voice a dry husk. "Get out of my way."

"It's not yours anymore. You gave up your home, and everything else, when you turned traitor."

"You're the traitor!" rasped Claybourne fiercely. "I warned you long ago that I would kill you if we ever met again."

"And you've been trying ever since." Barlow kept the pistol down by his side. "You're under arrest. Either put that pistol down, or use it."

Claybourne looked at the pistol in his hand—and smiled ruefully. "If you kill me, you'll be doing me a favor. You'll be making me a martyr."

"I don't want to kill you, Claybourne."

"The choice is mine, not yours."

He raised the pistol.

Barlow fired. At such close range he fully expected to feel the impact of a bullet. But he didn't care. He didn't care if John Claybourne killed him, just as long as Claybourne died, too, and no longer posed a threat to the woman he loved or the child she was carrying.

Yet Claybourne's pistol remained silent. As the powder smoke drifted away, Barlow saw Claybourne, clutching at his chest, rock on his heels for a moment. Then, glaring at Barlow with all the hate he could muster, John Claybourne died on his feet—and toppled backwards.

Barlow knelt beside the body, pried the pistol out of Claybourne's dead fingers, and checked it. The pistol was empty. So was the shot pouch on Claybourne's saddle. He had been out of cartridges. That hadn't deterred him from a confrontation with Barlow, though. Which made Barlow wonder if maybe the man had wanted to die. Or perhaps he had thought that by dying he would do more good for his cause than if he lived. Barlow shook his head. These were questions he would never have an answer for. One thing was certain, however. John Claybourne had been a lot of things, but a coward wasn't one of them.

He looked up to see the slaves coming through the fields toward the road. Rising, he took one final look at Claybourne—and felt both vague regret and vast relief. He had a feeling that what he'd done today would somehow come between him and Rose. Of course, he hoped fervently that this would prove not to be the case. But he had slain her brother. That was not something she would be able to overlook entirely.

But at least now he'd be able to sleep.

He turned and started back for the big house as the slaves gathered silently around the body of John Claybourne. Their faces were stoic, revealing no hint of their feelings. Barlow wondered if they were relieved, too. But a lifetime in bondage had taught them not to show joy at the death of a white man, no matter who it was.

He looked toward the big house and saw Jericho and Rose on the veranda. She started to raise her arm to wave at him, then lowered it, and came towards him, walking at first, then breaking into a run.

Barlow quickened his stride.

Look for these reissued ebook titles by Jason Manning:

HIGH COUNTRY SERIES
- High Country
- Green River Rendezvous
- Battle of the Teton Basin

FLINTLOCK SERIES
- Flintlock
- The Border Captains
- Gone To Texas

TEXAS SERIES
- The Black Jacks
- Texas Bound
- The Marauders

MOUNTAIN MAN SERIES
- Mountain Passage
- Mountain Massacre
- Mountain Courage
- Mountain Vengeance
- Mountain Honor
- Mountain Renegade

FALCONER SERIES
- Falconer's Law
- Promised Land
- American Blood

ETHAN PAYNE SERIES
- Frontier Road
- Trail Town
- Last Chance

THE WESTERNERS
- Gun Justice
- Gunmaster
- The Outlaw Trail

TIMOTHY BARLOW SERIES
- The Long Hunters
- The Fire-Eaters
- War Lovers

APACHE SERIES
- Apache Storm
- Apache Shadow
- Apache Strike

OTHER TITLES
- Showdown at Seven Springs
- Texas Helltown
- Texas Gundown
- Gunsmoke on the Sierra Line
- Revenge in Little Texas
- Robbers of the Redlands (originally titled Texas Blood Kill)